MARK MORRIS

VAMPIRE CIRCUS

HAMMER

AN EXCLUSIVE MEDIA COMPANY

Published by Arrow Books in association with Hammer 2012

2 4 6 8 10 9 7 5 3 1

Based on the classic Hammer film *Vampire Circus*, directed by
Robert Young and released in 1972

First published in Great Britain in 2012 by
Arrow Books in association with Hammer
Random House, 20 Vauxhall Bridge Road,
London SW1V 2SA

www.randomhouse.co.uk
www.hammerfilms.com

Addresses for companies within The Random House Group Limited can be
found at: www.randomhouse.co.uk/offices.htm

The Random House Group Limited Reg. No. 954009

A CIP catalogue record for this book
is available from the British Library

ISBN 9780099556275

The Random House Group Limited supports The Forest Stewardship
Council (FSC®), the leading international forest certification organisation.
Our books carrying the FSC label are printed on FSC® certified paper.
FSC is the only forest certification scheme endorsed by the leading
environmental organisations, including Greenpeace. Our paper
procurement policy can be found at
www.randomhouse.co.uk/environment

Typeset in Palatino by Palimpsest Book Production Limited,
Falkirk, Stirlingshire
Printed and bound by CPI Group (UK) Ltd, Croydon, CR0 4YY

VAMPIRE
CIRCUS

Mark Morris became a full-time writer in 1988, and a year later saw the release of his first novel, *Toady*. He has since published a further sixteen novels, among which are *Stitch*, *The Immaculate*, *The Secret of Anatomy*, *Fiddleback*, *The Deluge* and four books in the popular *Doctor Who* range. His short stories, novellas, articles and reviews have appeared in a wide variety of anthologies and magazines, and he is editor of the highly acclaimed *Cinema Macabre*, a book of fifty horror movie essays by genre luminaries, for which he won the 2007 British Fantasy Award.

His most recently published or forthcoming work includes a novella entitled *It Sustains* for Earthling Publications, a *Torchwood* novel entitled *Bay of the Dead*, several *Doctor Who* audios for Big Finish Productions, a follow-up volume to *Cinema Macabre* entitled *Cinema Futura* and a new short story collection, *Long Shadows, Nightmare Light*. He also writes under the name of J. M. Morris.

To find out more about Mark Morris visit his website at www.markmorriswriter.com

Foreword

Vampire Circus was my first movie and the most pleasurable and memorable. I was having lunch with Hammer's managing director Michael Carreras and my agent. The agent asked Michael what he was going to do next and Michael said, '*Vampire Circus.*' 'And who is going to direct it?' 'He is,' said Michael, pointing at me. It was quite a moment and the start of a glorious period in my life.

I then met the producer, an American called Wilbur Stark. He had a flat in Warwick Avenue and invited me over for many suppers to discuss the script by Judson Kinberg. We had a fun time and Wilbur taught me a lot. His great reply to 'How are you?' was 'No pain.' Both he and Michael Carreras were of the old school of producers. They looked after the director and saw that he did his job and that he received no interference from anyone else.

There were several incidents which, to a first time director, stay in the memory forever. We were starting the shoot in Black Park near Pinewood Studios. We had been allotted our piece of the forest and we had recce'd and planned. On the Sunday before the start on Monday I found myself driving out to look, yet again, at the location. Where had it gone? Had it disappeared in the two days since I last walked it? I had first night nerves in a big way. As I drove up to the site I found the ground covered in fake snow, the trees covered in fake snow and the area roped off ready for a Shirley MacLaine shoot. After explaining to the location manager for the MacLaine shoot that this was my piece of allotted ground and that I was supposed to be shooting mid-summer in the forest of Liechtenstein as opposed to mid-winter in Siberia, I was told that it was not his problem. 'Easier, mate,' he said, 'for you to find another piece of forest than for me to wash the snow away and start afresh somewhere else.' Minor panic ensued but a new forest was found and Monday dawned with all systems go. Or not . . .

The first set up was a wide shot with John Moulder-Brown, who I had seen as the brilliant young lead in *Deep End* with Diana Dors. John was mounted on a horse ready to gallop towards the camera. Suddenly klaxons blew and above the tree tops appeared the biggest camera crane I had ever seen. It was Shirley again and she was filming a high shot. A very, very high shot. A runner was sent to negotiate. Would they lower the camera so it did not appear in my shot? No, we had to wait for them to finish.

We waited as our location managers swore they would get even, our production managers saying the allocation department at Pinewood would answer for this in blood. At last I shouted my first 'Action!' as a director. After two galloping strides, John promptly fell off the horse. He got up, yelled he was sorry, mounted again and fell off again. He apologized, again, and admitted he said he could ride just to get the part. We got a double at the double, and started again. Although it seemed as if we would never catch up on the schedule the wily Wilbur had anticipated delays and put that into his planning.

There is an erotic scene where the actress Serena Weber imitates a tiger and her husband, Milovan, plays the trainer cracking a bull whip. It was the first time body-painted nudity had been filmed, the inspiration coming from the famous 1960s model, Veruschka, who posed in a similar way.

I found it a little disconcerting that Serena would remove all her clothes to rehearse. 'Why not,' she said. 'Why not indeed . . .' I replied.

Another first was using live bats and not models. The 'bat man' arrived at my flat with several bats which he let loose. He explained that all the bats were marked under their wings and must be returned to the same areas they had been taken from. The bats were a success and added to the atmosphere of the film. But the star bat was a magnificent fruit bat with a wingspan of over three feet.

He was large in every department and aptly named 'Balls'. His owner/handler would carry him inside her jacket with Balls hanging upside down from her neck like an exotic necklace. Every so often he would twist up and peer through the jacket opening to check what was going on. Satisfied, he would settle back into his handler's jacket. In a scene where the stake had pierced Count Mitterhaus' chest he was persuaded to fly and cling to the stake. Balls stayed long enough for the shot and then, as if on command, flew off in my direction and settled round my neck. I was ridiculously pleased. I have been fond of bats ever since and have no fear of them. It is, of course, the fear people have of bats that protects them.

The Hall of Mirrors was a feature in the film. All the mirror scenes were done in camera and no CGI was involved. Many hours were taken planning those shots and they worked.

I admired many of the actors and actresses that I worked with in the film, and it was such a fun part of film making to get to meet them. Adrienne Corri, Laurence Payne, Elizabeth Seal, Thorley Walters, Anthony Corlan and newcomer Lynne Frederick were all delightful and a dream to work with.

I auditioned David Essex for the vampire Count. He was magnificent and I remember how bright and blue his eyes were. His charisma came right through the lens and onto the screen. I told him he would be a star one day but he was not right for the vampire role. He thought I was trying to let him down lightly but I meant it. And he did become a star. Another lad I turned down was Robert Fox. He went on to become one of our most successful theatre producers.

Vampires do not like the cross or signs of the cross. Imagine the disquiet I had when I walked into the beautifully built church set to find the walls decorated with small crosses. This was going to be the location of the execution of the vampire who would not be seen dead in such a place. 'Don't worry,' said the designer, 'no one will notice.' And so far as I know no one has.

The most fun part of a movie is the music. Where it sits in the movie and what the music contains. Most of the Hammer films' music was organized by Philip Martell, and he suggested composers who scored under his aegis. At one stage, as Philip was conducting the huge orchestra to the image on the screen in front of him, he stopped the orchestra with a loud bellow and put down his baton. 'What is "God Save The Queen" doing in this score?' he asked David Whitaker, the composer. 'Bit of a joke,' said David, 'I thought it was covered with enough layers of counterpoint to hide it. I just liked the idea.' 'Not in any music I'm involved in,' said Philip. 'Rewrite it and I want it finished by this afternoon to record.'

I had not noticed it at all but as I played and replayed the piece there it was and, once heard, sat on all the other melodies. By the evening the music had been re-written and re-recorded and the Queen's signature tune was erased from my movie.

Robert Young,
Director

Prologue

Ten Years Ago

Mitre House had stood for two hundred years and might stand for two hundred more. It perched atop the hill overlooking the newly built Shettle Estate like a panther poised to spring upon its prey. Seen from below, it seemed to deflect light, to draw shadow into its stonework and timbers, to wrap darkness around itself. Its windows, always shuttered, were like sightless eyes. And yet it seemed forever watchful.

In the valley below, on a road flanked by woodland on one side and farmers' fields on the other, a single-decker bus, painted maroon and silver, halted with a wheeze of brakes. Its doors concertinaed open and a gaggle of children wearing the blue and grey uniform of Wenthorpe Primary School spilled onto the sliver of pavement. Most of them turned left, heading back along the country road that would lead them to the south of the newly formed community, but two girls – Jenny Peterson and Lynette Michaels – waited for the bus to pull away in a splutter of dust and exhaust fumes before they crossed over and started along a lane that intersected the road at right angles.

Jenny, the taller of the two girls, was snub-nosed and freckle-faced, her straw-coloured hair woven into plaits. Her friend Lynn was dark-haired and dark-eyed, as pretty as Jenny in her own way, but more sombre and thoughtful, less prone to smiles and chatter. In a few more years Jenny would no doubt have been thought of as 'vivacious', whereas Lynette would be more likely to be described as 'sultry' or even 'mysterious'. For now, though, they were simply two nine-year-old girls, enjoying the autumn sunshine and each other's company.

Their friendship was still in its infancy. Lynn had moved to Shettle with her parents three months ago after her dad's successful application to become inaugural editor of *The Wenthorpe and Shettle Times*. It had been a gamble for him, moving from a city newspaper with a circulation of 50,000 to a local rag that was starting from scratch, but he had liked the challenge not only of being in charge of his own paper but of building something up from a grass-roots level. Jenny, whose parents had bought one of the brand-new retail units lining Shettle's modest High Street and had subsequently opened it as a soft-furnishings store, had moved to Shettle only a week before the start of the new school year. Both girls had found themselves thrown together in a strange new environment and so, seeking mutual comfort, they had automatically gravitated towards one another. Now, a month later, they were riding a little easier in the saddle but had remained firm friends. It helped that they lived only a few minutes' walk from one another to the north of Shettle, an area which contained wide leafy streets and the majority of the community's larger, more expensive properties.

'Do you think it really *is* haunted?' Jenny said, nodding at the house on top of the hill, which loomed over the valley.

Lynn wrinkled her nose. 'Course not. I don't believe in ghosts.'

'I bet you wouldn't dare spend the night there, though,' Jenny said, a smile playing around her lips.

Lynn shrugged. 'Wouldn't bother me.'

'Yeah, right.'

'It wouldn't,' Lynn insisted calmly.

'Who do you think lives there?' Jenny asked.

'I don't know. Maybe nobody.'

'We ought to go up there one day to explore.'

'Why?'

Jenny rolled her eyes. 'Because it'd be fun. Exciting. Maybe a gang of psychos live there, and they chop off people's heads if they get too close and put them on spikes to warn others to stay away.'

'I doubt that,' said Lynn, deadpan. 'If they did, I think the police would know about it.'

'Oh, you're no fun,' said Jenny, pouting. But she grinned to show she didn't mean it.

The lane up which the girls were walking was flanked by drystone walls, beyond which were farmers' fields. Another half-mile's walk would bring them to a T-junction, at which they would turn right onto a road that ran downhill to Shettle itself. The track was barely wide enough for a single vehicle so both girls were surprised to hear the sound of an approaching engine. They turned, saw pale sunlight glinting off the green bodywork of a sporty-looking car and moved across to the grass verge. However, it wasn't until the car had halved the distance from the main road to where they stood that they recognised the driver.

'That's Mrs Miller,' said Jenny, shielding her eyes.

Mrs Miller was a teacher at their school, as was her husband.

Lynn pulled a face. 'I don't like her much.'

'Why not?' said Jenny, surprised. 'She's all right. I think she's pretty.'

'Yes, but she looks at you funny. She sort of stares. Haven't you noticed? It gives me the creeps.'

Jenny gave a dismissive frown and shook her head. 'You're just weird.'

'*She*'s the weird one, not me,' Lynn said, her voice tailing off as the car came to a halt beside them.

The passenger window lowered with a hum. Mrs Miller was a thin-faced, chestnut-haired woman, and Lynn would probably have liked her if it wasn't for the way she stared around the class when she thought no one was watching, like a cat trying to decide which little chick to gobble up first. Now her pale blue eyes were hidden behind square black shades, which gave her the look of a movie star from an old film.

'Hello, girls,' she said. 'On your way home?'

'Yes, miss,' said Jenny.

'Want a lift?'

'No, that's all right, miss,' said Lynn quickly before Jenny could reply. 'It's not far.'

'Far enough,' said Mrs Miller, glancing along the road. 'Come on, hop in.'

Lynn hung back, but Jenny stepped forward. 'Okay,' she said brightly. 'Thanks, Mrs Miller.'

Lynn felt a moment of dismay she couldn't quite explain as her friend settled herself into the passenger seat of the car and clicked her seat belt into place.

'Come along, Lynette, jump in the back,' Mrs Miller said.

Openly disobeying a teacher's instructions went against Lynn's every instinct, but she found herself backing away from the car, shaking her head.

'N-no, thanks,' she stammered. 'I think I'll walk. I like walking.'

Mrs Miller, half-leaning across Jenny's body, stared at Lynn for several seconds, her mouth set in a terse line. With her dark glasses her face looked like a hovering skull above Jenny's shoulder. Quietly the teacher said, 'I don't think that's a good idea. Do you?'

Unable to speak, Lynn could only shrug.

'I mean,' Mrs Miller continued, 'you *have* heard that several children have gone missing in the area recently?'

Lynn nodded. Of course she had heard. It was the biggest story that her dad's fledgling newspaper had thus far tackled. In the space of just under four months, eleven children, ranging in age from four to thirteen, had disappeared within an area of roughly twenty square miles. Seven of the children had disappeared in broad daylight – either walking to or from school, or out playing with friends – and four had seemingly been snatched from their beds in the dead of night. Despite an extensive inquiry, the police still had no leads and a search of the surrounding district had yielded nothing of value. It was as if the victims had vanished from the face of the Earth – which was why schools and local authorities were currently advising children not to be outside on their own, no matter how close to home they were, at any time of the day or night.

Logically, therefore, Lynn knew she was being foolish by declining her teacher's offer – and yet every instinct screamed at her not to get in the car. She wished she could transmit her feelings to Jenny, but how could she without looking foolish and offending Mrs Miller?

'Well, then,' Mrs Miller said reasonably in response to Lynn's nod, 'there's really no argument, is there? Come on, in you get.'

Although Lynn felt horribly conflicted, she knew there was *no way* she was getting in the car, and that nothing – no amount of persuasion or coercion – would change her mind.

'It's okay,' she said in a voice that she was surprised to find didn't tremble as much as she was quivering inside, 'I'll walk. I'll be fine.'

'You *won't* be fine,' Mrs Miller all but hissed. 'Get in.'

Lynn shook her head. 'I'm not allowed. My mum and dad told me not to accept lifts from strangers.'

'I'm not a stranger, you silly child,' Mrs Miller said coldly. 'I'm a teacher. You *know* me.'

Lynn put her hand into her school bag. 'I'd still better call my mum first,' she said. 'I'll ask her if it's okay for you to bring me home. I'll tell her I'll be there in ten minutes.'

A strange look crossed Mrs Miller's face. Although Lynn couldn't see her eyes, the teacher suddenly looked not just furious but somehow *trapped*. Curling her lip, she all but snarled, 'Oh, don't bother. If you're going to be silly, then forget it.'

Mrs Miller lunged across Jenny, and at first Lynn thought she was about to make a grab for her. But instead she simply grasped the top of the opened window and yanked the passenger door shut. A second later the engine revved and the car tore away in a cloud of dust, spraying Lynn's shoes with gravel.

Feeling sick, shaking all over, Lynn watched the car fade into the distance. She was grateful that Mrs Miller hadn't called her phone-call bluff. Her mum had told her that she wouldn't be allowed her own mobile until her twelfth birthday. Lynn was grateful, too – and somewhat surprised – that Jenny hadn't said anything. But maybe her friend had picked up on how strongly she was feeling about not accepting a lift and hadn't wanted to undermine her.

Thinking of Jenny gave Lynn a pang of anxiety; she hoped her friend would be all right. No reason why she shouldn't be, of course – and indeed later, when Lynn was at home, she hoped she would be able to look back on this and wonder why she had had such an extreme reaction to what would probably (no, almost *certainly*) turn out to be nothing but an innocent, even generous offer on their teacher's part.

Sighing, Lynn repositioned her school bag on her shoulder and set off along the lane again, trudging in the wake of the green car. She had gone no more than thirty or forty metres when she heard another engine approaching from behind her, and stepped off the hard-packed ground again and onto the grass verge.

This car was a Cavalier, like the one her dad drove, but dark blue or perhaps black. As it drew level with her, it slowed down and the driver turned his head towards her. From what Lynn could see he was sandy-haired with a long, sallow face, and like Mrs Miller he was wearing shades, which gave the impression that his gaze was blank but somehow penetrating. Lynn shivered, and for a split second wondered whether she had made the wrong decision by not accepting a lift after all.

But then, with a growl, the slowing car picked up speed once more. The driver turned his head to face forward again and the Cavalier sped away on a cushion of billowing dust.

Chris Blaine put his foot down, eager not to lose sight of Anna Miller's leaf-green MX-5. The woman stopping to pick up the schoolgirl was a puzzling development. He had slowed down next to the blonde girl's friend to ask her what the deal was, but the poor mite had looked so nervous that he had decided against it. The last thing he wanted – especially in light of all these kids going missing in the area – was to frighten the girl to death. Besides, he could probably work it out for himself. Anna Miller was a teacher at Wenthorpe, and the girls had both been wearing the school uniform, which meant that they were probably pupils of hers. Maybe, therefore, the blonde girl lived somewhere en route to Anna's destination . . . wherever that might be.

If her husband's suspicions were anything to go by, it would be a meeting with her lover. Nick Miller was convinced that his wife was having an affair and had employed Chris to either confirm or disprove his suspicions. As Chris was fond of telling his own wife, Caroline, 'It's a dirty job, but someone's gotta do it.' Besides, the money was good and although the news he delivered was not always welcomed by his clients it was Chris's belief that it was better to know than to stay ignorant.

He followed Anna Miller's car as it climbed towards the junction at the end of Hobbes' Lane. He fully expected her to take a right there towards Shettle, but she surprised him by turning left. He tracked her at a discreet distance, wondering where she was leading him – and wondering too what her intentions were towards the young girl she had picked up.

The road wound upwards between thick, high hedges and densely packed rows of gnarled and twisted trees. The uppermost branches of the trees formed an arthritically skeletal arch overhead, from which brown and yellow leaves drifted down, forming a loose covering on the ground. Bleak autumn sunlight flickered between the branches, dappling the Cavalier's windscreen. And then, quite suddenly, the trees retreated and the road levelled out, and on his right Chris saw the valley falling away below. Directly beneath him was Hobbes' Meadow and the toytown jumble of Shettle bisected by Hobbes' Lane. He was disorientated at first and then he realised that the road, as it had climbed, had brought him round in a loop. Which must mean that coming up on his left . . .

Yes. Here were the black iron gates of Mitre House. They were standing open like an invitation. Chris was about to drive straight past, unable to suppress a shudder, when a glint of metallic green snagged the edge of his vision. Turning his head, he was just in time to see the back of Anna Miller's car disappearing around a corner of the twisting, weed-choked drive. He brought his own car to a halt, then reversed into a lay-by opposite the gates and cut the engine.

He had a crawling feeling in his gut, a sense that something was very wrong here. Why would Anna Miller bring one of her young pupils to a seemingly abandoned house? He hesitated for a moment, then took out his mobile and thumbed in Nick Miller's number.

'I want to go home.'

Jenny was on the verge of tears. She glanced fearfully at the straggly trees at the edge of the forecourt. They screened the leering, blind visage of Mitre House from the road. Her arms were tightly folded and her knees drawn up, as if she was trying to make herself as small as possible. Beside her, Mrs Miller leaned back and smiled.

'And you *will* go home. I promise. I just thought you might like an adventure first.'

Jenny looked uncertain. 'What kind of adventure?'

'It's always better to show than tell. Come and see.'

Mrs Miller opened the car door and stepped out, allowing something else to curl in to take her place. It was an odour of dampness and decay, of loneliness and neglect, which seemed to reach out from the scabrous building a dozen metres away. Like a clammy hand it probed at Jenny's bare legs and exposed face. She shivered.

'I don't want to see. I want to go home.'

Mrs Miller laughed, a high, tinkly sound, which in the suddenly dank air sounded a little too shrill. 'You sound like your dreary friend. I thought you had more about you than that.'

'*Please* take me home,' Jenny pleaded.

'All in good time.'

Mrs Miller walked away from the car, towards the imposing front door of the house. It was an oak door, sturdy but pitted, with elaborate hinges that curled across the wood like black iron tentacles.

'*Please*, miss,' Jenny shouted again.

'Don't be a crybaby,' Mrs Miller called back over her shoulder.

Jenny watched as the teacher took an iron key from her pocket and pushed it into a huge lock beneath the handle. The key turned with a grinding click and the door yawned open. Mrs Miller looked back once and gave Jenny a mocking smile. Then she went inside.

Alone, Jenny sat in the car and stared at the front door, which her teacher had left ajar. Her eye was drawn to the band of darkness between door and frame. She gazed at it so intently, willing her teacher to emerge, that after a while she began to imagine that the darkness was writhing, twisting, like a bulging mass of black snakes. She blinked, looked away, and suddenly realised that a little of the autumn daylight had seeped from the sky. She wondered what time it was, whether her parents would be getting worried, whether Lynn was at home now. She wished *she* was at home, watching TV with a glass of milk and a biscuit, or lying on her bed listening to music on her headphones. Would she tell her parents where she'd been if they asked? She imagined her dad getting angry, stomping up to the school to complain, making a scene. She'd be embarrassed, but right now she didn't care; she just wanted to see her parents again, wanted it more than anything. She jumped and turned as something moved at the edge of her vision. But it was only the trees, nodding in the breeze like hunched old men.

How long would it take to walk home from here? An hour? Maybe two? Jenny decided to count up to a hundred, to give Mrs Miller until then to come out of the house. She started, slowly at first and then gradually speeding up, as it suddenly occurred to her that in less than an hour it would be dark.

'. . . a hundred,' she said, breathless, and opened the car door. Though she felt vulnerable without the metal shell of the vehicle to protect her, she planted her feet on the gravel and stood up. She gritted her teeth as the small stones shifted with a crunch beneath her. Glancing over her shoulder, half-expecting something fearful to peel from the band of darkness between door and frame and come shrieking and flapping towards her, she began to walk away from the house.

As she approached the skeletal trees that lined the curving drive the wind gusted again, causing the topmost branches to scrape against one another. Jenny glanced up to see shards of failing daylight trapped like pale and distorted kites. She saw something else, too; something black crouched within the lattice of branches. It was the size of her head, and roughly spherical. She halted for a moment as she gazed up at it. What was it? A hive? A nest? The light was getting too dim for her to be able to tell.

She took a deep breath and began walking again, the trees appearing to reach out with spindly arms as she neared them. Passing beneath the tree which contained the spherical black shape, she heard rustling above her. Her head snapped up.

As if alerted to her presence the shape was moving, stirring, shifting from side to side. As Jenny watched, saucer-eyed, she saw it unfurl, saw it stretch out leathery membranous wings.

It was a bat. But it was not a normal bat, the kind that could comfortably sit curled in the palm of an adult's hand like a winged mouse. No, this bat was *huge*, its brown-furred body the size of a large cat's, its outstretched wings as long as Jenny's own arms. Its eyes shone red, reflecting the setting sun, in its hideous wrinkled walnut of a face. It opened its mouth wide and let loose a raucous squeal, exposing a jutting jaw packed with rows of needle-sharp teeth.

Jenny screamed and ran, outstretched branches scratching her arms and snagging at her hair. Behind her she heard a series of ponderous cracks, like heavy wet sheets snapping in the wind, and the next moment something large and black wheeled out of the darkness and swooped down at her.

Trying to duck, Jenny succeeded only in slipping on

the wet leaves scattered across the gravel drive and falling headlong. She landed on her front, skinning her knees and the palms of her hands. Out of the corner of her eye she saw the bat wheel in the sky like a pterodactyl, readying itself for a second attack. Amber light shone through the stretched membrane of its wings, exposing dark veins like cracks in smoky glass. Then it was swooping again, screeching as it came. Jenny pressed her face into the wet gravel, wrapping her arms around her head and drawing up her knees.

She whimpered as the clawed feet of the descending monster tugged and tore at the back of her school jumper. The instant it rose into the air again, climbing in order to circle round for a further attack, she was up and running, ignoring her stinging hands and bleeding knees, her legs pumping as fast as she could make them. However, she didn't run up the gravel drive towards the large iron gates several hundred metres away but back towards the closest shelter available to her – Mrs Miller's car. Behind her she heard the flapping of the bat's great wings fade as it gained height, curling away from her, and then grow louder again as it completed its parabola and targeted her for the third time.

She focused all her attention on the car, putting every last ounce of energy into reaching the vehicle before the bat reached her. Its attack cry behind her was terrifying, but she tried to put it out of her head and not let it distract her from her goal. The passenger door was still open. Jenny pistoned her arms and legs, her blonde hair flying behind her. She was twenty metres away . . . ten . . . the drawn-out screech of the bat filled her head like a pneumatic drill. A split second before she felt sure that the bat's claws would tear into her back, she dived forward.

She made it, her body sprawling across the car's front seats. She gasped as her bloodied knees scraped across leather and the gear stick punched into her like a fist, bruising her ribs. The jolts of pain, however, were nothing compared to the relief she felt. She was safe – for now, at least.

And then she screamed as she realised that this wasn't the case, after all.

She had assumed the bat would not follow her, that it would change direction, veer away, discouraged by the confined space of the car. But it swooped through the still-open door without a qualm, and suddenly Jenny was trapped with its shrieking, flapping presence, its clawed feet scrabbling at her, one of its wings scraping across the leather upholstery and the other stretching across the windscreen like a macabre sunshade.

Screaming in terror, frantic to escape, Jenny lunged across the front seats like a beached fish trying to propel itself across dry land. She kicked out in a vain attempt to defend herself and simultaneously stretched out an arm to claw at the door handle on the driver's side. Grasping the cold metal, she jerked at it until the door opened, and then scuttled forward and out, landing on the gravel below. Ignoring the sharp stones embedding themselves in her raw, bloodied knees, she scrambled into a kneeling position, twisted her upper body around and slammed the driver's door shut before the bat could squeeze out after her. She glimpsed the creature hurling itself furiously against the door and window, leaving smears of grease and spittle on the glass. Then she turned and ran shakily towards Mitre House, desperate to reach it before the bat realised that the door behind it was still open.

Gravel spraying up around her pounding feet, she crossed the distance between the car and Mitre House and plunged towards the band of blackness beyond the partly open door. For a split second she felt as though she was forcing her way through clammy black oil, and then she was inside and leaning her weight against the heavy door behind her. It swung closed slowly with a boom that echoed up through the gloomy interior. Panting and shaking, Jenny leaned against the door and looked around.

Mitre House had clearly once been grand and impressive but had now fallen to rack and ruin. Dust shimmered in the air; thick grey swathes of cobweb trembled in the corners of the high, sagging ceiling and hung in looping swags between the banister spindles of the expansive staircase. The walls were cracked like dry skin; in some places chunks of plaster had fallen off, exposing the wooden latticework beneath like brown, decaying ribs. As a result, the floor – many of its once-expensive tiles cracked or missing – was littered with rubble.

Overcome with reaction, Jenny began to sob. The tears ran down her face as her gasping breaths spiralled into the dusty air and were absorbed by the fabric of the house. Now that her adrenalin was ebbing, her hands, knees and ribs began to sting and throb. She wanted to go home. She wanted it more than she'd wanted anything in her life before. Surely Mrs Miller couldn't refuse to take her back now, not when she saw how hurt and upset she was?

Making an effort to swallow her tears, Jenny called her teacher's name. Her voice was weak, quickly smothered by the dank atmosphere. Taking a deep, shuddering breath she tried again. 'Mrs Miller? Where are you?'

'Here.' The reply was faint and muffled. It came from somewhere above her.

'Where?' Jenny shouted, but this time her enquiry was met only with silence.

She hesitated a moment, then pushed herself away from the door and started towards the stairs. Grit crunched beneath her feet. Shadows shifted around her, making her nervous. She reached the bottom of the wide staircase and looked up.

'Mrs Miller?' she called again.

Silence.

Jenny placed her foot on the bottom stair, wincing as her skinned knee took her weight. She hobbled halfway up the staircase. 'Mrs Miller?'

The silence was so profound she could only imagine that her teacher was crouched somewhere in hiding, holding her breath.

Licking her lips, which tasted of salt and dust, Jenny ascended the stairs to the first landing. She had an idea that if she made no sound, that if she moved slowly enough so that she barely even disturbed the air, then no harm could come to her. She looked up and down the length of the corridor, which stretched off into the gloom in both directions. She saw firmly closed doors, peeling walls, a gaping hole in the floor a few metres to her left. She could see daylight through the hole and shuddered at the thought of crashing through the ceiling of a ground-floor room, falling twenty feet or more to the floor below. If she broke her leg or spine here, who would help? The thought rose in her mind before she realised that, of course, Mrs Miller would help. Despite the silence, her teacher was still here somewhere and, whatever her motives for bringing Jenny to this place, the girl felt sure she wouldn't be abandoned.

Reluctant though she was to draw attention to herself, Jenny called her teacher's name again. Once more there was no reply, though this time she heard a brief scraping above her – like someone dragging their foot an inch or two along a gritty floor. Instinctively she looked up, as if in the hope that the ceiling would suddenly become transparent. 'Mrs Miller?' she called once more, but there were no further answering sounds.

Still limping, she ascended a second set of stairs to the landing above. It was darker up here, less light leaking in from outside, shadows clotting like black scum on the surface of a pond. The air was cloying, dank, as if the walls were bloated and mouldy with moisture. Maybe they were. Maybe rain had been leaking through the roof and seeping into the fabric of the building for years. She would have to watch her step, ensure that the floor was solid before putting her full weight on it. Jenny started along the landing, probing with her toes, her fingers trailing lightly along the wall as if she was blind and using it for guidance.

Because of the gloom, she didn't realise there was a right-angled bend in the corridor ahead until she was almost upon it. She turned the corner.

At first she thought she had seen a ghost, a flickering golden phantom at the far end of the corridor. But almost immediately she realised that it was the glow of a candle flame, visible through the crack of a partly open door. The light made the surrounding corridor look blacker than ever. Jenny moved cautiously towards it.

'Mrs Miller?' she said again, too nervous now to raise her voice above a murmur. 'Mrs Miller, are you there?'

She reached the door and slowly pushed it open. The room beyond was a bedroom, once opulent but now long fallen into decay. On the left-hand wall a vast fireplace with a black marble mantelpiece was choked with a rotting heap of leaves and twigs, which spilled over the hearth. Above the fireplace a portrait of a young man in a loose old-fashioned shirt with puffy sleeves and lace cuffs stared down at her.

The portrait made Jenny shiver. The young man was handsome, with flowing dark hair, but there was something unsettling about him. His skin was too pale, his lips too red. His dark, depthless eyes seemed to stare out hungrily from the wall and there was a cruel slant to his mouth.

Beyond the fireplace and the portrait, jutting from the opposite wall, was a four-poster bed. The velvet drapes hanging from it were now colourless, tattered and, like the rest of the fixtures and fittings, swathed in cobwebs. The fluttering yellow light was coming from a three-branched candelabrum perched atop a bedside cabinet. A trio of fat red candles drooled wax down the tarnished silver stem and on to the dust-coated surface of the cabinet.

The door continued to swing open, revealing the remainder of the room. But it wasn't until it had opened all the way, squeaking on rusty hinges, that Jenny saw Mrs Miller. The teacher was sitting in a high-backed armchair, an almost vulpine smile on her face. It wasn't this, though, that caused the girl to gape in amazement and consternation.

No. It was the fact that Mrs Miller was naked.

Jenny blushed, uncertain where to look. But mixed with her confusion and embarrassment was a crawling sense of dread. This was wrong – *deeply* wrong. There was something going on here that she was not aware of. She felt like the fly in that old rhyme, lured into the parlour by a fat black spider. For a moment she couldn't move, couldn't speak. She felt as if she was under some kind of spell.

'Hello, Jenny,' Mrs Miller said softly, as if there was nothing even remotely unusual about the situation. 'Won't you come in?'

'I . . . I . . .' Jenny wanted to ask what was going on, why her teacher was sitting there with no clothes on, but even now she felt too flustered to draw attention to the fact. 'I want to go home!' she managed to blurt. Her voice was wheedling, desperate. 'Mum and Dad will be worried.'

'Not yet they won't,' Mrs Miller said, and there was something about the way she said it that sent a spike of ice through Jenny's soul.

'They will,' Jenny whispered, backing away. 'Please take me home.'

She sensed, rather than saw or heard, a presence behind her. Spinning round, she was horrified to see a hunched, straggly-haired figure looming from the darkness. With a breathy scream she stumbled back into the bedroom, half-aware that Mrs Miller, naked in the throne-like chair, was giggling as if this was all such fun.

The hunched figure shuffled forward, shedding the shadows coiled around it. Candlelight played across its features, revealing the face of an old man, his sparse hair like wisps of white cobweb, his cement-grey skin raddled and flaking. Despite never having seen him before, Jenny couldn't help thinking that there was something familiar about him. Familiar and terrible.

Then she realised. The old man had the same cruel eyes and wolfish grin as the young man in the portrait. Although decades must have separated them, she felt certain that they were one and the same.

'Yes, that's me,' the old man confirmed as if reading her thoughts. His voice was a parched rasp; it made her think of a dusty sun-cracked desert strewn with bleached bones. As he shuffled closer, Jenny wrinkled her nose. He smelled not just unwashed but as though he was rotting from the inside out. 'What's your name, my dear?' he asked, his breath a belch of decay.

Though the old man terrified and revolted her, Jenny felt compelled to answer his question. His eyes mesmerised her. In the candlelight they seemed almost yellow, like a snake's, though shot through with iridescent flecks of colour – gold, amber, red.

'Jenny,' she murmured.

'Jenny.' He tasted the name, relished it. 'Pretty . . . pretty . . .' Turning to Mrs Miller he said, 'Thank you, my dear. You're far too good to me.'

'I'd do anything for you,' Mrs Miller purred. 'You know that.'

The old man smiled and, as his thin liver-coloured lips peeled back, Jenny gasped.

His teeth, slick with drool, were like bullets, each one tapering to a sharp point. Most prominent were his upper canines, which were long and curved like those of a wolf or a big cat. As the old man unsheathed them his yellow eyes began to blaze, and all at once Jenny found that, terrified though she was, she couldn't move a muscle.

'Pretty,' the old man muttered again. 'So, so pretty . . .'

Then, with a predatory snarl of triumph, he pounced.

'Where is she?'

Nick Miller was a nice guy, but Chris Blaine could tell he was on the edge. His fists were clenched, his thin, almost delicate face pinched and white and his eyes were wild behind his black-framed spectacles. Chris was not so hardened by his profession that he didn't feel sorry for him. Judging from the discreet enquiries he had made, up until a couple of months ago the Millers had been a devoted couple. Married with a seven-year-old daughter, Nick himself had told Chris that before Anna had started to 'go a bit weird' they had been talking of long-term plans – *life* plans.

22

Chris nodded at the open black gates. 'Still in there. But, like I said, she had a kid with her.'

'You're sure it was a child?' The question came from the man who had driven Nick here and was now crossing the road from the car he had parked on the verge just beyond the open gates. He was in his late thirties, tall and athletic-looking, with a neat beard and striking blue eyes under thick dark eyebrows. He looked *dependable*, thought Chris. He looked like someone you could rely on.

Chris nodded. 'A young girl. Maybe nine or ten years old. Wearing a school uniform.'

'You see?' the man said to Nick. 'This could all be perfectly innocent. Perhaps you're jumping to conclusions.'

Nick shook his head agitatedly. 'You haven't been living with her these past few months, John. You don't know how much she's *changed*.'

'But if she's got a child with her . . .'

'Why bring a child to an abandoned house?' Nick snapped, and then he looked confused, as if even *he* didn't know where that line of thought was leading.

Why indeed? Chris thought. He glanced at Nick's friend (John, Nick had called him) and saw by his troubled expression that he was wondering exactly the same thing.

Stepping forward, he stretched out a hand. 'Chris Blaine,' he said. 'I'm a private investigator.'

The bearded man took the proffered hand and shook it. His grip was every bit as dry and firm as Chris had expected it to be.

'Dr John Kersh,' he said. 'I'm a friend of Nick's. We were together when he received your call.'

'John insisted on driving me here,' Nick interjected, and then stretched his mouth in a ghastly grin that contained no humour. 'He thought I was incapable.'

'You were clearly anxious, Nick,' replied John Kersh calmly. 'You still are.'

'I just want to know what Anna's up to, why she's behaving like she is. Look, can we go up to the house now? We're wasting time here.'

Nick marched back to his friend's car. John raised his eyebrows at Chris. 'You'll follow us up?'

'If you want me there.'

John hesitated a moment and then said, 'It might be best. An impartial observer, as it were. That's if you don't mind?'

It wasn't within his remit to accompany the two men, but Chris was curious in spite of himself, not to mention being concerned about the young girl. 'Not at all,' he said.

John climbed into his car, backed it out into the road and swung in through the open gates of Mitre House. Chris followed a few metres behind. A minute later both cars were pulling up beside Anna Miller's MX-5.

The instant John cut the engine, Nick jumped out of the car, gave his wife's car an anguished look, as if seeing it was somehow proof of the indiscretion he had suspected, and approached the house at a stumbling run.

'For God's sake, Nick, wait,' John called, scrambling out of the driver's seat and going after him.

Not wishing to be left behind, Chris too jumped out

of his car. As he slammed the door and locked it with a quick jab of his key fob, he wondered briefly why Anna Miller had left the driver's door of her car open. Then he hurried across the gravel forecourt after the two men.

John caught up with his friend as Nick was hauling open the heavy front door of the house. He gripped his arm above the elbow with a large hand. 'I know how wound up you are, Nick,' he said, 'but I advise caution. There's nothing to be gained from going at this like a bull in a china shop.'

Nick glared at him a moment – then he relented and nodded. 'Okay.'

'So we do this quietly and methodically,' said John. 'If Anna *is* up to something – and I'm not suggesting for a moment that she is – then it would be better to surprise her, to catch her in the act as it were, rather than alert her to our presence.'

Nick nodded again and allowed John to take the lead. The taller man pushed the front door open cautiously and peered around the widening gap before stepping inside.

'All quiet,' he whispered, looking around. 'Clearly this place hasn't been occupied for a long time.'

As if to refute his words, there suddenly came a shriek from above.

All three of them froze, wondering what terrible things were happening above their heads. Then the shriek dissolved into a fit of giggling laughter. Outraged and miserable, Nick cried, 'That's Anna! That's my wife!'

'Nick—' John warned, but this time to no avail. Like a dog sighting a rabbit, Nick ran for the stairs.

John rolled his eyes and went after him, with Chris bringing up the rear. Overhead, seemingly oblivious to their approach, the shrieking and giggling continued. It was not difficult in the otherwise silent house to track the sound to its source.

The house was not just silent, however, it was also dark – and getting darker by the minute. By the time Chris arrived, panting, on the second-floor landing, having raced up two flights of stairs, he could see so little ahead of him that he was having to trust to luck that he wouldn't put his foot through a hole in the floor. He cursed himself for not grabbing the torch out of his car's glove compartment before following John and Nick. What kind of investigator *was* he?

The two men ahead were now little more than moving shadows. Chris was almost relieved when he finally turned a corner and saw that the corridor in front of him was dimly lit by flickering candlelight seeping through a half-open door at the far end. Nick had already reached the door and was pulling it open. His black silhouette sharpened as more of the yellow light outlined it. Then he went inside, followed by John.

In the few seconds it took Chris to join his companions he became aware of the atmosphere inside the room abruptly changing. The giggling shrieks became angry cries; Nick let loose a strangled howl; even the previously calm and composed John Kersh shouted 'My God!' in a voice that was raw with horror and repugnance.

When Chris entered the room the reason for their reaction immediately became clear. The sight facing him was so terrible that it was like being punched in the stomach. The body of the young blonde girl whom Anna Miller had picked up in her car earlier was lying like a broken doll in the centre of the room, still in her school uniform. She had been viciously attacked, her throat torn open with such savagery that her head had been all but ripped from her shoulders. She was awash with her own blood – it was matted in her hair, trickling from her gaping mouth, pooled in her sightless eyes. Her clothes were slick with it, her pale face and sprawled limbs painted with thick red streaks and spatters.

But in some ways even *more* horrifying than the sight of the butchered girl were the actions and attitude of the couple on the bed. Despite – or perhaps because of – the presence of the mutilated corpse, they had clearly been rutting furiously, their naked bodies and the bedclothes beneath them smeared copiously with the girl's blood. The lower half of the young man's face was like a red mask that had dribbled into the sparse, wiry hairs on his muscular chest. The truth was so awful that Chris didn't realise the implication of this at first – and then it came to him in a rush. Evidently the man had killed the girl by tearing her throat out with his teeth.

Horror and outrage overwhelmed him – and his companions, too. As Nick ran forward with an anguished, almost inhuman screech, the man sprang up onto all fours like an animal and bared his teeth.

Chris stumbled back against the wall, his legs and

guts turning to water. The man's teeth were long and pointed, and the look of fury on his face was bestial, almost demonic. As Nick, blinded by rage and jealousy, rushed at him, the man leaped forward with terrifying speed. With an almost casual sweep of his arm he smashed Nick aside. Chris watched in horrified disbelief as his slightly built companion flew through the air as if he'd been struck by a car and crashed into a throne-like chair opposite the fireplace with enough force to shatter it into pieces. As Nick lay among the debris, groaning, John stepped forward as if to take his place.

Physically he looked more of a match for the blood-smeared child-killer, but the man dodged his first attempted punch easily and then shot out a hand, clamping it around John's throat. Temporarily frozen by the violence, Chris could only watch as the man lifted John into the air as if he weighed no more than a kitten. Sliding from the bed with the litheness of a snake, the man padded across the floor, leaving a trail of bloody footprints behind him, and slammed John up against the wall.

John, his face turning blue, scrabbled at the hand that was throttling him. Realising that if he didn't do some-thing he would witness the doctor being strangled to death, Chris forced himself into action. Glancing at the naked Anna Miller, who was perched on the bed, watching proceedings with a rapt and lascivious expres-sion, he ran across to the bedside cabinet and snatched up the candelabrum. Flames danced and jerked as he swung round with it, turning the room into a kaleido-scopic whirl of swooping light and leaping shadows.

Not entirely sure what he was doing, he leaped forward, jabbing the candelabrum towards the child-killer's naked back like a three-pronged rapier. The flames sizzled against the man's skin, but he barely even flinched. Still holding John – whose feet were now beginning to kick frantically – he turned his head and hissed at Chris. Then he swung his free arm in an arc, smashing the private investigator against the marble mantelpiece.

Chris felt as if he'd been struck by lightning. One second he was sailing through the air, still clutching the candelabrum, the next he was slamming into a hard surface, pain exploding in his shoulder and hip. The candelabrum flew from his hand and he crashed to the floor, landing in a mound of soot-blackened twigs and ancient birds' nests. Dazed, he looked up and, in the flicker of the single candle that was still burning, he saw the child-killer, clothed and unbloodied now, leering down at him – before realising that it was only a portrait.

Then he sensed movement at the periphery of his vision and turned his head groggily to see someone else enter the room. This new arrival was a portly man with a florid complexion, dressed in a baggy brown suit. He halted briefly in the doorway, eyes wide as he peered around. He was clearly shocked by the carnage before him, but to his credit he didn't allow it to faze him for more than a second or two. Side-stepping the girl's corpse, he hurried across the room and snatched up a metre-long spar of splintered wood from the chair that Nick had crashed into. Hefting it in his hand, he crossed to where the naked man was still squeezing the life out of John, swung the spar over his head and brought it crashing down on the child-killer's skull.

Chris winced, knowing that if *he* had been on the receiving end of that blow he would have been unconscious by now. However, although the murderer's head jerked forward, the attack seemed only to enrage him. Dropping John, who slid to the floor like a rag doll, his throat livid with bruises, he spun round on the balls of his feet, snarling and hissing. Fixing his stare on the portly man, he pounced like a tiger, arms outstretched, fingers hooked into talons. More through instinct than design, his opponent stepped back, thrusting the length of wood defensively out in front of him.

Unable to halt his forward momentum, the child-killer promptly impaled himself upon it. The sharp, splintered end of the metre-long spike slid through the flesh, muscle and bone of his chest as if it were putty. Surprisingly dark and foul-smelling blood gushed from the wound. The still-advancing weight of the killer caused the portly man to stagger back against the bed, still gripping the spar grimly. As he fell its other tip lodged against the floor, forcing the business end yet deeper into the child-killer's body. So *much* deeper, in fact, that it erupted from his back in a gout of blackish blood. As the portly man went down in a heap, the murderer, leaking blood onto his suit, collapsed on top of him.

Watching all this through a dream-like haze, Chris suddenly became aware of heat, accompanied by an angry crackling sound, washing over his back. Twisting his head he saw that the flame from the sole candle which had remained alight when he had dropped the candelabrum had spread, first to the threadbare carpet and then to the wallpaper above. The fire, unchecked, had now become so intense that it was already uncontrollable. It was climbing the wall and licking at the bedside cabinet, which was blackening and blistering in the heat.

Scrambling to his feet, Chris staggered over to John. The doctor's badly bruised throat was starting to swell, but he was alive, gulping down thick, guttural breaths, his eyelids flickering as he slowly regained consciousness. Though Chris was worried that the man might have been deprived of oxygen long enough to suffer brain damage, he knew that if the four of them – five, with Anna – didn't get out of the house within the next few minutes, that concern would rapidly become a moot point.

Leaving John for the moment, Chris turned his attention to the portly man. He was attempting to crawl out from beneath the body of the child-killer, and Chris hurried forward to help, grabbing the naked man by the shoulder and hauling him onto his back. As he did so, he was repulsed to find that the murderer's body was decomposing – or at least ageing – beneath his touch, the skin drying out, losing its lustre.

'Thank you,' gasped the man he'd helped, his chest and stomach glistening with the killer's blood.

'Thank *you*,' replied Chris, grasping the man's hand and hauling him to his feet. He jerked his head towards John, who was still slumped against the wall. 'I don't know who you are, but, if it wasn't for you, he'd be dead.'

All at once there was a screech from the bed and Anna hurled herself at the portly man. Though small and naked, she was like a wildcat, hissing and clawing and scratching. She raked her nails across the man's cheek, opening three parallel stripes of blood before anyone could react.

'You killed him!' she screamed. 'You took him from me!'

As the portly man staggered back, Nick seemed to appear out of nowhere. He stepped between Anna and the man and slapped his wife across the face hard enough to jerk her entire body sideways. Even before the startlingly loud crack of flesh on flesh had subsided, Nick was hurling an armful of bloodstained clothes at his wife.

'Get dressed!' he roared, his face like thunder.

She spun to face him, the handprint on her cheek red and blazing. 'You're not my master,' she sneered. 'You're nothing to me.'

Chris could see that this hurt Nick far more than if Anna had slapped him back. But in a low voice he repeated, 'Get dressed, or I swear I'll kill you.'

Meanwhile the portly man, one hand still pressed to his own wounded cheek, had stepped forward again. 'Oh my God,' he breathed.

Chris followed his gaze. He was shocked to see that the young man, the child-killer, was now young no more. Impossibly, he had aged so much and so swiftly that he was now all sags and wrinkles and grey parchment-like flesh. His thick dark hair had thinned to a few white wisps that clung to his mottled skull. But his poison-yellow eyes were still blazing, full of hate.

'Your community will die,' he hissed. 'Your children will die . . . to give me back my life.'

Then his head fell back, his muscles relaxed and the sickly yellow light went out of his eyes.

'We need to go,' said Cluis. He placed a hand on the portly man's arm and gestured towards John. 'Will you help me with him?'

'Of course.' The two men moved across to the semi-conscious doctor.

Anna had made no attempt to get dressed as her husband had ordered. Instead she was kneeling on the bed and rocking back and forth on her heels, keening like an animal as she grieved for her dead lover. Her blood-smeared skin glowed in the light from the blaze, which was now burning furiously, rolling along the ceiling, giving off dark billows of smoke.

Grabbing her wrist, Nick yanked her from the bed. 'Come with me,' he said.

Abruptly she began to screech and spit and claw again. 'No!' she screamed. 'I won't leave him!'

'If you stay you'll die,' he snapped.

'Let me die, then. I *want* to die. My life is nothing without him.'

Ignoring her, defending himself as best he could against her kicks and slashing nails, Nick dragged his wife from the room. He hauled her down the stairs too, in the wake of the two men who were carrying John, her naked body bumping down the steps as the fight went out of her and she went limp.

By the time the five of them made it out onto the forecourt, coughing and spluttering, thick black columns of smoke were rising from the upper windows of the house. As Chris and the portly man laid John across the back seat of Chris's car, Nick dragged Anna towards John's car, his wife unprotesting as her legs and buttocks scraped across sharp gravel.

'Stand up,' Nick ordered, and was surprised when she obeyed meekly. Looking over at Chris, he called, 'Could you look in John's pockets for his car keys? I'll drive—'

And that was when Anna attacked him.

Catching him unawares, she wrenched her arm from his grip and slashed at his face with her free hand. He ducked, though her trailing fingernails raked across his face, dislodging his spectacles. Off balance, he staggered against John's car, which allowed Anna to turn and run back towards the now-blazing building. By the time Nick had recovered enough to go after her she was slipping in through the open front door.

'Anna!' he yelled. '*Anna!*' He ran across the forecourt in pursuit but was only halfway there when he was intercepted by Chris and the portly man. They grabbed and clung to his arms, forcing him to a standstill.

'Let go!' he yelled furiously. 'Anna's in there!'

'If we do you'll both die!' shouted Chris. 'It's too late, Nick!'

As if to confirm his words, there was an ominous rumble, like an approaching earthquake, and seconds later the roof collapsed inwards with an almighty crash, spewing out ash and smoke and debris. As roaring flames leaped triumphantly into the air, Chris and his colleague dragged Nick away from the burning house. Nick screamed his wife's name over and over, but he knew it was no use; she was gone. Overcome by shock and grief and exhaustion, he couldn't help but think that the black, stinking flakes of ash spiralling down around him were the charred remains of his once-happy life.

One

Dr John Kersh closed the door on his last patient of the day, sank into the chair behind his desk and lowered his head into his hands.

He was exhausted. Not just physically, but mentally. At the very least he had always considered himself a competent doctor – sympathetic, knowledgeable, occasionally insightful – but just lately he had felt like a man floundering out of his depth. He was no closer to pinning down the cause of the strange malaise that was currently sweeping through Shettle than he had been several weeks ago when it had first reared its ugly head. He had prescribed all manner of treatments in an effort to find at least one that might make a difference, but if anything the demand for appointments was becoming greater with each passing day – and not only from patients newly struck down by the affliction but from those returning for a second or even third opinion.

Being a dedicated soul, John had been working increasingly longer hours in an effort to see as many of the patients demanding his attention as possible. But try as he might to meet the backlog, his surgery was always full. The main problem was that the damned illness was so hard to pin down. It took the form of an accumulation of symptoms rather than just one – symptoms which, taken in isolation, might ordinarily have been seen as entirely unrelated.

Headaches, digestive problems, chronic lethargy, depression, paranoia, nightmares . . . it was a cocktail of modern ailments, albeit one that was linked by a common theme. And that theme was the conviction, repeated time after time, by patient after patient, that something bad was coming; that a black cloud was sweeping across the community, dragging a terrible storm in its wake.

Collective hysteria or something more physical, like a virus or a chemical in the water supply? Blood and urine samples that John had sent away to be analysed had revealed nothing untoward. Yet there was *something* wrong, he knew it. And if he didn't identify it soon he couldn't help but feel that his reputation would be irreparably damaged. From the rumblings in the community it was already clear that those under his care were now beginning to lose faith in him.

If he hadn't known better John would have said that the *real* reason the people of Shettle were getting ill was because they were part of a community which itself was in a state of irreversible decline. A decade ago the place had been new and shiny and bright with promise, a rural idyll where people could live in peace and contentment, surrounded by fresh air and green fields.

But then something had happened, something to do with . . . with the house up on the hill, the one that wasn't there any more. John grasped at the memory, but it slithered away from him, leaving a lingering disquiet, a sense that he *ought* to be able to remember. All he could recall was that something bad had happened, something *terrible*, and that since then it had been as if the community was blighted, as if the poisonous energy of whatever awful deeds had been perpetrated there had been contained within the ash (because, yes, there *had* been ash, hadn't there? But why?) that had floated down like black snow.

Bad deeds. Ash. The house on the hill. John rubbed at his face, frustrated and alarmed by his inability to remember details. He told himself it was because he had been under a lot of strain recently, that due to his workload he hadn't been sleeping or eating properly. But deep down he sensed that it was more than that. He had the notion that whole chunks – *important* chunks – of his memory were simply missing. Oh, there was nothing that affected his ability to function as a doctor, nor even as a husband and father – he wasn't forgetting his wife's name or how to do his job – but something had been excised all the same. Something specific and vital and fundamental.

The most annoying thing was that he got flashes, tantalising glimpses, now and again. But like exotic fish rising briefly to the surface of a murky lake, they were fleeting, there one minute and gone the next. Take just now, for instance. What had he been thinking of? How Shettle had been affected by . . . by what? Something bad that had happened in the past. Something that had left its mark. Something to do with . . .

But no. It had gone again.

It was the glue between thoughts. The connections. That was what was wrong with him. His thoughts were not adhering to one another. But why? Was he ill? Suffering from some degenerative mental illness? But if so, why did it only affect *certain* memories? What illness was *so* selective?

Perhaps he had been brainwashed? Or hypnotised? Was that it? But, again, why? And how? And when?

John thumped the sides of his head in frustration. Oh, what was wrong with him? Was he suffering from the malaise too? He had certainly been having bad dreams lately. Dreams about . . .

About . . .

With a grunt of anger, he jerked his head from his hands and sat bolt upright. It was getting dark outside, shadows spreading like stains in the corners of his unlit consulting room. He stood up, shrugged on his jacket and stalked through the corridors of the surgery. It was a small practice, and everyone else – Drs Pope and McCardle, who were just as snowed under with patients as he was, and Janice on Reception – had gone home, leaving him to switch off the lights and lock up.

Driving through Shettle's streets, John tried not to look at how much the estate had sunk into disrepair and disrepute over the past decade. He tried not to look at the graffitied walls, the broken windows, the boarded-up shop units, the vandalised playground, the ragged scraps of litter clinging to fences and skulking in gutters. He tried not to stare at the hunched figures shuffling through the streets, at the blank-eyed faces that looked up briefly, turtle-like, to watch him drive past. He tried not to glance at anything until he was pulling into the driveway of his home.

Home. His sanctuary. His place of safety. He gazed up at the double-fronted, three-storeyed house enclosed by trees and high hedges and breathed a sigh of contentment and relief. Two minutes later he was closing the front door, shutting out the night.

'Hello?' he called.

'In here,' came the reply from the kitchen.

Lis, his wife, was sitting at the kitchen table, sipping a mug of tea and doing the crossword in *The Independent*. Her lips were pursed and her spectacles were perched on the end of her nose as she puzzled over a clue. Seeing her pushing back a strand of chestnut hair as it tumbled over her face, John felt a wave of love that was almost frightening in its intensity.

'Tea?' she said, glancing up.

He forced a smile. 'I'd prefer something stronger.'

'You all right, sweetheart?' Lis asked. 'You look as if you've swallowed a lemon.'

He smiled and lowered himself into the seat beside her. 'Hard day. This bloody virus, or whatever it is.'

'Doom-and-gloom merchants been getting to you again, have they? Well, never mind. There's a lamb casserole in the oven and a G&T on the way. You can relax and forget your woes until tomorrow.'

She got up to fix him a drink. As she chinked bottles and glasses, she said, 'See if you can get eight down. It's driving me up the wall.'

John smiled. He and Lis had met at college thirty

years ago. Now in her late forties she was still a fine-looking woman. She kept herself trim, even taught yoga twice a week at the local leisure centre. And she *glowed*. That was the thing about her, the thing that captured the eye and that people always commented on. She glowed with life and health and energy.

'I bloody love you,' he said as she carried his drink to the table.

Lis raised her eyebrows, her reading glasses still perched on the end of her nose. 'I should jolly well think so.'

He took the G&T from her and patted his thigh. 'Come here a minute.'

Her eyebrows raised another notch. 'Are you sure? I wouldn't want to rupture anything – of yours, I mean.'

John chuckled. 'You're as slim now as you were when I first met you.'

'Hmm,' she said, perching herself on his knee. 'If you think that, then you definitely *do* need to get your eyesight tested.'

'Not a bit of it,' he said. 'Twenty-twenty vision, me.'

Lis stroked his sideburns. 'Going a bit grey at the temples, though. Aside from that, you'll do.'

As he squeezed her, making her laugh, their son Anthony walked into the kitchen.

'Get a room, you two,' he said, rolling his eyes good-humouredly.

'You look nice,' said Lis. 'Going somewhere special?'

'I'm taking Kate out for a meal. We thought we'd try that new tapas place in Wenthorpe.'

'Special occasion?' asked John, winking at Lis.

Anthony, tall and athletic like his father, his blond

hair tousled just so, shrugged. 'Not really. Just fancied a night out, that's all.'

'So you're not thinking of, er . . .' there was a twinkle in John's eye '. . . popping a certain question?'

Anthony looked at him, aghast. 'Dad! Do I *look* like an idiot?'

'Oh, that's charming, that is,' Lis said. 'Kate's a lovely girl.'

'She is,' said Anthony. 'But she's seventeen and I'm twenty. It'll be a long time before we get hitched – if ever. What are you two *like*?'

John laughed. Then another of those fleeting memories flashed through his mind: Kate Miller's father, screaming and struggling as ash swirled around him. Suddenly sombre, he asked, 'How's Nick at the moment?'

'He's fine. Why?'

'I just thought . . . well, I haven't been in touch with him for a while.'

'You ought to give him a call, go out for a drink,' said Lis. 'It'll do you both good.'

John wasn't sure of that, but he nodded. 'Yes, maybe I will.' To Anthony he said, 'Give Nick my regards, won't you? Tell him . . . tell him I'll be in touch.'

'Will do,' said Anthony, and raised a hand. 'Right, I'll see you both later. Don't do anything I wouldn't do.'

'I'm not sure we'd be up to it even if we could,' said John.

'Speak for yourself,' Lis replied indignantly.

'Guys, *please*,' said Anthony, a pained look on his face.

As he left the room John called after him, 'Don't forget to tell Nick what I said.'

Two

Nick Miller couldn't stop thinking about the bottle of Bell's in his kitchen cupboard. He imagined the satisfyingly gritty sound of the cap being unscrewed; the oily swirl of the liquid, shimmering with amber light, splashing into a glass; the sweet, eye-watering sting at the back of his throat when he took his first swallow . . .

Most of all, he imagined the effect the whisky would have on him – the way it would numb his brain, take the edge off his fear that he was losing his mind. Ten years ago his wife Anna had died. He knew that. *Knew* it. And yet sometimes he forgot it. Sometimes he even forgot he had ever had a wife at all.

And that wasn't all that he'd been forgetting recently. Even on the occasions (like now) when he remembered not only that he had had a wife, but also that in three days' time it would be the tenth anniversary of her death, he still couldn't, for the life of him, remember *how* she had died. That particular memory was like a limb that had been amputated. It just wasn't there any more. And that was crazy. Crazy. How *could* he have forgotten?

He would have asked Kate about her mother's death if it wasn't for the fact that, oddly, when they were together it simply never crossed his mind. Although Kate was his and Anna's daughter, he never even gave Anna a thought when Kate was around.

Why was that? Was it self-denial or was it plainly and simply that he was going gaga, losing his marbles? If he didn't know any better he'd say that he was being *made* to forget, that his memories were being repressed in some way. But if so, by whom? The government? Aliens? The ghost of Elvis fucking Presley?

Although Nick couldn't remember *how* his wife had died, as he sat there brooding one fact about her did suddenly pop randomly into his head (a fact that he would no doubt forget again later), and that was that when she'd died there had been no body to grieve over. Her funeral had gone ahead with an empty coffin (why, he had no idea), and ever since then, aside from his beautiful Kate, seven at the time of Anna's death and seventeen now, his life had felt just as empty.

His reverie was interrupted by a pounding on his front door. Wondering briefly if it was Kate coming back early, and then immediately dismissing the notion (she simply wouldn't hammer on the door like that) he stepped into the hall.

'Hold your horses – I'm coming,' he called as the pounding came again. Through the half-moon of frosted glass at eye level he saw a hulking shadow and felt a shiver of apprehension. Then he took a deep breath, twisted the catch and pulled the door open.

The man on his doorstep was stocky and red-faced,

his stringy hair pulled back into a loose ponytail. He had a scar in the shape of a letter M across the bridge of his bulbous nose and a dark fuzz of stubble on his square chin. He was wearing greasy-looking jeans and a baggy tracksuit top, white with maroon stripes down the arms.

Ten metres behind him, hovering in the shadows, was a rangy man, a little younger, with a scarred, shaven head, holding a straining pit bull on a leash.

Before Nick could say anything, the stocky man jabbed a finger in the air, a few inches in front of Nick's chest.

'I want a fucking word with you,' he barked.

Nick instantly became aware of a fluttering pulse in his throat. 'Evidently,' he murmured.

'Why have you been picking on our Darren?' the man said.

Nick instantly made the connection. The man, presumably the boy's father, was referring to Darren Blackstock in Year 6, officially labelled a 'disruptive influence' on school reports and interdepartmental documents. An inveterate bully, Darren's extensive cata-logue of misdemeanours included pouring paint into a tank of tadpoles in the science lab, cutting off a sizeable chunk of a female classmate's hair, throwing a plate of baked beans at a dinner lady when she refused to give him more chips, and vandalising a teaching assistant's car after she had told him not to run in the corridor.

Trying not to let his voice betray his nervousness, Nick said, 'Now is not the time to discuss this, Mr Blackstock. If you would like to ring the school and make an appointment I'd be happy to—'

'Fuck that,' Blackstock interrupted. 'All you fucking need to know is that if you don't leave our Darren alone you're fucking dead.'

Though he was scared, Nick felt anger flare inside him. 'I don't take kindly to threats, Mr Blackstock,' he said curtly.

Blackstock's face crunched into an ugly mass of scowl lines. 'You think I give a shit? You've been fucking warned, cunt.'

Pit Bull Man's face, flooded with shadows in the dim light, was bisected by a cadaverously leering grin. Nick had the disconcerting impression that it was splitting in two.

'I don't have to listen to this and I won't,' Nick said, pushing the door closed. But Blackstock, having said his piece, was already turning away.

As the door shut with a click – a sound that Nick should have found reassuring, but instead made him think how flimsy the physical barriers which people constructed around themselves were – Blackstock said something to Pit Bull Man, who sniggered in a way that was more to do with spite than humour. The sound, even more than the encounter that had preceded it, depressed Nick more than he felt it ought to. As he walked back along the hall he clenched his fists, annoyed to discover how much he was shaking. Reaching the door to the sitting room, he abruptly changed direction and veered towards the kitchen. Fuck it, he *would* have that drink, after all. He bloody well *deserved* it.

Three

Chris Blaine didn't realise he'd been dreaming until he snapped awake, shaking and sweating. The instant he did so the dream dropped away, like a rock swallowed by a well. He was left only with a lingering feeling of dread, a sense of something imminent and inescapable. He was aware of movement beside him and then screwed up his eyes as they were abruptly flooded with light.

'What's happening? Are you all right?'

Caroline's voice was thick with sleep, her widely spaced chocolate-brown eyes blinking at him in alarm. Thick, glossy tresses of mahogany hair tumbled around her exquisitely boned face as she sat up.

Even now, at the age of forty-two and after seventeen years of marriage, her effortless beauty often took Chris's breath away. Though her modelling days were long past, she still scrupulously maintained the diet and exercise regime that she had followed since her teens. Though Chris was a little thicker around the middle than he had been in his twenties, he knew he would have run to seed long ago if it hadn't been for Caroline.

Staying in shape became progressively harder the older he got, but she was worth making the effort for. Not only was she the most beautiful woman he had ever met, she was also the sweetest and kindest.

Once the glare had faded from his vision, Chris glanced at the alarm clock on his bedside table and saw that it was 4:13 a.m.

'Chris,' Caroline prompted him, 'what's wrong?'

He became aware that beneath her voice was a sound – a tinkling, sinister sound.

'Shh,' he urged.

'What—' she began.

'Listen,' he said.

Surprised by his brusqueness she lapsed into silence. For several seconds the two of them sat motionless, heads cocked slightly as if that might enable them to hear better. Finally, tentatively, Caroline whispered, 'What am I supposed to be listening for?'

Chris frowned. 'I'm sure I heard music. Like fairground music. Didn't *you* hear it?'

She shook her head, her expression suggesting that she was sorry to disappoint him.

Before Chris could elaborate, the door to their bedroom opened and a figure lurched into the room.

For a split second Chris tensed, a bolt of fear shooting through him. The figure, momentarily in silhouette, was bulky, shaggy-haired, and his instant fleeting thought was that here, somehow, was a manifestation of his unremembered dream.

Then the figure took another step, yawning and blinking as light fell across it, and abruptly reality re-established itself, leaving Chris feeling both relieved and a little embarrassed at the wild vagaries of his imagination.

It was only Sam, their seventeen-year-old daughter, her corkscrew curls frizzy from sleep, the baggy knee-length T-shirt she slept in billowing around her. Tall, slim and almost as beautiful as her mother, she had looked bulkier than she was because her brothers, twelve-year-old Matt and fourteen-year-old Kieron, were flanking her like bedraggled, pyjama-clad courtiers.

Already pulling up her legs to create space for the children to sit down, Caroline said, 'What are you three doing up?'

'We heard a noise,' Matt said.

'We heard Dad shouting,' elaborated Kieron. He looked almost accusingly at his father. 'We thought you were being murdered.'

Chris glanced at Caroline, surprised and a little shamefaced. 'I wasn't shouting. Was I?'

She nodded. 'That was what woke me. You didn't give me a chance to say. Scared the life out of me.'

'Us too,' said Sam. 'What were you shouting about, Dad?'

'Not sure,' replied Chris. 'I was having a dream, I think. A nightmare. Sorry to wake you all up.'

Matt, his eyelids half-drooping as if he was still more asleep than awake, asked, 'What was the nightmare about?'

The question prompted Chris to try to remember. But it was as if a steel shutter had slammed down in his mind, as if the memory was too dreadful to recall. 'I don't know,' he said, trying not to sound as disturbed as he felt. 'As soon as I woke up it was gone.' To avoid the curious looks that his family were giving him he swung his legs out of bed and padded over to the window. He had no idea why but he had a sudden urge to look out into the night, to make sure there was nothing in the darkness, prowling around the house or staring back at him. As casually as he could he tugged one of the curtains aside and leaned forward, trying to penetrate with his stare the layer of seemingly almost solid darkness which was pressed against the other side of the glass.

He could make out thrashing movement, but it was only the tops of the wind-blown trees at the bottom of the garden.

'Wild out tonight,' he said.

Caroline shivered. 'Close the curtain and come back to bed.'

Chris was about to comply, but the sight of his washed-out reflection in the glass suddenly prompted another shard of memory from his dream. It wasn't an image, exactly, but more of an impression, a brief emotional flashback that seemed nevertheless to *form* an image. In his mind's eye he was face to face with himself – looking at his reflection in a mirror, perhaps? – and unable to move. Although he couldn't recall *why* he was unable to move, he had the overwhelming sense that he was rooted to the spot by sheer terror. He was sure that there was nothing behind him but vague and swirling darkness – and yet he was nonetheless gripped by the sudden, crushing certainty that there was *something* there. Something bleak and terrible. Something that was rushing out of the blackness towards him.

Four

'**D**ad?' The instant that the word was out of her mouth Lynn Michaels regretted speaking it aloud. Standing in the doorway of the conservatory, the coldness of the stone floor seeping through the bed socks she had pulled on over her bare feet, she wished she had found some other way to confirm the identify of the black hunched shape by the window. What if it *wasn't* Dad? What if it was . . . but that was when her thoughts became muddled, still half-tangled in the nightmare that had woken her. Of *course* it was Dad. It *had* to be. Things didn't come out of nightmares into the real world, did they? If this was the middle of the day and not the dead hours before dawn, she would realise how bloody daft that idea was.

Even so, she wished the black shape would say something. *In for a penny, in for a pound*, she thought, and took two further steps into the glass-enclosed room. Back when she'd been a girl, round about the time that . . . that her friend Jenny had died, the door she had just come through had led straight into the back garden.

The conservatory had been a later addition. Her parents had had it built the summer before Mum . . .

Her thoughts tailed off. Her recollection of the past had sparked a half-memory from her dream, an echo of the utter devastation she had experienced that night over six years ago. The guts had been torn out of her life back then, or so it had seemed at the time. If the emotions she had felt in her dream had been anything like as extreme as those, she was surprised she couldn't now recall any of the details. Of course, it could be that her mind was shielding her from the trauma of remembering, though she had never been unduly affected by her dreams before; had never felt anything other than a normal sense of relief when she had woken, even from the worst ones.

The black hunched shape a few metres away shifted position slightly, raising something to its face. Lynn's first thought was that it was feeding itself, but when the rounded end of the stubby limb made contact with the black blob of the head it created a brief flare of orange light, circular in shape but smaller than a penny. The orange glow lit up the plump contours of her dad's features, making what had initially seemed bizarre entirely mundane. Her dad was staring out of the window – or more likely into space – and smoking a cigarette. And the reason he hadn't looked round when she had called his name was because his ears were plugged by the small white buds of his iPod earphones. He was most likely listening to one of his beloved prog-rock bands: Can or Yes or Pink Floyd.

More relaxed now, Lynn shuffled into his line of sight,

waving slowly so as not to startle him. Despite her good intentions, the instant he caught sight of her he jerked in his seat, his head snapping round swiftly enough to make his jowls wobble.

'Sorry, Dad,' she muttered with a grimace of apology as he yanked out the earphones with a single tug.

'Lynn! You nearly gave me a heart attack! What are you doing up?'

'I might ask you the same question.' She crossed the floor and sat in the chair opposite him, bending her legs and tucking her cold feet underneath her.

'I couldn't sleep,' he said. 'Bad dreams.'

'Again?' said Lynn, concerned. 'What about, this time?'

His eyes, oily and yellow in the light from his cigarette, swivelled to stare at her. Looking at him, Lynn felt a pang of anxiety mixed with a protective love which had become more acute these past couple of years. Her dad had always been a big man – overweight and red-faced. As a hard-nosed news editor who liked a drink and smoked too much he was maybe a bit of a cliché, but he was still her *dad* and, cliché or not, he was a real person to her, with all the complexities and vulnerabilities that that involved. He had his bad points, yes – he could be brash, dismissive, occasionally insensitive – but they were far outweighed by his good points; traits that a lot of people never saw. He was loyal, and brave as a lion, and a big softy at heart. Lynn knew that he loved her to bits and would do anything to protect her, and she knew that he had loved Mum too, and that not a day had gone by in the past six years when he hadn't blamed himself for not being there to save her when she had needed him.

His gaze flickered away from hers, though whether that was because he was troubled or ashamed she couldn't tell.

'The usual,' he mumbled.

'Mum, you mean?'

He gave such a tiny nod that it might have been an involuntary twitch of the head. 'I've been thinking about her a lot lately. Or more specifically about *that* day.'

He didn't need to elaborate for Lynn to know which day he was referring to.

'Do you want to talk about it?'

'It's not something you'd want to hear.'

'I'm nineteen now, Dad. I'm a big girl. I'll never be a good journalist if you wrap me in cotton wool.'

'You're already a good journalist,' he said.

'Trainee,' Lynn reminded him.

He dismissed the word with a roll of his eyes. 'It's in your blood. I can tell.'

'Which is why I'm a nosy git.' She saw him smile and said softly, 'So talk to me. Share your burden.'

Her dad sighed and said, 'Just lately I've been finding it harder to repress the bad memories. It's as if . . . as if for years I've kept them locked in a box. But now the lock of the box has rusted off, allowing the memories to escape. I keep thinking about having to go and identify your mum's body, how awful that was. In my dreams I keep seeing her lying there, and the image is every bit as vivid and terrible as it was that day. It's like I'm being forced to relive it over and over again . . .'

His voice had become a rasp and now it faded altogether. He lifted his cigarette to his lips, and Lynn saw how much his hand was trembling. She could barely imagine how horrific it must have been, having to identify the broken body of the woman he loved.

Mum had been in her car, waiting at traffic lights, when the scaffolding encasing the building alongside where she had stopped had collapsed without warning, crushing her and the vehicle. She had died from multiple injuries. It had taken firemen almost three hours to free her body from the wreckage. There had been something else, a few years before that, which her dad had taken a while to get over (weird that she couldn't remember the details, especially as she had the feeling that she had been involved somehow). But when Mum had died it had reduced him – temporarily, at least – to a shell of the man he had once been.

That had been a terrifying time for Lynn. It had been bad enough losing her mum at the age of thirteen, but for a while she had thought she was about to lose her dad too, mentally at least. He had retreated into himself, became obsessed with the idea that Shettle was cursed in some way, that he was being punished for something.

Something to do with . . .

But again the memory slipped away from her.

Slowly, bit by bit, her dad had pulled himself together. He had a strong spirit, an indomitable spirit, and without recourse to medication or therapy, without even taking a break from his editorship of *The Wenthorpe and Shettle Times*, he had eventually stepped back from the edge of the abyss. Lynn liked to think she had played a small part in his recovery, though she knew that the biggest help had come from his friend Nick Miller. Nick had lost his wife Anna (again, Lynn couldn't remember the details, though she felt strongly that she ought to – Mrs Miller had been one of her former teachers, after all) and Dad had taken strength from his fortitude, from the way he had . . . well, not so much bounced back, but at least come to terms with his loss and carried on.

Thinking of Nick, and more particularly of his wife Anna, prompted a brief flash of memory in Lynn's head. She remembered having a feeling of dread in her stomach; she remembered a man in dark glasses slowing his car to look at her; and then she remembered running. Running and running. All the way to her dad's newspaper office to tell him what she had seen.

But what *had* she seen? That was the bit she couldn't remember. She could picture her dad listening intently to her. She could remember the look on his face – a look of dawning realisation. She could remember him telling her to go straight home. And after that . . .

Her mind was an odd and frustrating blank.

What Lynn *did* know, however, seeing her dad sitting there, insomniac and shaking as he puffed on one of his 'cancer sticks', as he called them, was that perhaps he hadn't quite been able to escape the past, after all. Uncurling her legs from beneath her, she pushed herself from her chair and padded across the short distance between them. She dropped to her knees, put her arms around his thick neck and pressed her cheek to his. His skin seemed to sizzle against her cool flesh; his breath stank of stale cigarette smoke.

'Don't worry, Dad,' she whispered, catching a glimpse of her white-faced reflection in the dark glass over his shoulder. 'Everything will be okay.'

He grunted, clearly unconvinced. His voice was a rumble against her ear.

'I hope you're right, love, but I'm not so sure.' His jowly cheek rasped against hers as he turned to peer out at the night briefly before shifting round again to face her. 'Call me an old fool, but I can't help feeling there's trouble on the way.'

Lynn leaned back so she could look into his eyes, her hands still resting on his shoulders. 'Trouble?' she asked. 'What kind of trouble?'

Her dad looked evasive. 'I don't know.' And then, almost reluctantly, he mumbled, 'Unfinished business, perhaps.'

Five

Calliope music.

Nick paused, tilting his head to one side, uncertain whether he had even heard it. Maybe it was nothing but an echo, bleeding from his subconscious. Certainly, despite the uproar in the classroom, it instantly transported him back to his night of broken sleep; to nerves made raw by dreams that he couldn't remember but which had unsettled him regardless.

It was those same raw nerves that now gave his voice a shriller edge than he had intended. 'Darren Blackstock, if you don't sit down and shut up *this instant* you'll start the day with a visit to the headmaster's office.'

Darren, standing beside Colin Sturrock's desk and eliciting squeals of protest from the smaller boy by punching him, continually and lackadaisically, in the shoulder, squinted at Nick from beneath a thick fringe of greasy brown hair. Twisting his lumpen features into a leer, he said, 'I don't think so, *sir*.'

Nick knew that the ten-year-old was alluding to the visitors that Nick had received the night before and to the threatened consequences should Darren once again fall foul of the teacher's attempts to maintain discipline. Knowing that he couldn't allow this to affect his professional judgement, he said sharply, '*I* think so, Darren. *Nothing* will prevent me doing my job to the best of my ability. Do you understand that?'

Darren stared at him sullenly.

Nick raised his voice a notch. 'I *said*: do you understand that?'

The pre-registration hubbub quietened as the stand-off simmered. Darren narrowed his eyes.

'Well? I'm waiting.'

Finally, with a look of pure hatred, Darren said, 'Yes.'

'Good. Now sit down, keep your hands to yourself and speak only when you're spoken to. If you do that we'll all get along much better.'

Darren slouched across the aisle and sidled into his seat. As he did so he muttered what sounded like, 'You are *so* dead.'

Nick kept his expression and voice neutral despite the hot jab of outrage in his belly. 'Are you *still* talking, Darren?'

Darren glanced up at him, and Nick was reminded of that old phrase: *If looks could kill . . .* 'No,' the boy muttered and bowed his head, staring down at his desk.

'Delighted to hear it,' said Nick, clapping his hands together. 'Now, let's try and get registration done before we all die of old age.'

The class was settling to silence when he heard it again – a drift of calliope music on the air, sugary-sweet and yet creepy enough to send feathery fingers dancing across his back.

Trying to ignore it he opened the register – then noticed that Rosie Pardew was waggling her hand in the air.

'Can it wait, Rosie?' he asked.

'Sir, I just wondered what that music was.'

There was a buzz of chatter – clearly others were wondering, too. Nick swallowed his initial response: *You mean you can* hear *it?* He was formulating a more appropriate reply when Jack Barber, sitting by the window, said, 'Sir, there's a little man in the playground.'

Immediately the other children on that side of the room were craning to see, while others, further away, were rising from their seats and gravitating towards the window.

'Sit down!' Nick barked.

'But sir—'

'I said sit down!'

There were grumbles of protest, but most of the children did as he ordered. Nick glanced at Darren Blackstock and was grateful that at least *he* was not taking advantage of the situation to be disruptive. On the contrary, he was sitting at his desk with his head lowered between his outstretched arms, as though asleep.

Sighing, Nick stalked over to the window, trying not to betray the fact that he was as curious about the 'little man' as most of the children were. Looking down into the playground, he saw a capering, chalk-faced dwarf in a multicoloured but shabby jester's outfit, scattering what appeared to be litter from a waste-paper bin tucked under his arm. For a moment Nick's dream came roaring to the forefront of his mind once more, then slipped back into the darkness before he could grasp it. Blinking to clear his head, he suddenly realised that it wasn't litter the dwarf was hurling into the air, but flyers of some kind. The wind was snatching them up and swirling them far and wide. Nick imagined them spreading across the community, drifting to earth like ashes. Like the ashes from . . . from where? The thought caused him a stirring of unease.

The dwarf, his head thrown back, now began to bellow up at the windows of the school, where doubtless dozens of startled faces were peering down at him. Nick tried to make out what he was shouting (Sir Custard Nice? Circle of Knives?), but his voice was thick and raucous and tinged with an odd accent – Eastern European, perhaps? The presence of the little man was unsettling in a way that Nick couldn't define, and he was about to tell the children to ignore him in the hope he would go away when another figure appeared. In contrast to the squat and clownish dwarf, this newcomer was tall, thin and white-haired, and dressed in a steel-grey suit. It was the headmaster, Mr Kingston, and he was cutting diagonally across the playground like a shark towards its prey.

'Wait here and be quiet,' Nick said.

'Where you going, sir?' Lee Weir piped up.

'To give Mr Kingston some moral support.'

'Sir, what's moral support?'

'I'll explain later.'

'Oh, sir, can't we come too?' pleaded Bethany Stiles, her frizzy hair standing up in anticipation.

'No, you can sit quietly until I come back. I'll be telling Mrs Lancaster to keep an eye on you.'

Ignoring the groans from behind him, Nick left the room. After sticking his head round the door of the next-door classroom to make his request he hurried towards the stairs. As he descended he wondered why he was abandoning his class merely to stand at the headmaster's shoulder. After all, it wasn't as if the dwarf was a physical threat. The only reason he could come up with was a ludicrous one: he wanted to ensure that the trespasser was *real*. There was genuinely a part of Nick that wanted to get close enough to the dwarf to reassure himself that the little man was flesh and blood, like everyone else. He wasn't sure where this odd idea had come from, and neither did he want to analyse it too closely. All he knew was that for the last few weeks he had been trying to ignore the feeling that the world had shifted slightly out of phase. He had begun to think of it like a rock on a beach that had become dislodged by the tide, and from beneath which dark and unpleasant things were crawling.

As soon as he stepped into the playground, a chill breeze ruffled his hair, bringing with it the wheezing, sinister jangle of the calliope music he had heard minutes earlier. Out here it was unmistakable and unceasing, a melancholy accompaniment to what was already turning into a very strange day. Ahead of him, through a blizzard of swirling paper, he saw Mr Kingston attempting to remonstrate with the dwarf, growing increasingly red-faced as the little man capered around him like a naughty child, laughing uproariously. Nick began to stride towards the two men and as he did so one of the flyers swooped at him like a bird of prey, plastering itself to his chest. Peeling it off before the wind could pluck it away, he held it stretched between his hands so he could read it.

CIRCUS OF NIGHTS the flyer announced in gaudy red letters above a lurid and rather macabre drawing of a snarling panther and a grinning clown. Unease stirred in Nick's belly as he noted that the Big Top would be setting up in Hobbes' Meadow, which was directly beneath the blackened ruin of Mitre House (something bad had happened there – but what?), for the next three nights. The final performance would be on Friday, 14 October – a date that caused Nick further unease, though he couldn't recall why. Trying to put the troubling thoughts from his mind, he scrunched the flyer in his fist and dropped it to the floor, where the wind immediately snatched it away, propelling it along the ground like a scuttling, lopsided crab.

The dwarf was still dancing around the spluttering and enraged headmaster as Nick drew closer. Only when he was a dozen steps away did the little man glance up, looking at him directly for the first time. As the dwarf first leered and then did a comical double take, as though for the benefit of the watching children, Nick saw that his white make-up was peeling like dry skin and that his teeth were brown and rotten.

'Oo-er!' the dwarf exclaimed, his gravelly voice raised in exaggerated alarm. 'It's the cavalry!'

He turned tail and fled, his thick bowed legs giving him a pronounced waddle.

Ignoring the dwarf for the moment, Nick asked, 'Are you all right, Malcolm?'

Malcolm Kingston was clearly flustered. His face was red and his feathery white hair was fluttering in the wind like a trapped bird.

'I ought to call the police,' he muttered. 'Have that . . . horrible little man arrested for trespass and littering.'

Nick glanced at the fleeing dwarf, and saw that beyond him, outside the school gates, was a halted procession of horse-drawn caravans and other vehicles. It was from here that the calliope music was coming. Indicating the procession, he said, 'Perhaps we ought to go and talk to that lot first. We don't want to create any more trouble for the school than we have to.'

Malcolm scowled and vainly attempted to smooth his wayward hair back over his scalp with a trembling hand. Nick thought he was about to veto the idea when he sighed and said, 'Perhaps you're right. But if you think I'm running after that little . . .'

'Of course not,' said Nick as the older man's voice tailed off. 'We'll walk, with due dignity.'

As the two men strode along the path which cut through the expanse of lawn at the front of the school grounds, Nick half-expected the line of carriages to rumble into motion, forcing Malcolm and himself to either hurry in pursuit or give up the chase and return to the school. But the procession remained stationary, which gave Nick the surely fanciful idea that this was what the circus people had wanted all along, that they had sent in the dwarf simply to draw them (*him?*) out.

As he and Malcolm approached the column, Nick took the opportunity to absorb its many and varied details. Pulled by massive shire horses, the caravans were of the traditional Romany style, painted in bright but fading colours. The one at their head was driven by a woman whose age and identity was impossible to determine. She wore a black headscarf from beneath which straggly russet hair cascaded to curtain her face and cover her shoulders, and large black glasses which reflected the overcast sky. Her body was swathed in a black shawl over a thick red velvet dress, and a clay pipe jutted from between her teeth. Even her hands, holding the reins, were encased in dainty black felt gloves.

The dwarf was perched on the driver's seat next to the woman, leering at them. Further along the procession, Nick saw a bearskin-clad strongman, nearly seven feet tall and almost as wide, staring at him with bland hostility. A number of young people, lithe and sinewy, all wearing the skintight silky sequinned costumes favoured by acrobats and trapeze artists, gazed at them with dreamy half-smiles. Beyond the caravans Nick saw a number of trailers, one draped in red velvet curtains and bearing a dangling plaque which read 'Mirror Of Life', and towards the back of the column a number of old-fashioned wheeled cages containing wild animals – a chimpanzee, a tiger, a black panther – which surprised him. He had assumed that circus animals were banned in these supposedly enlightened times.

But that was just it, he thought. That was what was so strange. The circus seemed to be an anachronism; it was as though it had slipped into being from a bygone age. It was small, shabby, ramshackle, and Nick couldn't see how it would possibly entice the children of Shettle away from their Xboxes and PlayStations. For a moment he felt almost sorry for the gaudy yet threadbare circus troupe. But there was something disquieting about them too . . . disquieting and yet weirdly enticing.

Unable to reconcile these seemingly contrary feelings, Nick glanced at Malcolm and was surprised to see that he appeared to be feeling the same way. The headmaster looked both eager and uncertain; his eyes were sparkling and he was licking his lips almost obsessively, like a child anticipating candyfloss and toffee apples.

'Malcolm, are you okay?' Nick murmured.

The headmaster looked startled, as if he hadn't realised he was not alone. 'What? Oh, yes. Of course. I'm fine.'

They reached the gate and opened it with a squeal of hinges. Malcolm stepped onto the pavement, Nick just behind him. Looking up at the woman in the headscarf he said, 'Are you in charge here?'

The woman snorted, as if this was the stupidest thing she had ever heard. Removing the pipe from her mouth, she tapped the bowl on the side of the wooden seat to dislodge black shreds of burned tobacco. 'I'll speak for everyone, if that's what you mean,' she said.

'In that case perhaps you'd care to explain yourself. What do you think gives you people the right to trespass on school property and litter the playground?'

The woman looked at him, nonplussed. 'We weren't littering,' she said. 'We were advertising.'

'Call it what you like. The fact is, there are bits of paper *everywhere*. Who's going to pick them up, do you suppose?'

Despite her dark glasses, Nick could tell from the woman's posture and pursed lips that she was looking at the headmaster with disdain. 'Who do you think? Children. It's children that like circuses. Children who'll want to come – dragging their parents behind 'em, I shouldn't wonder.'

Malcolm huffed in exasperation. 'I could have you prosecuted,' he said.

The woman simply shrugged, and the dwarf sitting next to her hooted with laughter.

Standing at the headmaster's shoulder, Nick glanced once again along the row of cages. Suddenly he blinked. In the panther's cage was no longer a panther, but a young man with long sleek black hair, shimmering black clothes – silk, maybe, or something similar – and dark, staring eyes. The young man was reclining on a bed of straw. Catching Nick's eye he sneered, exposing catlike fangs.

Startled, Nick stepped back, the bulk of the strongman now blocking his view of the cage.

Malcolm turned. 'Whatever's the matter?'

'I . . .' Nick stepped forward again. In the cage, reclining on its bed of straw, was not a young male human at all, but a black panther, its head half-raised in lazy contemplation of its surroundings, yellow eyes staring at him unblinkingly.

Nick shuddered. 'Nothing,' he said firmly. 'I'm fine.' Looking up at the woman he asked, 'Why have you come? Why now, I mean?'

The woman laughed – which seemed to be a signal for the dwarf, the strongman and the acrobats to laugh too.

'To steal the money from dead men's eyes,' she replied.

'What's that supposed to mean?'

But the woman simply laughed again and gave the reins she was holding a flick. The shire horse, which had been patiently nibbling grass from the verge, began to clop slowly forward, pulling the trundling, creaking caravan behind it. A moment later, with a steadily rising clatter, the rest of the procession was moving too.

'Hey!' Nick stepped forward and raised an arm. 'I haven't finished.'

Before he could take another step, the strongman clumped forward and placed a massive hand against his chest. He gave Nick only the slightest of shoves but it was enough to send him staggering backwards. He might have slipped and fallen if Malcolm hadn't reached out to steady him.

Regaining his balance, Nick watched the procession pass by and felt a coldness pierce through him. He averted his gaze when the panther's cage rattled past, afraid of what he might see. From his elevated perch at the head of the procession, the dwarf began to hurl his flyers into the air again. They swirled and spiralled in the wind, like tiny inverted tornados, carrying news of the circus far and wide.

Six

'What's this?'
Kate Miller plucked a flyer from the well between the front seats of Anthony's car. 'Circus of Nights.' She shuddered. 'Sounds creepy. We ought to go.'

Anthony took his eye off the road for a split second to arch an eyebrow. 'Sounds lame, you mean.'

She pushed out her bottom lip in a mock-pout. 'Oh, don't be such a spoilsport. *You* need to connect with your inner child once in a while.'

He laughed. 'Why do I need an inner child when I've got you?'

'Oi!'

Kate sounded indignant, but she was laughing too. It was one of those mornings when life seemed endless, full of hope. And why shouldn't it? She was seventeen years old; it was a sunny (albeit windy) day; her gorgeous, funny, sweet, smart boyfriend was taking her out for lunch . . . Seriously, did life get any better than this?

There *were* clouds on the horizon, of course. She was

worried about her dad, for one thing. And then there were her exams, and which universities to apply for, and what she'd do if she didn't get her grades, and how being away from Shettle would affect her relationship with Anthony . . .

But Kate was an optimist. And right here, right now, none of those problems seemed insurmountable. *Que sera, sera*, she thought. *Whatever will be, will be.*

She glanced across at Anthony as he drove confidently through the country lanes. He was only a few years older than her, but he seemed so much more mature sometimes. Perhaps it was because he had always had a definite goal in life. He was determined to be a doctor just like his dad, and was currently doing his medical training at the big hospital over in Wenthorpe. Unlike a lot of guys his age, he always dressed smartly, often in suits, and like his dad he had something about him – a likeable sense of authority and reliability. He was the kind of person who could take charge of a situation without seeming arrogant or bossy.

It was rare that their time off during the week coincided. As a student doctor, Anthony worked all sorts of odd shifts; sometimes Kate wouldn't see him for days on end. So when they did manage to get some time together they always made the most of it. Last night Anthony had taken her out for dinner, and today it was lunch in Wenthorpe followed by a bit of shopping, maybe a walk, maybe even a movie if there was anything worthwhile on at the little two-screen cinema.

Or maybe, she thought, realising she was still holding

the flyer in her hand, they would spend the evening at the circus. It would be fun. She hadn't been to a circus since . . .

All at once Kate began to feel strange.

It started with a pounding in her head, and then a wave of the most intense and debilitating nausea washed over her. Within seconds she was sweating and shaking and black spots were dancing in front of her eyes. Blindly she groped at the air, intending to tell Anthony to pull over, that she needed to be sick.

But it was as if he had read her mind. He was already slowing the car, pulling onto the grass verge.

Kate was fumbling for the door handle when she realised that he had already thrown open the door on the driver's side. Next second she heard him retching, and in bewilderment thought, *You too?* Then the passenger door fell open and she leaned out and vomited onto the grass. She did it again, and again. By the time her stomach was empty she felt wrung-out, boneless, and no less terrible than before.

Head spinning, stomach grinding, hovering between consciousness and unconsciousness, she felt a hand gently and clumsily patting her leg.

'You okay?' Anthony's voice was faint, wavering.

'I feel awful,' Kate whispered.

'Me too.'

'Must have been something we ate last night.'

For a moment all she could hear were his groaning gasps for breath, and then he said, 'Can't be. Too sudden. Too much of a coincidence.'

She felt too ill to argue. 'What, then?'

'Not sure. Let's get on our feet . . . get some fresh air. We can't stay here.'

Kate begged to differ. She would quite happily have stayed where she was until she either died or recovered; both options seemed preferable to the way she was feeling right now. She closed her eyes and tried to distance herself from the waves of nausea still rippling through her body, until she felt weak hands tugging at her arms.

'Go away,' she muttered.

Anthony sounded drained but determined. 'Come on. On your feet.'

Groaning and protesting, Kate nevertheless tried to help him as he dragged her from the car. She couldn't remember ever feeling *so* ill *so* suddenly. This was worse than the worst bout of flu she'd ever had; worse than the food poisoning she'd once got from eating three-day-old rice. Her feet felt like weighty lumps on the ends of legs made of string or spaghetti, but with Anthony's help she managed to plant them on the ground. And then together, leaning against one another for support, they staggered away, back in the direction they had come from, feeling so ill that nothing else mattered – not Anthony's beloved Spitfire with its doors left open; not lunch in Wenthorpe; not the cloudless sky overhead.

And then, miraculously, she suddenly began to feel better. Maybe it was the fresh air filling her lungs; or maybe she had got all the poison out of her system when she had thrown up. Whatever the reason, she suddenly felt stronger, felt the pounding in her head begin to fade, her stomach settling.

'I'm . . . okay now,' she said, straightening up.

Beside her, Anthony was frowning. 'Me too. But it doesn't make sense.'

Kate raised her eyebrows. 'Who cares if it makes sense? As long as we're feeling better . . .' She blew out a long breath. 'God, I never want to feel like that again.'

Anthony halted, turned, looked back at the car, a troubled expression on his face. 'But it's not right,' he said. 'There's got to be a reason why we both felt so ill at the same time, and why we both feel better now.'

'Maybe we breathed something in,' she suggested. 'Fumes from the petrol or something.'

'Chemical warfare?' he said wryly. 'Terrorist attack?' He shook his head. 'No, there's nothing airborne I know of whose effects can come and go so suddenly.'

'Well, let's just put it down to one of life's mysteries and be thankful we're okay.'

Anthony smiled at her. 'Maybe we should get checked out.'

'Oh, do we have to? We're fine now. Let's just go and have lunch.'

'You sure you still want to?'

'Definitely. I'm starving. Especially after . . . you know.'

He grimaced. 'Could do with brushing my teeth.'

'Let's stop at a garage, get some water and mints.'

They started walking back towards the car. They were less than halfway there when Kate stopped and put a hand on her stomach. 'Oh.'

'You too, eh?' said Anthony, wrapping his arms around himself.

'What's going on?'

Anthony looked pale; his jaw clenched and unclenched. Through gritted teeth he said, 'I want to try something. Go back about . . . half a dozen steps.'

She looked puzzled, but did as he asked.

'*Now* how do you feel?'

'Fine,' she said in a kind of wonder. 'Much better again.'

'Right, now I'm going to walk forward. If I'm right it'll have the opposite effect.'

A little unsteadily he began to walk towards the car. After seven or eight steps he stopped and doubled over.

'Anthony!' Kate said, hurrying forward. 'Are you—'

But she couldn't finish her sentence. After half a dozen steps she began to feel ill again. A couple more and the feeling intensified. Ahead of her, Anthony leaned over and retched, then waved an arm shakily.

'Go back,' he ordered, his voice wavering.

She did so. With each backward step she felt better again.

A dozen or so paces in front of her, Anthony slowly straightened up. She could see that he was in distress, but making a valiant effort to fight it. 'Going to try and . . . get to the car,' he said haltingly. 'Reverse it back to you.'

'Do you want me to—'

'No! You stay there.'

Kate watched, nibbling her lip anxiously, as Anthony staggered to the car. With each step he seemed to become weaker. She gasped when, less than five metres from his destination, he dropped to his knees like a dehydrated man in the desert. He crawled the rest of the way, seemingly unconcerned about the knees of his nice suit and the toes of his meticulously shined shoes. Finally he reached the open driver's door, where he paused to retch a string of bile onto the ground before hauling himself, inch by painful inch, into the car.

He sat motionless behind the steering wheel for so long that Kate became concerned that he might have passed out. She was bracing herself to venture forth on a rescue mission when the engine roared almost angrily to life. The noise dwindled, roared again, and then the vehicle began, jerkily and erratically, to move. As it reversed in short, growling bursts it veered from side to side, and Kate moved warily to the side of the road, pressing herself against the stone wall at her back.

But her caution was unnecessary. The further the car reversed, the smoother Anthony's handling of it became. By the time it halted beside her, he was driving as assuredly as he always did. The driver's-side window lowered and he leaned towards her, smiling weakly. He looked washed-out, but even now she could see the colour returning to his cheeks.

'I don't think we'll be going to Wenthorpe today,' he said. 'It's like an invisible barrier across the road. The more you try to push through the sicker you get.'

'But that's impossible,' Kate said.

'Yes,' he agreed with no trace of irony, 'it is.'

She scanned the road ahead. 'What do you think would happen if we ignored the effects and just kept going?'

'I don't know. I expect we'd eventually black out. I don't fancy trying it. Do you?'

'No,' she said, with a shudder. 'I don't.' She looked at him, suddenly afraid. 'What if this stretches all the way round Shettle in a circle? What if we can't get out at all?'

Anthony's face was as composed as ever, but Kate thought she saw a flicker of fear in his blue eyes.

'What indeed?' he said quietly.

Seven

'Sorry, kids, I think I'm gonna—'
Those were the last words Matt Blaine heard before the school bus slammed to a halt, throwing him against the seat in front. As his face collided with the headrest, not badly enough to bruise but certainly hard enough to bring tears to his eyes, he was vaguely aware of screams and groans around him, of other kids being thrown around too. A few of them – big Will Fenning, for instance – fell sideways into the aisle. Bags went tumbling, scattering their contents.

As Matt picked himself up, he heard the sound of retching from the driver's cab. Looking in that direction, he saw Joe, the bus driver, leaning out of the side window, throwing up onto the road. Almost immediately, as if the sound of his vomiting had set off a chain reaction, most of the other kids around Matt began to puke too. Within seconds the stomach-churning stink of vomit was filling the bus.

Beside him, Kieron, his older brother, said, 'This is gross. Let's get out.'

He emphasised his words with a shove. Matt

staggered into the aisle, wrinkling his nose. Stepping over school books, pencil cases and Miranda Kent, who was hunched into a ball, shivering and whimpering, he made his way to the front of the bus. Behind him were Kieron and a handful of other kids, all eager to get out into the fresh air. It wasn't until later that it would occur to Matt that these kids, the only ones *not* puking, were from Shettle. The others – the sick ones – all lived further afield.

Reaching the front of the bus, Matt said, 'Uh . . . Mr Acklam? Joe?'

The driver, his head still hanging out of the window, was a big guy, his beefy arms sleeved with tattoos of dragons and mermaids. He had a shaved head, a ginger goatee and several facial piercings. He always wore studded wristbands and black T-shirts emblazoned with the names of thrash-metal bands. The kids loved him.

When Joe didn't immediately respond, Matt said, 'Joe, we need to get out. Can you open the door?'

Joe swung his head round. His eyes were bleary and Matt tried not to grimace at the sight of vomit in his beard. 'Wha'?' he said.

'Can you let us out? We can walk from here.'

Nervously Kieron asked, 'Did you hit something, Joe?'

That possibility had not occurred to Matt until now, but suddenly, like his brother, he was wary of what they might see when they got off the bus. Maybe it was the sight of whatever – or *whoever* – the bus had collided with that had made Joe throw up. Matt wondered whether he'd respond in the same way, or maybe even faint, if he saw someone mangled in the road, blood and guts everywhere. He was therefore relieved when Joe – the movement uncoordinated, as if his skull was as heavy as a bowling ball – shook his head.

'No, just suddenly felt . . . feel . . . really ill.'

'Open the door!' someone yelled from halfway down the aisle. 'It stinks in here! We want to get off!'

Joe blinked, his head lolling again. He looked, thought Matt, as if he was battling desperately to stay conscious. Then he lurched forward, and at first Matt thought he'd lost the battle. But when the doors opened with a hiss, Matt realised that Joe must have been going for the button or lever or whatever it was that activated them.

Matt, Kieron and the others spilled out into the chilly autumn afternoon. After the foul, cloying atmosphere of the bus, the air seemed unbelievably crisp and fresh. Matt sucked it in so deeply that after a few seconds he started to feel dizzy. He stood, hands on knees, and closed his eyes to stop the world from spinning. By the time he recovered, most of the other kids had drifted away. Only Kieron, a head taller than he was, was still there, but he was looking not towards Shettle but off into the trees to his left.

'Do you wanna go and look for conkers?' he said.

Matt nodded towards the bus. Joe was leaning out of the window, throwing up again. 'What about Joe?'

'What about him?'

'We ought to help him.'

'How?'

'I dunno . . . call someone?'

Kieron shook his head. 'We'd only get him into trouble. He'll be all right. Come on.'

Matt supposed his brother was right, but he felt bad all the same. Kieron began to walk away and after a moment, raising his hand in an apologetic wave that he was pretty sure Joe didn't even see, Matt followed.

The two brothers climbed carefully over the barbed-wire fence at the side of the road and trudged down a short incline, through a thick brown carpet of autumn leaves shed by the gnarled trees around them. Within seconds they could no longer see the road, nor even hear the soft growl of the bus's idling engine. Not that they were worried; they had been playing in these woods for years and knew them like the backs of their hands. Like most kids who lived in Shettle, Kieron and Matt had heard tales of the child-killer who had lived in the big house on the hill, and who had died when his house had burned down. Course, there were local rumours that the killer's ghost haunted these woods. There were even kids who claimed to have seen him, his face and hands burned, smoke rising from his clothes. But such stories didn't bother Matt, at least not when he was with his brother or his friends. If he'd been alone it might have been different, but Matt never came here unless he had company and neither did anyone else he knew.

Now that they were both in 'big school' he and Kieron didn't play conkers any more. Such simple pastimes were regarded as lame, the province of little kids and retards. Matt still liked the tradition of *looking* for conkers, though – and so did Kieron, though he would never have admitted that to any of his Year 9 friends. What Matt particularly liked was finding a conker that was still in its spiny green shell but almost ready to split. He loved peeling the shell away and exposing the hard seed beneath. However many times he did it there was still something magical in that. A newly hatched conker, smooth and gleaming and chestnut-brown, was the most beautiful thing in the world. He and Kieron would fill their pockets, and when they got home they would line up their booty, like nuggets of treasure, along the windowsills of their bedrooms where they could catch the light. All too soon, though, the conkers would wither, turn dull and hard, and as the golds and reds of autumn decayed to the grey mulch of winter they would invariably be scooped up and thrown out with the rubbish, their brief, shining moment of glory over again for another year.

It had been Dad who had first started the conker-hunting tradition, Dad who had first led the boys through the woods to the huge horse-chestnut tree when Matt was four and Kieron six. Back then the sun-dappled clearing had seemed to Matt like a fairy-tale realm: a wonderful, secret place known only to them.

He knew now how dumb that idea was, just as he knew how dumb it was to believe in Father Christmas and the Tooth Fairy. And yet sometimes – especially on bright, clear days like this – the magic of the place still clung to him. Secretly he still liked to believe that he and his brother were following an ancient, mystical path through the forest, a path known to no one but themselves.

It took them ten minutes to reach the clearing. Ten minutes of pushing through brambles and slithering down slopes and weaving between trees whose trunks, from a distance, appeared to form an impenetrable barrier.

'Here we are,' Kieron said unnecessarily once they had pushed the final stand of bushes aside. The familiar tree reared above them, its outstretched branches hanging down like dozens of arms trying to draw them in. Those same branches were laden with spiny green seeds, so many that they seemed to be weighing the tree down, forcing its trunk to bend at the waist like an old man with heavy bags of shopping. Occasionally, in the past, when the boys in their eagerness had arrived too early in the season, they had had to throw sticks and stones up into the branches to dislodge the conkers. Not now, though. Now they knew all about patience and timing. Now they only came when the conkers were in the process of falling, when the ground was strewn with them.

For the next twenty minutes the years disappeared and the brothers became four and six again. As they scrabbled on the ground, looking for the fattest, shiniest, most perfect specimens, their inhibitions vanished and their surroundings melted away. They whooped and yelled and laughed; they crawled about like toddlers; they stuffed their pockets; they threw handfuls of leaves at one another. Finally, grinning, pockets bulging, they stood up and dusted themselves down.

'We ought to get back,' said Kieron.

Matt nodded. 'I'm hungry. Wonder what's for tea.'

Kieron walked across to where he had dumped his school bag. 'One of Dad's curries, I hope. Or maybe Mum's lasagne.'

Matt screwed up his face, mentally judging one against the other. 'Mum's lasagne is good, but Dad's curry is better.'

'I'll tell her you said that.'

Matt looked horrified. 'You'd better not!'

'How much is it worth?'

'Shh.'

'Don't shush me, you little—'

'No, really, *listen*,' said Matt urgently. He looked at his brother, wide-eyed. 'I *heard* something.'

Kieron looked sceptical, but there was a hint of wariness in his voice. 'What kind of something?'

'I'm not sure,' said Matt. 'Something moving. Just shush and listen.'

The boys stood stock-still, holding their breath, heads tilted towards the sky.

Eventually Kieron murmured, 'I can't hear anything.'

'I *did* hear something,' insisted Matt.

'Where did it come from?'

'I don't know. Over there, maybe.' He pointed towards a clump of bushes at the far side of the clearing, but he didn't look entirely sure.

Dismissively Kieron said, 'It was probably just a bird or something. Or even the wind. The problem with you is—'

Then his voice cut off. Across the clearing, precisely where Matt had pointed, the bushes shook violently, as if someone had grabbed them at the bases of their woody stems and was trying to uproot them from the ground.

The boys looked at each other, fear in their eyes. Matt had always felt safe here, protected from the world, but for the first time it occurred to him how far away from home he and his brother were. If they shouted for help, no one would hear them. And if anything happened . . .

'Let's go,' he said nervously, and began to move in a brisk walk towards the far side of the clearing, grabbing his school bag as he passed it. He didn't want to run, because that would be like admitting there was something to run *from* – not to mention that it might encourage whatever was on the other side of the clearing (spying on them?) to give chase.

For once Kieron didn't argue. Glancing behind him, he followed his brother, sticking close to him as if for protection.

'We'll be okay,' he gasped as they hurried along, pushing through the bushes, scrambling up the slope on the other side. 'Whatever it was, it's probably more scared of *us* than we are of *it*.'

'Yeah, I know,' said Matt. Then, a few seconds later, 'What do you *think* it was?'

Kieron paused before replying, 'Just a deer or something.'

They crested the rise. In front of them trees sloped down to a blue trickling thread of a stream; beyond that more trees were interspersed with tangles of undergrowth and thick bushes. In the wind leaves drifted down constantly, like dry flakes peeling from the decaying sky. Through the swirl of leaves, between two pillar-straight tree trunks on the far side of the stream, Matt saw a dark figure watching them.

His body jerked so violently that he slipped on the carpet of leaves, and had to grab at his brother's arm to stop himself sliding down the slope. For once Kieron was neither irritated nor scornful.

'You okay?'

Matt pointed with his free hand. He was so scared that he could barely speak, but with an effort he managed to blurt, 'There – look.'

Kieron followed the direction of his brother's pointing, trembling finger. But in the few seconds since Matt had seen it, the figure had gone.

'What am I looking at?' Kieron asked.

'There was someone there. A man.'

Kieron frowned. 'Are you sure?'

'*Yes!*'

'Well . . . what did he look like?'

'I don't know. Just a dark figure. All in shadow. But it was definitely there.'

Kieron licked his lips. He scanned the trees for a few moments, eyes narrowed, then cupped his hands around his mouth. 'Hello?' he shouted.

Horrified, Matt gripped his brother's sleeve. 'What are you *doing?*'

'If there's someone there, they'll answer us.'

'But what if it's . . .' Matt hardly dared say it '. . . a *bad* person.'

'Then he already knows we're here,' Kieron replied almost calmly, before shaking his head. 'But it won't be. There's probably no one there at all. All those leaves and shadows and trees make you imagine things, that's all.'

Matt bit back on his response. He didn't want to insist that there *had* been someone there, in case his conviction somehow made it so. And maybe Kieron was right. Maybe he *had* imagined it.

'Come on,' Kieron said. 'Let's keep going. In five minutes we'll be back on the road.'

They slithered down the slope and jumped the stream, both of them unable to help glancing nervously at the spot where Matt claimed to have seen the figure. Around them trees and bushes rustled, but only because of the wind. When a hand reached out and caressed Matt's face, he cried out in terror and swung round. But it was merely a drifting leaf. They were two, maybe three minutes from safety, when Kieron jerked aside so violently that he bumped into Matt, sending him staggering sideways.

'*What?*' Matt snapped.

Kieron was glaring at the foliage several metres to his right.

'What?' Matt asked again, more quietly this time.

Slowly Kieron raised a hand and pointed. 'There's something there.'

For the second time in ten minutes the boys stood motionless, staring and listening. It didn't help that the wind had now picked up a little and was buffeting them, flapping their clothes, causing the surrounding trees and bushes to whisper and shudder and rattle. The clump of foliage that Kieron was pointing at was a particularly thick tangle of plants and brambles, full of indeterminate shapes and clots of shadow.

'What did you see?' Matt whispered after a few seconds.

'Something moving.'

Matt peered hard at the mass of foliage but could see nothing. 'Where do you think it is now?'

Kieron glanced at his brother, and Matt was shocked at the stark fear in his eyes. Hoarsely the older boy said, 'I think it's still there.'

As if to confirm his words there was a stealthy but prolonged bout of rustling from the foliage and then a dark shape rose slowly from behind it. It was still mostly concealed by an overlapping collage of twigs and leaves, and so was more an impression of a figure than a figure itself. In the split second before he yelled and ran, Matt was reminded of a shark rising from the depths of the ocean, of the dark stain of its presence in the water widening and lengthening ominously as it got closer to the surface.

Only half-aware that Kieron was beside him, Matt slithered and scrambled up the slope, towards the daylight that the trees and bushes appeared to have shattered into fragments and trapped between their branches. He had no idea whether the dark shape was giving chase, or of how close it was. Fear had given him tunnel vision and he could hear nothing but the pounding of blood in his head and his own ragged breathing.

Clawing for handholds, his feet slipping and sliding, he somehow managed to make it to the top of the slope.

Grabbing bushes and clumps of brambles, ignoring the thorns scratching his skin and drawing beads of blood from the palms of his hands and the pads of his fingers, he hauled himself through the last straggly barrier of trees and into the light. Ahead of him was the barbed-wire fence and then the dusty road, beyond which were farmers' fields and eventually home. Barely even acknowledging that the school bus was no longer there, Matt ran at the fence like a sprinter towards the tape, fear-fuelled adrenalin giving him the impetus to leap.

Despite his heavy school bag and the conkers spilling from his pockets, he almost made it. His leading leg cleared the fence by a good six inches, but the toe of his trailing foot was snagged by a twist of barbed wire, which ripped through the leather of his shoe and halted his momentum as surely as a hand around his ankle. He crashed to the ground, the impact skinning his knees and knocking the breath from him. Winded, he tried to rise to his feet, but could manage only to drag himself a few inches along the ground. Then he felt hands gripping his arms, and screamed.

It was Kieron. His brother was wild-eyed and had a three-inch scratch from a thorn across his cheek and the bridge of his nose.

'Keep going!' he yelled into Matt's ear, and somehow the raw panic in his voice gave Matt the ability to do so. Almost side by side the brothers ran across the road, scrambled over the wall on the other side and fled in a hobbling run across a farmer's field. Three-quarters of the way across, Kieron, red-faced and struggling for breath, gasped, 'Hang . . . on . . . a minute . . .'

Fearfully Matt glanced behind him, half-expecting to see some terrible dark shape flailing towards them. But there was nothing. The field behind them was clear, and so was the road beyond that. And on the other side of the road . . .

Matt squinted. Was that a dark figure, standing between two trees at the edge of the woods? With his head pounding, and the light from the vast white autumn sky half-blinding him, it was difficult to tell. As Kieron sank to the ground, sweat pouring down his face, Matt blinked, rubbed his eyes and looked again.

There was nothing. No figure, nor even a suggestion of one. If there had been one there at all, it had now melted back into the trees.

Eight

That calliope music again. As soon as he heard it, drifting on the wind, Nick began to feel queasy. He halted, trying to shake the muzziness from his head.

'Dad? Are you okay?'

He blinked at Kate who was looking up at him, her face looming in his vision. For a split second he saw not his daughter's face but Anna's and he felt a jolt go through his body. His heart began to race. Then her features seemed to settle, to subtly transform, and he realised that it *was* Kate, after all; of *course* it was. Her face was rounder than her mother's, her features softer.

'Yes, I'm . . . fine,' he said distractedly. It was a cool night, the wind still gusting, but all at once he felt hot, hemmed in by the crowds around them, streaming down the lane towards the distant big top.

'You sure, Mr Miller?' Anthony appeared concerned too. 'You look a bit pale.'

I could do with a drink, Nick thought but didn't say. Instead he forced a smile. 'Just the light from the moon, I suppose.'

They all glanced up. The moon was fat and yellow.

A gibbous moon, thought Nick. *Is that what they call it? Not quite full, but bloated. Like a boil filled with pus.*

'You *sure* you're all right, Dad?' Kate asked.

He barked a laugh, trying to make it sound convincing. 'Yes, just a bit tired. Wondering why the hell we're tramping out here on a freezing cold night instead of staying inside, in front of the telly, where it's warm.'

For a moment Kate looked distracted too. Someone bumped into her, muttered an apology. The contact seemed to prompt an answer from her.

'You can sit in front of the telly any night of the week. It's not every day that the circus comes to town. And look around you, Dad. Everyone's here. That can only be good for the community.'

'Besides – free tickets.' Anthony waved them in the air to prove his point.

Nick frowned. 'Yes, but don't you think that's odd? Giving away so many free tickets for the first night?'

'It's just a promotional thing, to get people in,' Kate said vaguely.

'But how do they make any money? If everyone comes for free on the first night then the place will be empty for the rest of the week.'

'Well, the circus people rely on the audience to . . . tell their friends, I suppose,' Kate said.

Nick sensed from her troubled expression that she was still thinking about what had happened earlier. As soon as he had arrived home from school he had been able to tell that there was something on her mind. But when he had asked her about it she had simply told him that her lunch date with Anthony hadn't gone quite as planned.

'Sorry to hear that,' he had said. 'Difference of opinion?'

She had shaken her head vigorously. 'No, it's . . .' She paused for a long time, and then eventually said, 'This is going to sound stupid, but we couldn't get out of Shettle.'

She told him what had happened, about how she and Anthony had felt so ill that they had been unable to make it past a certain point on the road. Then the two of them talked vaguely for a while about why that might have been, rehashing the unsatisfactory theories that she and Anthony had come up with – food poisoning, fumes or gas of some sort leaking from somewhere. Yet although they had discussed the matter there had been something awkward and fractured about the conversation. Throughout it Nick had been unable to shake the unsettling impression that there was some unknown factor that was making both of them tiptoe around the topic, as if there was something dangerous at its heart, something to be avoided.

Not for the first time he felt as though his thoughts were being directed, manipulated in some way. It was a similar situation with this ticket business. As soon as free tickets for the Circus of Nights had landed on his doormat (and it was weird that he hadn't heard the clatter of the letter box, as he usually did) there had been no question at all that he *wouldn't* go. Despite the fact that he wasn't a particular fan of circuses, and that this circus seemed even less attractive than most, the free tickets had acted almost like a royal summons. However much Nick told himself he didn't *want* to go, however much he queried his motives for going, there was no question that when it came to the crunch he would be there.

He tried to justify his decision by convincing himself that he was here out of curiosity; or even that he was here purely in order to get to the bottom of . . .

But that was where his thinking again went off the rails. The bottom of what?

Something was happening in Shettle: he knew that. But he couldn't seem able to grasp exactly *what* that something was. There was a sickness in the town – bad dreams, bad thoughts – and a little voice deep inside was telling him that it was all tied up with the circus, and with Kate and Anthony's inability to leave town that day, and with . . . with . . .

With what? He felt that he ought to be able to see it – the pattern, the connection. But he couldn't. Something was clouding his brain; the links were there but he couldn't fit them together. It was all too confusing, too much of a jumble. He hadn't had a drink today but his mind still felt dulled, as if by alcohol.

Despite the sickness in the town – lots of absenteeism at work, lots of kids off school – it seemed as if the entire community was making the effort to attend the first performance of the Circus of Nights. It was like a pilgrimage, like the children of Hamlyn pouring from their homes to follow the music of the Pied Piper.

It was wrong, Nick *knew* it was wrong – but he went along with the flow, all the same.

The red-and-white-striped big top in Hobbes' Meadow seemed almost to pulse with light. It was a vast and billowing beacon, which made the darkness that surrounded it all the darker. The constant flow of people compacted into a slow-moving crush as Nick, Kate and Anthony neared the open gate into the field. A pair of grotesque-looking clowns were taking tickets, while another juggled skittles and pretended to collapse unconscious on the muddy ground when they clattered down on his head, making children giggle nervously as they clung to their parents' hands.

'Welcome, welcome,' the clowns said in high scratchy voices as people streamed through the gate. When Anthony proffered their free tickets, one of the clowns, his fat face as orange as a Halloween pumpkin, his green hair standing up in wild tufts, all but snatched them out of his hand. 'Hope you enjoy the show!' he shrieked, sticking out a fat purple tongue.

'Rufus! Don't be rude to the nice people!' the other clown, its face white, its eyes and mouth cancelled out with thick black crosses, scolded.

'I'm not being rude!' the clown called Rufus protested.

'You *are* being rude!'

'Not!'

'Are!'

'Not!'

As soon as they were out of earshot, shuffling with the rest of the crowd towards the snout-like entrance jutting from the main bulk of the big top, Kate murmured, 'Well, *that* was hilarious.'

'Hmm?' said Nick, distracted. He was looking beyond the big top, to Mitre House perched atop the hill that reared up behind Hobbes' Meadow. Or rather, he was looking at the *absence* of Mitre House, because there was nothing left of the place now but a big black hole in the ground, like a gaping cavity that had once held a rotting tooth. The house was no longer there because . . . because . . .

'The clowns,' said Kate, scattering his thoughts. 'Bit creepy, don't you think?'

Nick sighed; the connection was gone. 'Clowns are always creepy,' he said.

'What's that place in aid of, do you think?'

Anthony was nodding towards one of a row of shabby trailers that were parked in a line leading up to the big top's entrance. Most of the trailers were selling food – candyfloss, toffee apples, burgers that stank of boiled blood and greasy onions – but one, set a little apart from the rest, had an entrance composed of two long red velvet curtains and a sign above, its swirling letters painted in red and gold, which proclaimed 'Mirror Of Life'. Remembering it from that morning, Nick saw that the dwarf who had scattered flyers in the school playground was standing at the entrance, doing a 'Roll up, roll up' routine in his sand-paper-rough voice.

'Who dares to face the truth?' he was shouting.

The answer seemed to be no one. Though he felt a little ashamed of his uncharitable thoughts, Nick felt a savage satisfaction at the sight of the little man failing to attract a single customer.

As if he could read Nick's thoughts, the dwarf suddenly spotted him. 'What about you, friend?' he bellowed. 'Will you be the first to see the light?'

Embarrassed to be the centre of attention, Nick shook his head. 'No, thanks.'

'There's nothing to be afraid of,' the dwarf said mockingly.

'I'm not afraid,' muttered Nick. 'I just don't want to, that's all.'

'Maybe next time,' the dwarf said, and gave Nick a leering grin. 'Don't think you can escape me that easily.'

'Hard sell or what?' muttered Anthony as they shuffled on.

The calliope music jangled as they entered the big top. The rising tiers of benches circling the ring were already three-quarters full. Despite the chill night air, the interior of the tent was warm with body heat and buzzing with excited chatter. The air was redolent with the smell of sawdust and raw earth, fried onions and sickly-sweet candyfloss. There was something else too, a darker, muskier scent underlying the others that set Nick's nerves on edge.

Anthony pointed. 'There's Mum and Dad. They've saved us seats.'

John and Lis Kersh were sitting to their left, about halfway up the rows of benches, waving at them. There was a space next to them over which they had draped their coats. Nick, Kate and Anthony picked their way through the crowd. As Nick settled himself on the bench next to John, his friend leaned towards him.

'You too, eh?'

Nick looked at him. 'What do you mean?'

'Dragged out on a night like this. What the hell are we doing here, Nick?'

Nick shrugged and almost didn't say anything. But eventually he replied, 'I felt I had to come.'

'Me too,' said John. 'Now, why should that be, do you think?'

Before Nick could formulate a response, Lis Kersh leaned across her husband, looking as radiant as ever. However he was feeling, Lis's smiling face and the warmth of her personality never failed to lift Nick's spirits. 'He's not being a curmudgeon, is he, Nick?'

Nick half-laughed. 'Of course not.'

Lis reached for her husband's hand, laced her fingers through his. 'He doesn't know how to enjoy himself, this one. Free tickets and he still moans.'

'Well, it's hardly sophisticated entertainment,' said John. 'Pratfalling clowns and people swinging about like apes.'

'Since when did you become so hoity-toity?' Lis teased. 'You're such a grumpy old man these days. You sound eighty-eight, not forty-eight.'

John rolled his eyes at Nick, but Nick knew he was not as exasperated as he was pretending to be. John was a contented husband playing the role of long-suffering spouse. Seeing him and Lis so happy together gave Nick a pang. He was delighted for them, of course, but he still found it tough. It reminded him of what he had had, and what he had lost.

As the last of the stragglers trickled in and took their places, Nick looked around. Not far away he saw Chris and Caroline Blaine and their three children (Chris raised an almost cautious hand to him and Nick reciprocated), and on the far side of the ring was the unmistakable figure of Alan Michaels, together with his daughter Lynn. It was the first time that Nick had seen Alan for a while and he was shocked at the news editor's appearance. He had always been a big man, but now he looked positively corpulent, his face both flushed and waxy. He seemed to be struggling for breath, his mouth opening and closing like that of a goldfish, and he kept dabbing at his damp face with a large white handkerchief.

A thought rose unbidden in Nick's mind: *So here we all are, together again at last.* The thought disturbed him in a way he couldn't define, but before he had time to ponder on it the lights went down and the show began.

In the darkness a spotlight formed a bright white circle in the centre of the ring. Into the spotlight, as if appearing from nowhere, stepped a female ringmaster. In her red jacket, crisp white shirt and shiny black knee-high boots, she cut an impressive and glamorous figure. But it wasn't until she cracked her whip and swept off her top hat with a flourish, causing masses of ruby-red curls to cascade over her shoulders, that Nick recognised her.

It was the woman he had spoken to that morning, the one who had been driving the leading carriage. Divested of her pipe, her shawl, her headscarf and her dark glasses, she was now unrecognisable from the hunched, swaddled figure he had encountered earlier. Transformed though she was, however, her true identity remained elusive. Her face was heavily made-up – chalk-white skin, bright red bow lips and black-ringed eyes framed by long curling lashes.

'Ladies and gentlemen,' she cried in a clear, ringing

voice, 'the Circus of Nights is honoured to present to you an entertainment which has thrilled and staggered not only the crowned heads of Europe but of the world! We are an ancient troupe of travelling players, ladies and gentlemen, our history steeped in folklore and tradition. Our feats of physical artistry and spectacular legerdemain are guaranteed to take your breath away! Prepare to be amazed by our opening act – Milovan and Serena!'

The lights blazed up and a broad-chested man in a pink silk shirt, high-waisted black breeches and a curling handlebar moustache stepped into the ring. He cracked a whip, there was a shower of sparks, and suddenly a writhing, feral female creature, her bald head, long limbs and lithe, muscled torso painted or tattooed in tiger stripes, sprang upwards as though she had burst from beneath the ground. She began to dance frenziedly and erotically, her body twisting and bending, turning cartwheels and flipping head over heels with incredible speed and dexterity.

Nick leaned forward in his seat, mesmerised. Because the woman was a blur of movement she was impossible to focus upon, but even so he could have sworn that she was naked. He had an impression of small bouncing breasts and a tightly muscled bottom. And between her legs . . . well, the glimpses he had of what appeared to be a smoothly shaven vagina were agonisingly brief and tantalising, but all the more exciting for that.

The man cracked his whip again and, with a feline snarl and an animal-like leap that had the crowd gasping, the woman jumped on him, causing him to stagger backwards several paces. She wrapped her limbs around him in what could easily have been construed as an act of abandoned sexual congress and with a swipe of her clawed hands ripped his shirt open to expose a hairy chest scored with bleeding claw marks. With her legs still wrapped around his waist she leaned back, arms aloft and breasts exposed, and howled at the sky. Then she kicked away from him, propelling herself across the ring in a series of rapid backflips.

Tearing his gaze from the spectacle with an effort, Nick discovered to his embarrassment that he had a raging and very obvious hard-on. Folding his arms carefully over his lap he glanced around at his fellow audience members. He was a little unsettled to see that they were all, without exception, just as captivated by the tiger-woman as he was. Fathers and mothers alike were sitting open-mouthed, not in outrage but in hungry fascination, their eyes glazed and staring, their offspring forgotten. Even the smallest of the children looked hypnotised by the spectacle before them, though Nick assumed – hoped – that their thoughts were purer than those of their parents, that they were entranced not by the woman's display of overt sexuality but by her lightning-quick movements.

Even John, next to him, appeared to be under the woman's spell. He looked drugged, his eyes sleepy and lustful, his bottom lip wet and gleaming as his tongue moved slowly across it. Yet more disturbing was the realisation that Kate, on Nick's other side, was similarly affected. He touched her arm and her eyes flickered, as if she had been roused from a dream or a trance. When she looked at him her face wore a troubled, confused expression, though her eyes still swam with dark and forbidden thoughts.

The man cracked his whip a third time, and with another explosion of white sparks the tiger-woman vanished. The audience expelled a gasp of shock mingled with a groan of disappointment. The next moment they were all looking round confusedly, guiltily, as if not quite able to believe what had just happened and the effect that it had had upon them.

Before anyone could recover from the experience enough to question it, clowns were streaming into the ring. Instantly the heavily erotic atmosphere of moments before was punctured as the clowns began to leap and run and fall about, making the children in the audience shriek with laughter. One clown drove into the ring in a rickety yellow car, which collapsed around him before exploding in an eruption of coloured streamers. The adults in the audience watched the slapstick antics with slightly shell-shocked expressions, still trying to come to terms with the sudden change of mood. After the clowns had departed the ringmistress introduced a family of jugglers, who started by hurling skittles to each other, and progressed from there to flaming torches and finally to whirring chainsaws.

Next came a tightrope act; then a tiny girl in a tutu performing gymnastics on the back of a galloping horse. Then the strongman appeared and amazed everyone by dragging a cart packed with cackling clowns all the way around the ring, using only his teeth. When he left, the clowns stayed on for an encore and this time they were joined by a chimpanzee who kept stealing their hats and picking their pockets. Also present was the white-faced dwarf, who made the children scream by tearing his face off to reveal a grinning skull, only to then disappear with a loud bang and a puff of green smoke.

'Ladies and gentlemen,' the ringmistress announced once the clowns had lolloped and tumbled away for the second time. She strutted round the ring as she spoke, cracking her whip. 'Would you please now welcome Helga and Michael, otherwise known as . . . the Flying Twins!'

She gestured upwards with a flourish. Like the rest of the audience, Nick peered at the trapeze platforms high above the ring and saw a pair of fluttering shapes, like shreds of shadow that had torn loose from the darkness. As the shapes descended in lazy spirals he saw that they were bats, large and plump, with leathery semi-transparent wings and furry rat-like bodies. There were a few squeals from the audience as the bats drifted towards them, which then intensified as the creatures began to swoop over their heads, making people cower and duck.

The ringmistress laughed and stretched out her arms. Instantly the bats veered towards her, one alighting on her left arm, one on her right. They hung upside-down for a moment, wrapping their wings around their bodies. There was a drum roll and another flash, and suddenly the bats were gone. In their place, standing one on either side of the ringmistress, were a young couple, both about eighteen years old, the boy tall, handsome and dark-haired, the girl petite and pretty with straight golden hair that hung down her back almost to the base of her spine.

The couple smiled at the crowd – or rather smirked, thought Nick, as if they felt themselves superior in some way. Then, although the ringmistress had announced that they were twins, they stepped forward, embraced one another and then tilted their heads forward, their lips meeting in a lingering and lascivious kiss.

In a split-second display of optical trickery, which drew yet another gasp of wonder from the audience, the young couple then vanished abruptly and where they had been standing the bats reappeared, hovering like birds of prey before suddenly, in unison, ascending straight as arrows towards the ceiling of the big top far above.

Nick tried to follow their progress but lost their fluttering bodies in the shadows. Then people began to murmur and point and he realised that Helga and Michael, while the audience's attention had been distracted by the bats, had somehow scaled the tall wooden poles surmounted by the trapeze platforms, and were now standing, one on each platform, at either side of the ring. The twins' shiny red costumes gleamed in the darkness, and they had each now donned a silver mask that flashed and sparkled as spotlights swivelled to focus upon them.

Michael unhooked a trapeze from the vertical wire beside him and swung out across the ring. The audience gasped at the fact that he was performing without the aid of a safety net. For the next few minutes he and

Helga performed a series of leaps and twists and catches in the air, which had the audience on the edge of their seats. Finally the ringmistress appeared once again and announced that the Flying Twins would now attempt a quadruple twist, a feat which had never before been successfully performed without the aid of a safety net. Despite knowing that her words were just so much melodramatic flimflam, Nick couldn't help feeling as nervous as the rest of the audience appeared to be. He watched with clenched fists as Helga and Michael stood, motionless and straight-backed, facing each other on their respective platforms at opposite sides of the ring as a low, throbbing drum roll filled the air like an auditory manifestation of the audience's tension.

Then Michael, the trapeze hooked behind his bent knees, began to swing, and a split second later Helga did too. The two of them swung out across the heads of the crowd, on parallel but opposing trajectories, gaining height and speed with each arc. Finally, after five such swings, the moment came. At the apex of her swing Helga let go and began to spin and flip in the air – once, twice, three times. At the completion of her fourth twist, she stretched out her arms so that Michael could grab her wrists.

He swung towards her, reached out – and missed.

The audience screamed as Helga's body plummeted towards the ground. Hands covered mouths and turned children's heads away as she dropped like a stone, her limbs spinning, pinwheeling. When she was perhaps ten metres from the ground the lights in the big top abruptly went out. In the sudden and shocking blackness – blackness which seemed absolute, utterly impenetrable – Nick braced himself for the sickening smack of the girl's flesh hitting the sawdust-strewn ground, the terrible crunch of her breaking bones.

But it never came. In a silence that felt as if the darkness had smothered the sound of their screams, the audience waited. They waited for two seconds, five, ten, not daring to speak, barely even daring to breathe.

Then, as abruptly as they had gone out, the lights came back on . . .

. . . to reveal the ringmistress standing in the centre of the ring, with the two bats once again hanging from her outstretched arms.

For a few seconds there was silence, which was eventually broken by a small sound as if someone was stifling a sob. Then, slowly, hesitantly, a couple of people began to clap, which in turn encouraged others to join in. Gradually, like the roar of an approaching wave, the applause grew, intensified, until at last *everyone* was clapping, vigorously and enthusiastically.

Nick joined in too, aware that this was more an outburst of relief than celebration. He was grinning and slapping his hands together because of the simple realisation that Helga's fall had been a trick, a part of the act. For the moment he tried not to think about *how* she had survived; he was simply grateful that she *had*.

'Some act, eh?' John muttered into his ear. Nick nodded and raised his eyebrows.

'How did they do it?' Kate asked. 'Where did she go?'

'Magic!' said Anthony, with a magician's flourish.

Kate still looked troubled. 'No, but really? I mean, what just happened was impossible, wasn't it?'

Before anyone could reply, a woman in the front row let out a sudden high-pitched screech and their attention snapped instantly back to the ring.

The reason for the woman's distress was that a black panther – the same panther that had appeared to swap places with the dark-haired young man in the cage that morning – had entered the ring and was prowling its perimeter, regarding the audience with unblinking yellow eyes. The alarming thing was not that the panther was there, however, but that it was *alone*. There was no keeper accompanying it, no indication that it was tethered or restricted in any way.

The audience sat transfixed – the children fascinated, the adults terrified of moving a muscle in case they drew attention to themselves – as the big cat prowled round and round. Nick sat as still as everyone else, a little ashamed of his gratitude that there were at least a dozen rows between himself and the stage and that, if the panther *did* attack, it was unlikely that he would be the target.

After what seemed like several minutes – but was probably no more than one or two – his attention was snagged by a flicker above him. He glanced up and saw that a burning hoop, like a fiery messenger from the heavens, was slowly descending on a thin chain.

The panther saw the hoop too and seemed to bunch its muscles, to adopt a defensive stance. It snarled at this visitation from on high, its velvet muzzle curling back to reveal long sharp teeth. The hoop descended until it was no more than a metre or so above the ground. Then it halted, crackling a little as it burned, a thin black drift of oily smoke curling up into the darkness.

Without warning the panther suddenly sprang at the hoop. It sprang as though the hoop was prey, stretching out its forelegs and unsheathing its claws. Instead of tearing the hoop from its chain and bearing it to the ground as though making a kill, however, the animal sailed straight *through* the hoop, lifting its body in the same way that a racehorse rises to surge over a fence. As it did so, something extraordinary happened. With the fire rippling around its velvet-black form, the creature seemed to *change*. Nick, like the rest of the audience, was staring enraptured at the panther, and was just as astounded as everyone else when, emerging from the ring of fire, it suddenly became a man.

Beside him, Kate gave a shrill gasp, her body jerking. 'What just happened?' She sounded almost panic-stricken and looked at Nick with alarm. 'Dad, *what just happened?*'

Anthony, sitting on her other side, muttered, 'Smoke and mirrors.' But he looked startled too.

The man, who had emerged from the hoop, did a forward roll as he hit the ground and then sprang instantly to his feet. He raised his arms as though to embrace the adulation of the audience, but at first all that emerged from the seats around him was a muttered tumult of bewilderment and consternation. Then, as before, someone began to clap and within seconds the ripple of applause that followed surged into a wave, and then a tsunami, of whoops and cheers. The man bowed and rose, tilting his chin almost pugnaciously, his black curtains of hair falling away from his swarthy face. His eyes smouldered like coals as he scanned the audience. As the man's glare passed over him, or at least over the area in which he was sitting, Nick shuddered involuntarily. Then, like the panther before him, the man began to walk round and round the ring, to prowl, his stare sweeping the audience as if he was searching for someone specific.

Finally he stopped, his black-clad form poised almost on tiptoe, his head tilted coquettishly to one side. He appeared to be peering intently at someone in the audience. Slowly the house lights dimmed and a spotlight, soft but considerably brighter than the gloom around it, fell upon the subject of his attention. Nick felt an odd, almost weary sense of inevitability when he saw that the startled face that the light illuminated belonged to Chris Blaine's teenage daughter Sam. Like her mother, Sam was beautiful, her pale skin flawless, her lips plump and full, her hair a tumble of corkscrew curls.

Her eyes were wide, fixed on the man as he stared at her. Slowly he raised a hand to his mouth and blew her an extravagant kiss. Even from across the ring, Nick saw Sam's lips part as though to draw the kiss in, saw her shoulders rise and fall as though she was expelling a sigh of contentment.

Then the man in black wheeled away and sprinted back towards the hoop of fire. Raising his arms he dived through it again – and a panther emerged on the other side, landing lightly on its four black paws.

Once more the audience gasped in shock and surprise and wonder. Like a ripple of oil the panther bounded across the ring and disappeared, trailed by a stream of applause.

'Well-trained animal,' said Anthony admiringly.

Kate still looked anxious. 'How did they change like that? The panther into the man and back again, I mean?'

'I told you,' he replied. 'Smoke and mirrors.'

She frowned. 'It can't be that simple.'

'All right, so maybe it's not literally smoke and mirrors, but it's certainly misdirection. It's a classic magician's technique.'

'But I was *watching*,' she said, 'especially that second time.'

'You mean you *think* you were,' said Anthony. 'But really you only saw what they wanted you to see.'

Kate looked ready to argue further but slumped back into her seat as the ringmistress once again entered the ring.

'Ladies and gentlemen,' she said, her voice booming around the big top, 'that is the end of our entertainment for this evening. I trust you have all found something to suit your tastes, and that we will see you again tomorrow. Goodnight!'

She raised her arm and with a bang and a flash of white sparks she was gone.

'Tomorrow?' said John, puzzled. 'Why should we come again tomorrow?'

Perhaps because we won't be able to stay away, thought Nick, but the response seemed so peculiar, even to him, that he remained silent.

The audience trailed out in something of a daze, clearly preoccupied with all that they had experienced that evening. Nick too felt as if he had been cast under some kind of spell. At times the performance had been like a vivid and astonishing dream. He wondered how many of the actual dreams of Shettle's inhabitants that night would be full of people transforming into bats and panthers, of falling trapeze artists and leering clowns.

The cold night air outside the big top seemed to revive him a little. Kate slipped her arm through his.

'I'm not sure I liked that very much,' she admitted.

Overhearing her, Anthony said, 'Why not? I thought it was good fun.'

At that moment they became aware of a commotion off to their right. 'Jamie?' a woman was shouting in apparent distress. 'Jamie, where are you?'

Nick turned to see a woman stumbling towards the now dark and shuttered trailers, which had earlier been selling food, her head darting left and right. 'Jamie!' she shouted again, her voice becoming shriller, more desperate. 'Jamie!'

John and Lis Kersh were already hurrying towards the woman, and Nick, Kate and Anthony followed, as did several other people.

'Is there anything we can do to help?' John asked.

The woman turned to him, her eyes darting with panic. 'I've lost my Jamie. He's only six. One minute he was here and the next . . .' She ran a hand through her hair distractedly.

'Don't worry, we'll find him,' John said reassuringly. 'I'll ask the circus people to make an announcement.'

'I'll come with you,' said Nick quickly. For some reason he didn't like the thought of John going back into the big top alone.

John glanced at him. 'Right you are.' Turning to his wife he said, 'Lis, you stay here with Mrs . . .' He looked at the woman questioningly.

'Pasco,' she said, 'Barbara Pasco.'

'. . . with Mrs Pasco, and we'll—'

But suddenly the woman's head snapped up. 'Oh!' she shouted. 'Oh, there he is! Thank God!'

Nick turned to see a grotesquely tall figure with a disproportionately small head lurching towards him. Then he realised that he was looking at the black-clad panther man with a small boy sitting on his shoulders. From his elevated position the boy giggled down at the knot of spectators. As the woman rushed forward, a man who was clearly the boy's father pushed his way between Nick and John, shouting, 'You've found him! Thank God for that!'

The panther man lifted the small boy down from his perch and set him gently on the ground. Barbara Pasco smothered the boy in a hug and then turned to the panther man. 'Oh, thank you! Thank you! Mr . . .'

For the first time the panther man spoke. In a low, gruff, heavily-accented voice he purred, 'Emil.'

'Emil,' said the boy's mother dreamily, and then to everyone's astonishment she took the man's shaggy-haired head in her hands and kissed him long and hard on the lips. When she broke away she looked breathless and shocked at her own actions. Mr Pasco gaped at her.

'What the bloody hell do you think you're doing?' he said.

'I don't know. I . . .' Barbara Pasco looked at Emil with a combination of the sleepy-eyed lust that Nick had witnessed earlier, confusion and more than a little fear. 'I don't know,' she murmured again, and then she seemed to pull herself at least partly together. 'Thank you for finding my little boy,' she said almost primly. 'My husband and I are very grateful.'

Emil nodded once and then he turned and slipped away into the night. Watching him go, Nick wrapped his arms tightly around himself. All at once he felt very, very cold.

Nine

'I have to go.'

As they walked away from the big top, Sam Blaine had been falling further and further behind her parents and her annoying little brothers, who couldn't stop gabbling about the circus. Who *cared* about the stupid clowns and the trapeze artists? All that mattered was—

'What do you mean? Go where?'

Sam snapped back to reality, knowing how important it was to focus. She had to make this convincing. She couldn't take no for an answer. If her parents refused to let her go, she'd just *die*, she knew she would.

Looking her frowning father in the eye, she held up her iPhone, waggling it between her fingers. 'Gemma's just texted me. We've got some homework to finish for tomorrow. A project we're doing together.'

Now it was her mum's turn to frown. 'At this time? It's almost half-past nine.'

'I know, but this is the first chance we've had.' She waved a hand vaguely. 'If you hadn't made me come to the stupid circus . . .'

'I thought you wanted to come,' her dad said. 'You didn't raise any objections.'

'Well, that's because you and Mum were going on about how we don't get together for family outings that much any more because of our "independent lives".' Sam made little quotation marks in the air with her fingers as she said this.

'But if you had too much homework you should have said, sweetheart,' her mum replied.

Sam did her best to look contrite, submissive. The last thing she wanted was to make them angry at her. 'I know, but I didn't want to disappoint you.'

'Oh, for goodness' sake,' her mum said, but Sam could see she was softening. Her mum was the sort of person who couldn't stay cross for long and who was so nice that she always looked for the best in everybody. Ordinarily Sam would have felt guilty for deceiving her, but on this occasion she just wanted – no, she *needed* – to get away, and she knew that the end would justify whatever means she had to use to get there.

'How long will you be?' her dad asked.

'No more than an hour. And I'll get Gemma's dad to drive me home afterwards. I won't be wandering the streets at the dead of night or anything.'

'Well, where does Gemma live?' her mum asked. 'Do you need us to take you there?'

Sam shook her head and gestured back towards the big top, from which people were still streaming. 'No, she's been to the circus with her mum and dad. They're going to meet me by the entrance.'

Her mum glanced at her dad. There was still uncertainty on her face, but in that moment Sam knew that the battle had been won. 'What do you think, Chris?'

Her dad looked sternly at her and tapped his watch. 'An hour. No more than that. You've got school in the morning.'

'I know. That's why we have to finish this project tonight.'

Her mum stepped forward and kissed her on the cheek. 'We'll see you later, sweetheart. I hope you get your work finished.'

'Thanks. We will.' Sam knew that she should have been feeling guilty, but she was too excited, too desperate. She had never taken drugs but she guessed this must be what addicts felt like when they needed a fix – that the drugs were all that mattered, that they were the only important things in the world.

She turned and walked away, against the flow of people, back towards the big top. She tried not to look too eager in case her parents were watching, though she felt like running, tearing through the crowd, shoving people aside just so she could be with *him* again. With Emil.

How did she know he wanted her? She just did. How did she know he would be waiting? She just did. How did she even know his *name?*

A tiny part of Sam knew that this was wrong, that it didn't make sense, but that tiny part was like a rickety wooden shack facing a vast hurricane of obsession and need and desire. The moment he had looked at her, singled her out, a connection had been made between them. His mind had touched hers, and immediately she had known – just *known* – that he wanted her, and that they were destined to be together.

Once she was through the gate and back in the field the crowds thinned out and now she *did* begin to run. She couldn't help it. She could feel his pull. He was reeling her in, and nothing anyone could say or do now would have stopped her going to him even if she had wanted to. She passed the last of the stragglers fifty metres or so from the big top. Now all was silent, aside from the vast glowing tent itself billowing in the wind. As she neared the entrance porch she slowed to a walk.

'Emil?'

The huge tent was deserted. Sam walked forward into the main auditorium, stepped over the waist-high barrier into the ring. The sawdust felt soft beneath the thin soles of her shoes, like a sandy beach.

'Emil?'

The name drifted up into the darkness, a whispering echo.

He had to be here. *Had* to be. She closed her eyes, as if summoning him.

When she opened them again, there he was, standing in front of her. Those burning eyes, drinking her in, possessing her soul.

Beautiful.

'Emil,' she breathed, her voice clotted, husky.

His lips peeled back in a slow smile. His teeth were long, sharp. He raised his arm, inclined his hand almost formally towards her, like a suitor at the start of a waltz.

She took the hand. Gasped. His skin was cold. A charge went through her. Electric ice.

Sam tilted her head back and waited for his kiss.

Ten

Nick rolled his eyes and reached for a custard cream. Couldn't people talk about *anything* else? All morning he'd had it from the kids – those who had turned up for school, that was. Out of a class of thirty-two only nineteen had appeared for registration, presumably due to this bug that was going round.

But of those who *had* turned up, not a single one had seemed capable of thinking or talking about anything else but last night's bloody circus. Despite his attempts to restore order, they had gone on and on about it, until eventually he had been forced to yell at them to shut up and concentrate on their work.

He hadn't lost his temper simply because of irritation, however. Mostly it was because he was alarmed and disturbed. The way the kids were talking it was as if they were obsessed, as if the circus was the most exciting thing they had ever seen in their lives. All right, so it was a novelty, Nick accepted that – but had it really been *so* special? And did no one else feel the same way that he did? Did no one else, beneath their almost euphoric enthusiasm, feel that same crawling sense of doubt, even dread? Did no one feel their mind becoming clouded, confused, when they tried to analyse their emotions? And did no one feel the subsequent anxiety and frustration caused by the inability to think clearly?

Nick felt as if was living among the Pod People. He felt as if the whole of Shettle had been brainwashed and that he was the only one who had an inkling – vague and unfocused though it might be – that something was very wrong.

He had been hoping for a bit of sanity in the staffroom but his work colleagues were just as bad. Even Malcolm Kingston, who had been furious with the circus folk for littering the playground with their flyers yesterday, seemed to have fallen under their spell. He had burst into the classroom at break time, flushed and excited, almost childishly eager to share his views on how 'wonderful' and 'exciting' the circus had been, on how it was 'a breath of fresh air' and 'just what Shettle needed'.

Nick knew that it wasn't natural for people to be *quite* so effusive – but no one else seemed able to see it. When he expressed this viewpoint it was clear they thought he was being a spoilsport, a curmudgeon, a grumpy old man. Worse than that, *creepier* than that, was the mental shutter that would slide down behind his listeners' eyes when he voiced his doubts. His opinions just seemed to bounce off them, like a ball rebounding from a wall.

Sipping his coffee, warily watching his colleagues as they chatted about how *incredible* and *amazing* and *exciting* the circus had been, and feeling increasingly like a pariah in their presence, Nick felt his mobile throb in his pocket. He took it out and looked at the display screen: **John Kersh calling.**

Raising the phone to his ear, he said, 'Hi, John, how are you?'

'How am I?' said John almost brusquely. 'I'm hoping to find a voice of sanity, that's how I am.'

Immediately Nick felt a wave of relief wash over him. He stood up smartly, feeling that it might be advisable to take the call somewhere a little more private. 'The circus?' he muttered.

'The circus. The bloody circus. All day long patients, staff, even the other bloody doctors have talked about nothing else.'

'Hang on,' Nick said, striding towards the door, imagining – or perhaps not imagining – the disapproving looks as he crossed the room.

Leaning against a section of corridor wall between Malcolm Kingston's office and the staff toilets, Nick said, 'Okay, I'm out of earshot now.'

'Sounds like it's been the same at your place. What is this, Nick? Bloody mind control?'

'I don't know,' Nick said. 'But don't you feel . . .'

'Go on.'

'It's hard to express, but don't you feel like your brain's not working properly? Like this whole thing's a big jigsaw puzzle and for some reason you can't quite put the pieces together?'

'That's it exactly. Every time I try to think about what's going on – *really* think about it, I mean – I seem to get distracted; my mind wanders as if I'm too tired to concentrate.'

'Why us, do you think?' Nick asked.

'What do you mean?'

'Why are we the only ones who don't think the circus is the best thing since sliced bread? In fact . . .'

'Go on.'

'The circus frightens me. I don't know why, but it does. It fascinates me – I feel drawn to it – but it frightens me too; more than that, it *terrifies* me.'

There was a silence. Eventually Nick said, 'John? Are you still there?'

John's voice was sombre. 'I'm still here. And . . .'

'And?'

'And you're right. That's exactly how I feel. Fascinated but terrified. It's similar to how I felt when I went scuba diving in Hawaii a few years ago and a shark swam above us, a brute of a thing – six metres long from nose to tail. In that moment I felt so . . . small. So slow. So vulnerable. I thought, "If that thing comes for me there's nothing I'll be able to do about it. Nothing . . ."' His voice trailed off.

'What are you thinking?' asked Nick.

'I'm thinking about what you said, about us being the only ones who don't think the circus is the best thing since sliced bread. What if that's not the case? What if there are others?'

'What others?'

'I don't know. Maybe that's the answer. Maybe if we find the others we'll work out what this is all about. We'll overcome this . . . conditioning or brainwashing or whatever it is.'

'Strength in numbers?' said Nick.

'Exactly.'

Nick had a sudden flashback to yesterday, to when he had found the free tickets on his doormat and had been trying to justify to himself why he would go to the circus that evening. He would go because there were links to be made. Links between the circus, between Kate and Anthony not being able to leave Shettle, between . . . between Anna and how she had died. The links were there, he felt sure they were, and he felt that they were glaringly obvious too. And yet for the life of him he couldn't . . . quite . . . grasp them.

'Fuck it!' he said.

'What?' asked John. 'What's the matter?'

'I'm just trying to think, trying to make connections. But something's blocking me.'

'It's them,' said John. 'The circus people. They're doing this somehow.'

Nick knew it was true, knew that that thought should lead to another . . . but it wouldn't come. 'Did you speak to Anthony yesterday?' he asked.

'About he and Kate not being able to leave Shettle?'

'Yes.'

'I did. And apparently he and Kate were not the only ones. I've heard of other people who suffered the same symptoms when they tried to leave this morning. Apparently they simply couldn't do it. Got so far and had to turn back. And it works the other way, too. People who live outside Shettle can't come into it – the school bus included. As far as I'm aware, none of the kids from Shettle who go to school in Wenthorpe have been able to get out.'

'But that's . . . crazy. What does it mean?'

'It means we're trapped. It means no one can get in or out.'

'But it doesn't make sense,' Nick said. 'It's just impossible.'

'Hmm,' said John. 'And what makes even less sense is that people don't seem that worried about it. They're too obsessed with the circus to think of anything else. You know they're all planning on going again tonight?'

'Yes,' said Nick. 'It's the same here, too. When I ask them why, the attitude seems to be: why *wouldn't* we go again?'

'And what about you?' asked John. 'Are *you* going again?'

Nick paused. In truth the question startled him. Eventually he said, 'Maybe. But not because I *want* to. Because I feel I *have* to. Does that make sense?'

'Yes, it does,' said John. 'Remember I told you about the shark? Well, the last thing I would have done in that situation was to turn my back on it.' He paused and then said quietly, 'That's exactly how I feel about the circus.'

Eleven

The first thing Alan Michaels did after easing his Volvo to a stop beside the gate was to pull a handkerchief from his pocket and mop his sweating face. The second thing was to lean forward with a grunt and retrieve his Marlboros from the glove compartment. With a fat finger he pushed in the black button of the lighter on the dashboard and sat, breathing stertorously, unlit cigarette stuck between his lips, staring across the muddy, rutted field at the candy-striped big top. In the daylight it looked patched and shabby, streaked with dirt and bird shit. The trailers around it resembled squat hovels, hunched against the drizzle. His gaze flickered higher, to where Mitre House had once stood on top of the hill.

'I know why you're here,' he murmured, and said it again with more conviction, as if to lock the thought into place. *'I know why you're here.'*

The lighter popped out of its socket. Alan applied the glowing coil to the end of his cigarette and pulled smoke deep into his lungs. Down at the base of his throat he felt rather than heard a slight phlegmy rattle,

126

but he kept inhaling until the rattle became a tickle, making him cough.

At least the smoke slowed his uncomfortably rapid heart and stopped the tremors at the ends of his fingers. When he had regained his breath he took another pull, longer and smoother this time. On the passenger seat next to him was a reporter's notebook bound in black leather. Picking it up, he opened it to the last entry.

Nightmares-death-darkness-bad memories-premonitions-sickness-something coming-Mitre House-Nick, John, Chris, me-Anna-10 years ago-Karl Mitterhaus-Your community will die. Your children will die. To give me back my life.
CIRCUS OF NIGHTS!!

At first glance it appeared to be a collection of unrelated words and phrases, of random jottings. But Alan knew it was more than that. To him it was a web, each strand of which was seemingly separate but which together formed a pattern. He had begun to spin it a couple of weeks ago when the dreams had started. He had sensed that 'something' was coming; something bad. And he had felt that same 'something' filling his mind like smoke and stealing his thoughts away whenever he tried to focus upon it. And so, like a good journalist, he had jotted down thoughts and images and ideas as they had occurred to him, in the hope that if he could see them all in the same place they would make some kind of sense, that the whole would become more than the sum of its parts.

And so it had proved. Although he hadn't *consciously* been able to make the links – although he had been *prevented* from doing so – the simple act of recording the flotsam and jetsam of his struggling subconscious, of getting it down in black and white, had enabled him to pull the threads together. And once he had done so the pattern was obvious. *So* obvious. Although Alan still couldn't claim that his mind was clear, although whatever dark influence the circus was using still maintained its strange hold over his conscious thoughts, his accumulated scribblings had at least enabled him to grasp why the circus people – whoever or whatever they were – had come.

It was to fulfil the promise of Karl Mitterhaus's final words. It was to exact his terrible revenge. Alan wondered whether, of all Shettle's inhabitants, he was the only one who had been able to discern the terrible truth of the matter, the only one who could see that the community and its people were weak, declining, and that the Circus of Nights was the cancer that had come to finish them off.

Your community will die. Your children will die.

Lynn, he thought. *My beautiful Lynn.*

Your children will die.

'No,' Alan muttered, so vehemently that smoke gushed from his mouth. 'No fucking way. Not if I can help it.'

He had thought of calling the police, of calling his friends, but he had been afraid that he would not be able to make them understand. Like everyone else, he had felt the pull of the circus, had gone to last night's performance with Lynn in order to assess the enemy's strengths and weaknesses. And it had taken all his willpower – plus the words in his notebook, which he had read over and over, cementing them in his mind – to resist being bewitched, as everyone else seemed to have been bewitched, by the circus's deadly allure, its lethal glamour.

There was one more item in his glove compartment he would need today. Alan hoped he wouldn't have to use it – that the mere threat of it, coupled with a clear display of his determination, his conviction, would be enough to make them realise he meant business. But he *would* use it if there was no alternative; he would do whatever it took to protect his daughter. He opened the car window, threw his cigarette into the wet grass, closed the window again. Then, leaning forward over his fat stomach and grunting as air was forced out of him, he lifted the item out of the glove compartment and set it on the seat beside him.

Unwrapping the grey, slightly oily cloth, he exposed the dull metal gleam of the gun. His heart quickened again. The weapon – all Alan knew about it was that it was a Browning Hi-Power and that it was loaded – had been acquired for him by an ex-colleague, a crime reporter now based in Cardiff, who had 'underworld connections'. (Eschewing the habits of a lifetime, Alan had not asked too many questions.) The gun had cost him £300, though whether that had been cheap or expensive he had no idea. Again, he had handed the money over without question – and also with a sense of incredulity, a suspicion that perhaps, finally and irrevocably, he was going mad.

It didn't seem mad now, though. Now it seemed like foresight. Somehow – and he suspected that the idea had been planted deliberately, insidiously, in order to provoke a climate of fearful but unfocused apprehension – he had known that the Circus of Nights was coming. He hadn't known what form it would take, and neither had he even initially known whether the notion had come from outside himself or had been cooked up by his own delusional mind. But he had felt an overwhelming urge – an urge he had been unable to ignore – to ensure that when the time came he would be fully equipped to defend himself.

And now his instincts had borne fruit. Now that time was here. The Circus of Nights was his worst nightmares made manifest. It was loss and grief and wickedness and mortal terror, all rolled into one.

Alan picked up the gun almost with distaste and dropped it into his jacket pocket. He felt its weight pulling the side of his jacket down, making it tight across his right shoulder. He opened the car door and wheezed and struggled his way out into the bitingly cold October air. At the beginning of each year he vowed to lose a little weight, and by its end he was always heavier than he had been twelve months before. He knew that if he didn't cut down on his eating, drinking and smoking soon, and that if he didn't take a little exercise now and again, he would never make old bones. As he closed and locked the car door and pushed open the creaking gate into Hobbes' Meadow, the irony that, of all people, he was Shettle's representative, even its defender against evil, was not lost on him.

His heart felt like a trapped animal as he trudged up the muddy well-worn track towards the big top. His right hand rested gently on the bulge of the gun. He had no idea how he was going to play this. It had been pointless trying to prepare a speech when simply maintaining a sense of focus and purpose had been difficult enough. 'Your children will die,' he whispered to himself. 'Your children will die.' If his concentration started to slip he knew that remembering these words would snap his thoughts back to the matter in hand, that they would provide him with all the resolve and determination he would need to see this through. All the same, by the time he arrived at the first of the trailers flanking the final twenty-metre walk to the big top's entrance he was sweating and shaking and craving yet another cigarette.

Despite his nervousness, however, the place was so quiet that it seemed abandoned. Alan guessed that the caravans where the circus people lived, and the cages where they kept the animals, must be somewhere behind the big top, out of sight. Maybe there would be a bit more life round there – though he hoped there wouldn't be *too* much; he didn't want to have to face the entire troupe in one go. Best just to seek out their ringleader (or ringmistress) and make his feelings known.

He plodded past the trailers, his chest heaving with exertion, and arrived panting at the entrance to the huge tent. He could see that it was sealed up tight, but he gave the thick rope woven through the fist-sized eyelets of the entrance flaps, cinching them together, an experimental tug nonetheless. As he stepped back, he heard a throaty chuckle behind him and whirled round. Standing in front of the velvet-curtained entrance to the 'Mirror of Life' was the dwarf who had peeled off his face to reveal a grinning skull during last night's show.

'Think you might have dropped something,' the dwarf said, slowly raising his hand. Dangling from his thumb and forefinger was Alan's gun.

Aghast, Alan slapped his pocket. Sure enough, the gun was gone.

'In fact,' the dwarf continued, 'you've been very clumsy. Aren't you glad I'm here to pick up after you?'

He held up his other hand. Alan's car keys were hanging from his little finger, and pinched between the other digits was his black notebook.

Instantly Alan realised both how foolish he had been to come here alone and how easily he had been manipulated. Even so, he took a lurching step towards the dwarf, raising a pudgy hand.

'Give me those!' he snapped.

The dwarf reared back, cracks appearing in the white make-up on his face as he scowled. 'Didn't your mother teach you any manners?'

Alan paused, licked his lips. Despite the cold day he felt sweat trickle down his chest and stomach, the hot stuffiness of his muddled thoughts trapped inside his skull.

'Please,' he said. 'Let me have my things.'

'You want me to give you back your gun so that you can shoot me with it?' the dwarf said incredulously.

'I wasn't intending to shoot anybody,' said Alan.

The dwarf narrowed his eyes shrewdly. 'So why have a gun if you're not prepared to use it?'

'I brought it for protection.'

'Protection against what?'

Alan didn't want to be having this conversation, but he saw no alternative. He had been stripped of his advantages – if, indeed, he had ever had any in the first place, which he was now beginning to doubt. 'Against whatever . . . hostility I might find here.'

The dwarf grunted, clearly unconvinced. Gripping the gun more firmly and pointing it at Alan, he said, 'Perhaps I ought to shoot *you*.'

Alan held up his hands, palms out. The animal inside his chest kicked frantically for release. 'Please don't.'

'*Bang! Bang!*' the dwarf shouted, causing such a jolt of shock to go through Alan's body that he dropped to his knees in the mud.

The dwarf roared with laughter. 'Go away, *little man*,' he said, and then hooted again at his own joke. He half-turned, pushing at one of the velvet curtains behind him so as to open a gap large enough for him to slip through.

'Please,' Alan gasped. 'My things.'

'They're mine now,' said the dwarf.

'But my car keys,' replied Alan. 'I need them to get back.'

'You've got legs, haven't you?' the dwarf sneered and dodged between the curtains, beneath the sign reading 'Mirror of Life'.

'Please,' Alan said again.

He hated his own wheedling desperation, but he felt frantic, panic-stricken. He didn't care about the gun and the keys – not much, anyway – but he couldn't bear the thought of losing his notebook. Without it to focus his thoughts, to remind him why the Circus of Nights had come to Shettle, he would be helpless to protect Lynn when the time came. And so, knowing it was probably hopeless, but too desperate simply to walk away, he struggled to his feet and stumbled after the dwarf, following him through the curtains and into the 'Mirror of Life'.

Alan's first impression, as the red drape fell back into place behind him, was of a velvety soft-black darkness. Although he had barely even taken a step since entering the trailer, the atmosphere already seemed rarefied, completely at odds to the mulchy, cold autumnal day on the other side of the curtain. A little anxiously, he reached behind him to reassure himself that the real world was still only an arm's length away – but was shocked to discover that his grasping hand encountered nothing but air. As half-memories of recent nightmares sprang into his head, nightmares involving an endless darkness in which he floundered, lost and alone, a jolt of reaction caused his heart to lurch – a spasm of pain which set off a chain reaction of further rapid pulses in his fingers and throat. He swallowed and was suddenly aware of the meaty glottal sounds of his own corpulent body – the sluggish gurgle of blood through his fat-hardened arteries, the wheezing of air through his flabby tar-encrusted lungs.

It's a trick, he told himself. *An illusion. Don't let it get to you.* He took a deep, shuddering breath, which triggered a further pang in his chest, and yanked his handkerchief out of his pocket to mop his sweating face.

Alan considered calling out, but shrank from the idea of drawing attention to himself. Instead he took a couple of steps back through the darkness, the air so dense that he could almost feel it pressing against his face like something glutinous. He reached out, but the curtain through which he had entered was no longer there. *An illusion*, he told himself again. *A clever illusion, that's all.* His urge was to keep going back the way he had come until he found the exit, but he resisted; he wouldn't give them the satisfaction of revelling in his panic. Instead he would do what a proper journalist *should* do – he would remain inquisitive, receptive, detached.

Easier said than done, but he turned himself back around and began to walk forward. He took small, slow, careful steps, right hand out to prevent himself colliding with unseen obstacles. After half a dozen steps he paused. Surely he ought to be at the back wall of the trailer by now? As soon as the thought formed he felt his mind scuttling away from it, like a mouse fleeing from a potential predator. Alan knew that if he wanted to preserve his sanity he shouldn't try to analyse too closely what was happening to him. If nothing made sense, if physical laws became forfeit, then what would be left for him to cling to?

Just keep going, he told himself, and had a sudden memory of the way his first editor, Jock Pardew, would clench his fist and proclaim 'Onward!' whenever he came up against an obstacle. The recollection gave Alan a brief modicum of comfort, a fleeting sense of a simpler, happier time – and then his hand brushed against what felt like the furry hide of an animal and he was jolted back to the present.

He snatched his hand away so suddenly that his elbow flared with pain. For a few seconds he stood rigid, hands bunched defensively in front of him, feeling slow and blind and horribly vulnerable. He expected to hear a shifting movement in the darkness, to hear a grunt or a snarl, perhaps to be assailed by a reek of rank animal odour or hot, meaty breath. Alan wondered if he had somehow blundered into the panther's cage, or even whether the creature had been deliberately released into this dark space with him. But hadn't the fur felt too shaggy to belong to one of the big cats? And hadn't it been too high up, unless the thing was standing on its hind paws? A gorilla, then, or perhaps a bear? But neither of those animals had featured in last night's performance – which didn't necessarily mean, of course, that they weren't a hitherto unseen part of the circus's menagerie.

It was only when Alan had been standing motionless for ten, maybe fifteen seconds that he allowed himself to hope that maybe it hadn't been an animal, after all. Even so, he had to summon a huge amount of willpower to reach into the darkness once more. Although it was pitch black, he closed his eyes as if that might expel the mental image of wide jaws full of jagged teeth crunching over his wrist. When his fingers brushed the shaggy pelt for the second time he froze, but on this occasion resisted the urge to snatch back his hand. Instead he spread his fingers out slowly, applying more pressure, and when he felt the fur first ripple and then give a little as he pushed against it he released a long, shuddering sigh of relief. Facing him was not an animal, but a flimsy barrier of some kind.

Flattening his palm against it, he moved slowly forward. The barrier yielded under the increasing pressure of his hand, but it was only when he felt something brushing across his right arm that he realised it was one of a pair of thick, furry overlapping curtains, which were now parting in the middle. Slipping between them, and hearing them crumple softly back into place behind him, Alan was suddenly excited to see a sliver of light to his right. He moved towards it like a crab, in slow, shuffling, sideways steps.

As he got closer the band of light widened and brightened. It was a welcoming buttery-gold glow, and after the darkness it filled his eyes with such a coruscating radiance that he only knew he had reached the edge of the curtain when the heavy fabric slipped across his palm and fell away behind him, leaving his left hand clutching at air. With nothing to anchor him he stood for a few moments, squinting in the light as it spread and sparkled across his vision. He felt disorientated and exposed, but also pathetically grateful that the darkness had not proved to be as endless as it had seemed in his dreams.

As his eyes adjusted, Alan realised that someone was standing silently in front of him. Startled, he took an involuntary step back, and the figure, who seemed freakishly elongated, instantly and mockingly aped his action. Alan blinked frantically, and as he half-raised his right hand as if to ward off an attack he became vaguely aware that the tall, skinny figure was raising its left. Agonisingly slowly the dazzle faded and the figure came into focus, whereupon Alan blurted out a blubbery, gasping laugh. The figure standing facing him was his own reflection, monstrously stretched in a funhouse mirror.

Looking around, Alan realised that he was standing at the far end of a narrow corridor whose shimmering golden walls were lined with many similar mirrors. Each of them was warped in some way – horizontally or vertically concave or convex, or rippled like waves, or fashioned with speckles or swirls – that pulled some aspect of the body it reflected grotesquely out of shape.

Taking a couple of steps to his right, Alan rapped on the wall at the end of the corridor. From the way it absorbed the sound it seemed disturbingly thick and solid, as though it had stood for years. Turning back to face the corridor stretching ahead of him, he was shocked to find that the hanging or curtain through which he had entered this impossible place was no longer there, that it had been replaced by another mirror – one that tripled the glistening expanse of his sweaty forehead and caused his eyes to bulge into dark and fearful pools.

Trying to reject the idea that he was being pushed towards a specific destination as his exits were systematically sealed behind him, Alan turned his gaze towards the far end of the corridor. A wedge of shadow from beyond the right-hand wall suggested that a further corridor met this one at a ninety-degree angle. Fearful of where it might lead, but aware that the turning provided him with his only chance of escape, Alan moved forward cautiously. His bizarrely distorted reflections crept along with him but he tried not to look at them, tried not to think how they suggested that he was here purely to be manipulated, toyed with, pulled out of shape. Instead he thought of Lynn and clenched his fists.

Your children will die.

'No,' he muttered. 'No.'

The closer he got to the end of the corridor, the thicker the wedge of shadow spilling from the right-angled opening seemed to become. If he stared hard enough Alan could almost imagine movement within the darkness, like a mass of bees crawling over one another in a hive. He continued to creep forward, taking care to set his feet down slowly, so as not to alert anyone or anything to his approach. When he reached the final pair of mirrors facing each other across the corridor he stopped, the sweat pouring down him, his breath rattling deep in his chest. A pulsing behind his eyes, in tandem with his heartbeat, made the walls of the corridor appear to throb like a living thing.

Flanked by twin parodies of himself – one squat and wide as a bullfrog, the other with limbs as crooked as a lightning-blasted tree – he stood still and listened. Aside from the booming, wheezing, gurgling rush of his own body it was silent. Were they watching him? Somewhere out of sight? Were there hidden cameras in the mirrors, or concealed in the walls? His neck gave a gristly crackle as he looked around. He felt an urge to say something, to challenge them, but his courage deserted him.

Trying to appear nonchalant, Alan walked forward and into the wedge of shadow. It wasn't straining towards him like a long black snout, not really; neither did it seem to chill and sting his skin like something corrosive as he stepped into it. He had no idea what would be awaiting him around the corner, but he was nevertheless surprised when, after a couple of metres, the corridor widened out into a cavern-like room. He was immediately aware of a sense of echoing space, of a ceiling so high that it was lost in shadow. Had he somehow wandered into the big top? He had a feeling that he was underground, but perhaps that was an illusion too.

Though the walls and ceiling around him stretched away into darkness, the room wasn't entirely without light. Something glimmered a little way ahead of him, something tall and rectangular and silvery – a mirror, like the ones in the corridor. Alan glanced over his shoulder and was not surprised to find that the glow from the mirrored corridor behind him had disappeared, that only darkness now followed at his heels.

Facing front again he trudged slowly towards the mirror. *The Mirror of Life*, he thought, recalling the sign hanging above the velvet drapes. It seemed like a long time since he'd followed the dwarf in here. Back in the real world he imagined hours, days, months passing by while he blundered through endless corridors, lost and alone. He had the feeling that time here didn't exist, or at least that it was meaningless. He shook his head in an attempt to dislodge his dark and fanciful thoughts, but they continued to swarm in his mind like pulsing black parasites.

As he approached the mirror, his reflection plodded forward to greet him. It was an uncorrupted one this time, the glass smooth and clear, but it was no more reassuring for that. He looked ghastly, his skin the colour of overboiled potatoes, his suit rumpled and damp with sweat. There were dark circles beneath his eyes, and his thick, almost girlish lips – 'kissable lips', his wife had always called them – were as grey as old pastry.

Maybe I'm already dead. Maybe I'm dead and this is Hell. He should have been snorting scornfully at the idea, but he couldn't bring himself to do so.

What now? Alan wondered, staring at his reflection. And then an even more terrible thought occurred to him: *Is this it?* He put a hand on his chest, as if that could calm the kicking animal in there. And, seeking strength, he dredged up those familiar words yet again: *Your children will die.*

'Lynn,' he whispered, the first word he had spoken out loud since he had entered this place. Instantly the word seemed to take flight, to multiply, echoing off the walls around him. As though in response, a shape began to form in the mirror, just behind Alan's left shoulder. He tried to turn his head in the hope of reassuring himself there was nothing there, but was suddenly horrified to discover that he was paralysed. He could only watch as the shape, fluttering and black at first, continued to expand, to take on form and substance and colour. His eyes widened in terror as the shape elongated into a figure standing behind him, as a face with burning black eyes boiled whitely out of the darkness.

No, he said, *no*, though the words were only in his head; his lips and tongue and vocal cords were frozen.

Standing behind Alan, the image of Karl Mitterhaus grinned, his lips peeling back to reveal long white needle-sharp teeth.

And when he snarled, lunged forward and buried those teeth in the side of Alan's neck, Alan felt the pain not where Mitterhaus had bitten him but in his heart, which seemed to burst and tear and drown him in his own hot, gushing blood.

Twelve

Where are you? You ok?

Lynn hesitated a moment, then pressed 'Send'. She hoped her dad wouldn't read the text and think she was making a fuss. She knew that he still saw her as his little girl and was only trying to protect her from all the bad things in the world, but usually, when she asked him how he was, he would grunt and frown and say that he was fine, and why shouldn't he be?

The incident the night before last, when she had come downstairs to find him sitting in the conservatory, had been an exception to his usual rule of not burdening her with his inner thoughts and feelings. She was aware of the bad dreams he'd been having recently and, however much he still played the bluff and hearty boss at work, she had been able to tell by his manner that he had been overly preoccupied of late. But she had assumed that the dreams, and the memories they'd stirred, had been the *sole* cause of his preoccupation. And although it had occurred to Lynn to wonder what might have instigated them, she knew that the subconscious could be a strange beast, that it sometimes randomly threw up old obsessions and supposedly long-buried memories.

Two nights ago, however, her father had fazed her. She had thought his preoccupations were internal, but then he'd revealed his fear that something was coming, that there was 'trouble' on the way. 'Unfinished business,' he had said. But what did that mean? Had he been receiving threats? Had someone been dredging up dark secrets from the past? Or *was* it internal, after all? Had he been referring merely to his inner troubles, to the serious mental and emotional distress he had suffered after Mum's death? He had clammed up when she had pushed him to elaborate, but it had left Lynn feeling anxious, out on a limb, and even more worried about him than before.

She had hoped that a night at the circus might bring him out of himself but it had had the opposite effect. Maybe it had been a bad idea in light of the mood he had been in at work. He had spent most of yesterday locked in his office, and on the infrequent occasions when he had emerged he had communicated with his staff in little more than grunts and scowls. Not even Lynn had been able to get through to him. The longest sentence she had been able to prise out of him all day had been, 'I'm fine. I've just got things on my mind.' When she had light-heartedly offered the opinion that a problem shared was a problem halved, he had snapped 'Not this one,' and had shut the door on her. He had barely responded to her increasingly desperate stream of chatter on their way to the circus later that evening, and after the performance he had looked . . . *haunted*. Yes, that was the only word she could think of to describe the expression on his face.

'You all right, Dad?' she had asked. 'You don't look so good.'

'Yes, fine,' he had muttered, wheezing along beside her. 'I'm just tired, that's all.'

'You're sure there's nothing else?'

He had shaken his head irritably. 'No. What else *would* there be?'

Hesitantly she had said, 'I don't know. But you look as if you've seen a ghost.'

He had smiled at that, but it had been a ghastly smile – a *haunted* smile – after which he had refused to discuss the matter further.

Lynn had been hoping to speak to him again this morning, but he had somehow managed to avoid her. He had got himself up and out during the ten minutes she had been in the shower. She had come downstairs, ready for work, only to find a scrawled note on the kitchen table:

Sorry I couldn't give you a lift this morning.
Lots to do. See you later.
All my love, Dad xxxx

It was that 'All my love' which had bothered her, and those four kisses at the end. Her dad was affectionate, but he had never been a gusher. Even in birthday cards his messages were generally perfunctory. Anything more than 'Happy Birthday, Dad x' would be, for him, an uncommon display of emotion. This scribbled breakfast-time note, therefore, seemed particularly poignant. It was almost as if he was afraid he might not see her again.

No, that was ridiculous. How *could* she think that?

'See you later'. That was what she clung to. He wouldn't write 'See you later' if he didn't mean it.

As soon as she arrived at work that morning she knocked on the door of his office.

'He's on a job,' Jimmy Madison, the sports reporter, told her.

'What job? Where?'

'No idea. He came in early, went into his office, came out again two minutes later. Said he had to go out and didn't know what time he'd be back.' Eyes suddenly brightening, Jimmy said, 'Hey, did you go to the circus last night? Wasn't it amazing?'

Lynn nodded, distracted. 'Yes, it was . . . good.'

'Good?' Jimmy looked almost offended. 'It was more than good! What about that trapeze act, eh?'

His zeal unsettled her. He reminded her of one of those Christian fundamentalist nutters banging on about Jesus. Even more disturbing was the fact that as the morning progressed – and her dad *still* didn't show up – it quickly became apparent that Jimmy was not the only one spellbound by the Circus of Nights.

The circus, the circus, the circus. Her colleagues – normally so cynical, so hard to impress – were seemingly incapable of talking about anything else. Wondering if she had stepped into *The Twilight Zone*, Lynn spent the morning hunched over her computer, trying with increasing desperation to give the impression that she was too engrossed in the music and book reviews she had to write for Friday's round-up to indulge in idle chit-chat about the *fucking circus*.

Now it was lunchtime, and she had fended off Jimmy's offer of a pub lunch in order to grab a bit of time to herself. It was while sitting in the park, picking at a prawn sandwich and watching the swans on the lake, that she finally succumbed to the temptation to send her dad a text. She didn't want to irritate him by being over-solicitous, but she had reached the stage where even if he sent her a grumpy message back she would be happy.

But there was nothing. No reply. Despite the weather, which had turned cold enough overnight for her to see her breath on the air, she sat on the park bench for as long as she could before sighing and rising to her feet.

What Lynn saw and heard while walking back to the office through the centre of Shettle only confirmed how much the Circus of Nights had insinuated itself into the community. Their flyers were everywhere – plastered to lamp-posts and bus shelters, displayed in shop windows, even fluttering loose in the streets. Every conversation she had overheard since leaving the office had been about the circus. People had been talking about it in the sandwich shop, in the street, in the park. But the *really* weird thing was not simply that the circus had made such a positive impression but that everyone seemed to be planning to return there that night. Their enthusiasm (obsession) was downright creepy. She felt as if she was the butt of an elaborate joke. Either that, or as if she was one of only a tiny percentage of the population immune to some kind of mass hysteria.

But maybe not entirely immune. She still felt the pull. Somewhere deep down she heard the circus calling to her. Perhaps she was not as enamoured with it as everyone else because she was worried about her dad, or more particularly about the detrimental effect that the circus seemed to have had on him. Or perhaps it was something more than that. Perhaps on a deeper, more fundamental level, she recognised that the circus was . . . bad? Rotten in some way?

The idea was gone before she could grasp it, but the instinct was definitely there. Lynn thought again of her dad, of his assertion that trouble was coming. But it was the circus that had come, wasn't it? Could he have meant . . .

And then the notion, slippery as a fish, wriggled away again, splashed back beneath the surface.

What was the matter with her? She couldn't think straight. Couldn't seem to make even the most basic connections. She frowned as she turned off the main street and began crossing the plaza on the other side of which, beyond the fountain, stood the glass-fronted office block that housed *The Wenthorpe and Shettle Times*.

Lynn was so engrossed with struggling with her thoughts that she didn't look up until she had taken at least eight steps, maybe ten. When she *did* finally look up, the thoughts she had been trying to bolt together collapsed like a house of cards.

There was a police car parked at the bottom of the steps up to the main door. And in that moment she knew – she just *knew* – that they were here to see her, and that it was about Dad. And so she started to run, and she was so full of panic, of fear, that her limbs wouldn't work properly, and several times she stumbled and almost fell. And people turned to look at her curiously, disapprovingly – women in suits, men with briefcases. But she didn't care. She didn't care about anything except finding out that her dad was all right . . .

They must have seen her coming. Someone must have looked out of one of the big office windows that faced onto the plaza and seen her staggering and loping along. Because just as she reached the bottom of the steps the main door of the building opened and two police officers came out. They looked at her with carefully neutral faces.

'What's happened?' she gasped as she reached them.

One of the officers frowned. 'Miss Michaels?'

She nodded impatiently. 'It's my dad, isn't it?'

The policemen glanced at each other. And then, as if in response to some silent agreement, the one who had already spoken said, 'Yes, Miss Michaels, it is. He's in a stable condition, but I'm afraid he's had a heart attack.'

'Oh God,' she said, half-stifling the second word with the hand that she pressed to her mouth. But although she was shocked, there was a tiny part of her that felt weirdly relieved. A heart attack was such a normal thing. It was something she could understand and cope with. And then, more optimistically, she thought, *He's in a stable condition! That means he's alive!*

'How bad was it?' she asked.

'Quite severe, I understand. But he's comfortable now. And receiving the best possible treatment.'

Lynn felt suddenly flustered; her mind was going into overdrive. 'I need to go to him,' she said, half-turning away as if to search for a bus or a taxi. 'Which hospital is he in?'

'We'll take you there,' the more communicative policeman said, indicating the patrol car a few metres away, as if she might not have guessed it was theirs.

Once their journey was under way the policeman who'd been doing all the talking so far introduced himself as PC Johns and his colleague as PC Neal. They told Lynn that her father had collapsed during an interview with the circus people in Hobbes' Meadow.

Lynn jerked upright in the back seat, as if stung. 'The circus? What was he doing there?'

'A story for the newspaper, apparently. It seems he was chatting away and then he just keeled over. It was the strongman who saved his life. Gave your dad cardiac massage and mouth-to-mouth, got his heart going again. He even drove him into town in your dad's car and carried him into the surgery. Very public-spirited, I'd say.'

Lynn saw the two officers look at each other and smile. They had that same zealous gleam in their eyes that she had seen everywhere today. Her stomach crawled. Was there *anyone* left in Shettle who was immune to the circus's charms?

'Is he in Wenthorpe?' she asked.

PC Johns narrowed his eyes as if he didn't understand the question.

'My dad. Is he in Wenthorpe Hospital? That's where the local heart unit is.'

She knew that because Dad had worked on a newspaper campaign last year to keep the unit open when it had been faced with government cuts. Who would have thought that he would have required its services so soon? But both officers were shaking their heads.

'Wenthorpe is currently inaccessible,' PC Neal said.

'Inaccessible? What does that mean?'

Lynn sensed a tension in the car. 'There have been problems accessing the route,' said PC Johns.

Lynn was none the wiser but she decided to let it go for now. 'So where's Dad been taken?'

In lieu of a response, PC Johns indicated and turned left into the car park of Shettle surgery. It was a white stone building with metal grilles across the windows to deter drug thieves. The side wall was a mess of graffiti, fainter stains beneath indicating that in more prideful times there had been efforts made to keep the place looking presentable.

'He's here?' said Lynn, confused. 'But why isn't he in a proper hospital?'

Again the two officers exchanged a glance. 'He's being well looked after,' said PC Johns.

'I don't doubt it,' said Lynn. 'But they don't have the facilities here, surely?'

'They've got everything they need,' PC Neal assured her. 'It's the best place in Shettle.'

'Fuck Shettle!' snapped Lynn. 'What's wrong with Wenthorpe? What aren't you telling me?'

PC Johns, having parked the car, twisted round in

his seat to face her. 'It's not common knowledge yet,' he said, 'but it will be soon.' He paused, then said, 'No one can get in or out of Shettle. They just . . . can't.'

She looked at him incredulously. A centipede of absolute dread wriggled down her gullet and into her belly. She didn't know why she was so afraid, but she was. Instinctively she felt that it was to do with more than her dad's condition.

Faintly she asked, 'What do you mean, no one can get in or out?'

PC Johns told her about the localised but debilitating 'sickness barrier'; that was what he called it.

'But that's . . . crazy,' breathed Lynn. 'So what's happened to all the people who work outside Shettle? And all the kids who go to school in Wenthorpe?'

PC Neal shrugged. 'They've had to stay home today.'

'But I work at the newspaper. Why haven't I heard—' And then she broke off as a feeling of coldness went through her. She suddenly knew *exactly* why she hadn't heard. It had been because people hadn't been talking about it; they'd been talking about the circus instead. They'd been obsessed with the trivial and ignoring the impossible.

It was a feat of misdirection on a massive scale. For a second she clearly saw the full horrific implications of that – and then a dark cloud swept across her mind, obscuring her thoughts. But the fear remained, profound but directionless. Wrapping her arms around her body to stop herself from shivering, she said 'I'd like to see my dad now.'

He was lying on a leather examination table in the

nurse's office, swaddled in blankets, an oxygen mask over his face. Lynn was relieved to see that he was hooked up to a portable heart monitor and that the nurse was sitting by his bedside, providing him with constant attention. The spike of his heartbeat on the little screen looked strong and regular.

'How is he?' she asked in a small voice.

Nurse Collins smiled at her. She was a kindly woman of about sixty. She had given Lynn all the inoculations she had needed throughout her childhood, and had never failed to present her with both a sticker and a lollipop afterwards for being a brave girl.

'He's bearing up,' she said breezily, and then winked at Alan as if the two old-timers had been sharing a joke. 'But why don't you ask him yourself?'

Lynn had thought her dad was sleeping, but when she looked at him more closely she realised that his swollen, bruised-looking eyelids were slitted open and that the dark glints of his eyes were peering out at her. As she moved forward, Nurse Collins vacated her chair so that Lynn could sit down. Lynn took her dad's rough, cold hand in her considerably smaller one.

'Hello, Dad,' she said, tears springing unbidden to her eyes.

His face creased into what she assumed was a smile beneath the condensation-speckled oxygen mask. He reached up slowly, tiredly, and pulled the mask down to his chin. His face was sweaty beneath it; his lips, livid, almost blue, barely moved as he spoke.

'Hello, sweetheart.' His voice was a low, phlegmy

rumble. The unexpected endearment tugged a sob out of her. 'Sorry about this.'

'It's not your fault, Dad,' Lynn said, simultaneously smiling and weeping. 'How are you feeling?'

'Weak as a bloody kitten.' Then his slurred voice acquired a new urgency. 'But listen. There's something I have to tell you. Something you need to know.'

On the monitor screen his heartbeat seemed to speed up, to spike a little higher. Nurse Collins, who had been standing unobtrusively against the wall, glided forward.

'Now then, Alan,' she said with cheery calm, 'try not to get over-excited. We don't want another episode, do we?'

Alan scowled. Between rasping struggles for breath, he said, 'I'm not getting excited . . . but I have something important to tell my daughter . . . so please butt out.'

Before Nurse Collins could reply, Lynn held up her hands and said quickly, 'Don't worry, I'll keep Dad calm. If he's got something to tell me I think it's best he does it without any interruptions, don't you?'

Nurse Collins looked uncertain. Lowering her voice, she said 'Your father's in a very fragile state, Lynette.'

'I know that. But if we could just have five minutes alone?' Lynn presented her most appealing face, her eyes wide and wet with tears.

'Well . . . all right,' said Nurse Collins hesitantly. 'I'll be just outside if you need me.'

'Thanks,' said Lynn. 'I appreciate it.'

When Nurse Collins had gone, Lynn turned back to her dad, gripping his big hand firmly between both of

154

hers. 'Right, Dad, say what you need to say. But do it slowly, calmly. I'm not going anywhere.'

He swallowed, closed his eyes and opened them again, as if ordering his thoughts. Then quietly, haltingly, he said, 'They did this to me . . . the circus people . . . In a mirror I saw . . .' he frowned, as if struggling to recall the memory, then said '. . . *him* . . . Mitterhaus . . . they're trying to bring him back . . .'

Alan paused to fumble the oxygen mask back into place, taking several long breaths. Confused, Lynn said, 'Mitterhaus? The murderer, you mean? The one who killed all those kids?'

Her dad gave a single tired nod.

'But he's dead, isn't he?' said Lynn.

Her dad tugged the oxygen mask away from his face again. 'There's something . . . not right about them . . . not human . . . they're here for revenge . . . against the children . . .'

'What children?' asked Lynn. Then, when her dad seemed to tense and scowl with agitation, she said softly, 'It's okay, Dad, take your time. I'm listening.'

'*Our* children,' he said. 'The ones who . . . killed him . . . Me, Nick, Chris, John . . . our children are in danger . . . you're in danger . . .'

'They told you this?'

He shook his head, a quick, jerky movement. 'The pattern's there . . . but . . . but they do something to your mind . . . make you forget . . . you have to fight it . . . try to remember . . .'

Lynn glanced at the monitor again. The spikes of his

heartbeat were becoming jagged, erratic. 'Take it easy, Dad,' she soothed.

He gestured towards a table beside his bed. On it was a jug of water, medication capsules, a pen and notepad bearing the surgery's logo.

'Wrote it down for you . . . as much as I could remember . . . so I wouldn't forget . . . show the others . . . Nick and John and Chris . . . make them remember . . . make them see . . .'

Lynn reached across and took the notepad. It contained page after page of scrawled, spidery writing; random phrases, some repeated over and over; jottings from a confused mind:

Anna . . . Mitre House . . . 10 years . . . something coming . . . darkness . . . death . . . dreams . . . something bad . . . evil . . . Circus of Nights . . . dreams . . . Mirror of Life . . . the children . . . Nick Miller, John Kersh, Chris Blaine . . . Karl Mitterhaus . . . revenge . . . Your Children Will Die . . . 10 years ago . . . Your Children Will Die . . . To give me back my Life . . . Circus of Nights . . . Your Children Will Die . . . memories . . . protect the children . . .

'Promise me,' he whispered. 'Promise me you'll make them remember . . .'

Lynn stared at the words. Pages and pages of them. The same phrases cropping up again and again. They frightened her. She felt her mind trying to turn away from them, to blind her to their meaning.

'Promise me . . .' he hissed.

His heartbeat spiked higher, a jagged peak. She grasped his hand, as if to transfer some of her strength to him.

'I promise, Dad,' she said. Her voice was a husky wheeze. She cleared her throat, said it again, her voice stronger this time.

'I promise.'

Thirteen

Although Caroline Blaine was exhausted, she was up off the settee like a shot the instant she heard the stealthy click of the front door. She ran into the hallway to find Sam standing on the mat, trying to push the door quietly closed behind her.

Thank God, she thought, *thank God*. But as Sam turned and went rigid with guilt at the sight of her mother, Caroline's relief turned to anger.

'Where the *hell* have you been?' she snapped, her voice cracking on the last word.

Guilt and defiance chased themselves across Sam's face. 'I told you,' she said, 'I was at Gemma's. We had some work to finish. It took longer than we thought, so I stayed over.'

A gentle, trusting, honest woman, Caroline had always tried to instil her children with her own values. Until today she thought she had largely succeeded.

'That is a blatant lie!' she exclaimed.

Sam scowled. 'No, it isn't.'

'Yes, it is and you know it! Did you honestly think

we wouldn't phone Gemma's parents when you didn't come home? Did you really and truly imagine that we wouldn't find out?'

Sam shrugged sulkily, rolled her eyes. 'Oh, get off my case, Mum.'

Caroline was flabbergasted. She rarely lost her temper, but suddenly she was screeching. 'How *dare* you speak to me like that after what you've just put us through! Your father and I have been worried sick! We haven't slept a wink all night! We've had the police out looking for you!'

'Oh, for God's sake,' muttered Sam. 'Overreaction or what?'

'Over . . .' Caroline's voice trailed off. She gaped at her daughter, stunned into silence. For a few seconds she couldn't speak, and then with a mighty effort she managed to dredge up a voice that sounded to her own ears like cracking glass.

'I can't believe I'm hearing this. You lie to us. You stay out all night. You don't answer your phone. Nobody knows where you are. And you honestly don't expect us to be worried? What sort of parents would *not* be worried by behaviour like that?'

Sam shrugged. 'Cool ones?'

Caroline blinked. 'You really believe that? Do you *honestly* know what you're saying?' She shook her head. 'What's happened to you, Sam? This isn't the daughter I know.'

'Well, maybe you don't know me very well, then,' Sam muttered.

Caroline shook her head again. 'No, I'm not accepting

that. Something's happened, hasn't it? Something's changed.'

Sam scowled again, but she looked defensive. 'What's it to you? I'm old enough to make my own decisions.'

'You're *seventeen!*' Caroline's voice rose shrilly on the second word, partly in anger, partly in distress. 'Not eighteen. Seventeen! Your father and I are still responsible for you. For your well-being.' She waved a hand as if batting away a troublesome fly. 'But that's not the point. The point is, this isn't like you. This isn't who you are.'

'Maybe it is,' said Sam defiantly.

'No. I won't accept that. You've always been a model daughter. You've never given us any trouble before.' Caroline's tone softened. 'Can't you tell me what's wrong, darling?'

'Nothing's wrong.'

'Are you in trouble?'

Sam shook her head irritably. 'No.'

'What, then?' Caroline sounded desperate. 'Why won't you talk to me? If nothing else, we've always been honest with each other.'

Sam, her back still pressed against the front door, looked around as if seeking an escape route. Finally she murmured, 'Not that it's any of your business, but if you *must* know . . . I'm in love.'

Caroline looked puzzled. 'In love? With who?'

Evasively Sam said, 'No one you know.'

Trying to be understanding, Caroline asked, 'Well, does he have a name, this . . . boyfriend of yours?'

Sam sighed. Then, as if the name itself was some kind of incantation, she smiled dreamily. 'Emil,' she said.

'Emil? I've never heard you mention him before. How do you know him? Is he a school friend?'

Sam snorted with contempt. 'Don't be ridiculous! The boys from around here don't know anything. Emil, though . . .' her voice softened again '. . . he's seen so much.'

Caroline was puzzled. 'But if he's not from around here, where *is* he from?'

Sam looked at her mother as if she was being deliberately obtuse. 'The circus, of course.'

'The circus?' Caroline felt an odd mixture of emotions at the word – a strange yearning; a flush of almost sexual longing; a dark, primal fear. For a few seconds her mind swirled with confusion – and then she remembered the dark-eyed man, the panther-man, and her maternal instincts surged to the fore.

'No!' she said.

Sam's eyes narrowed. 'What do you mean, "no"?'

'You *can't* love him! You . . . you . . . don't know anything about him.'

'I know *everything*,' replied Sam, her face again softening into an almost euphoric expression. 'I knew everything as soon as he looked at me. I love him. We're meant to be together. I just know it.'

'You *don't* know it!' Caroline's fear – unfocused but intensely powerful all the same – was making her increasingly desperate. She had the odd notion that she was battling for her daughter's soul. 'You *can't* know it! I want you to keep away from him, you hear me? He's . . . he's . . .'

Sam's face twisted. She was a beautiful girl, but in that moment she looked ugly. 'He's what, *mother?*'

'He's *dangerous!*' Caroline was shocked by her own statement – but instinctively she knew it to be true.

Sam sneered. 'He's not dangerous. He's beautiful. And he's mine. And nothing you say will change that.'

She strode forward, shoving her mother roughly out of the way. The violence was so unexpected, and so uncharacteristic of her daughter, that Caroline was caught off balance. She staggered back, the base of her spine hitting the Victorian washstand which stood in the hall with enough force to topple a vase of flowers. The vase smashed, flowers and water scattering and spattering all over the carpet. Unremorseful, Sam swept past her and up the stairs.

Gulping back tears, unable to believe how much her beautiful, sweet daughter had changed, seemingly over-night, Caroline stumbled to the bottom of the stairs, glass crunching under her feet.

'*I won't let you see him!*' she screeched. '*I won't let you see him again!*'

At the top of the stairs Sam halted and turned slowly. Caroline took a step back. The cold intensity of her daughter's expression was terrible to see.

'Just try and stop me,' Sam hissed.

Fourteen

When Lynn walked into the fuggy warmth of The Fleece, Nick Miller and John Kersh were already sitting at a small table in the corner between the log fire and the bay window. They were hunched over like spies, hands curled protectively around bottles of Beck's. They didn't look up until she was standing close enough to cast a shadow over them.

'Can I buy any of you gentlemen a drink?' she asked.

Nick looked pinched and ill, blinking behind his spectacles. John was the first to respond, rising to his feet quickly enough to bump his thighs on the table.

'Let me get *you* one,' he said, gesturing at a stool which they had been saving for her. 'What'll you have?'

'Oh . . . er, thanks. Dry white wine please.'

'Nick? Same again?'

Nick looked at his bottle a little guiltily, and Lynn got the impression he was wrestling with his conscience. Then he nodded abruptly. 'Why the hell not?'

'Good man.' Turning back to Lynn, John reached out and briefly touched her arm. 'I'm so sorry to hear about your dad. And sorry that I wasn't there to attend to him. It was my day off today, but I'll be in tomorrow. How is he?'

'Oh . . . bearing up,' said Lynn, trying to muster a smile. 'You know what Dad's like.'

'I do indeed. If anyone can pull through he can. Can't imagine he'd let a little thing like a heart attack deter him.' John nodded and smiled with such brisk confidence that for a second Lynn felt that everything would turn out fine, after all. 'Right, I'll get those drinks.'

As he headed for the bar, Lynn settled herself, looking around. It was five p.m., the sky already bruising dark outside, and the pub was moderately quiet. She noticed a few flyers for the Circus of Nights here and there – one tacked to a floor-to-ceiling wooden beam just a couple of metres away.

'How are you, Nick?' she asked. Less than ten years ago he had been one of her teachers at Wenthorpe Primary, before he had moved (or perhaps 'retreated' might be a better word) to the smaller school in Shettle after his wife died, and it still felt weird to call him by his first name.

He gave a slightly strained smile. 'Oh, you know . . . not so bad.' But the expression on his face belied his words. He wore the same haunted expression as her dad had worn after the circus performance last night.

'Have you heard from Chris Blaine at all?' she asked. 'I left a message, but he hasn't got back to me.'

Nick nodded. 'I'm afraid he can't make it. Family problems, he said.'

Lynn felt a twinge of unease. 'Oh dear. Nothing serious, I hope?'

'I don't know. He didn't elaborate.'

'So he didn't say whether it was anything to do with his children?'

Nick frowned, as if she had awoken a memory that he couldn't quite grasp. 'No, he didn't. Why do you ask?'

Lynn reached into her shoulder bag and took out a plastic A4 document wallet, which she placed on the table. 'Let's wait till John gets back. It's part of the reason why I asked you to meet me here.'

Two minutes later John was back and they were all sitting with drinks in front of them. Nick immediately snatched up his bottle and took a long gulp from it. Lynn sipped her wine.

'So to what do we owe the pleasure of your company this evening?' asked John.

Lynn paused. Where to start? Finally she said, 'How have you both been feeling lately?'

John half-laughed. 'As a doctor, shouldn't *I* be asking that question?'

'I'm serious, John. How have you been feeling? Up here, I mean?' She tapped her head.

His smile faded. He looked at her seriously. 'To tell you the truth . . . pretty exhausted. Drained. Overworked. You're hale and hearty, so you may not know it, but there's been a lot of illness in Shettle just recently. Some kind of . . . well, I hesitate to say "virus", because the symptoms are myriad, and not even remotely linked with each other. But let's just say there's been a marked decline in the community's health of late.' He shrugged. 'It could just be the colder, murkier weather, I suppose, but . . .' He trailed off, looking troubled.

Lynn and Nick were both nodding. Nick said, 'A lot of kids are off school. Some of the staff, too.'

'Yes, we've been short-staffed at the newspaper as well,' said Lynn. 'But that's not what I'm getting at – or not entirely, anyway. As well as physical symptoms, have people been complaining of . . . bad dreams? Bad memories? Feelings of anxiety? Confusion?'

'All of the above,' replied John.

'And what about you two? Have you experienced any of those symptoms? Have you recently felt as if you've forgotten something important? Or as if you're not quite making the mental connections you think you should be making?'

John was frowning again. A little of the colour had drained from his face. 'What are you getting at?'

Lynn took a deep breath and said, 'As you know, my dad's a journalist.' They both nodded. 'Well, recently *he*'s been having these feelings. This afternoon, when I went to see him at the surgery, I had a long conversation with him, and he really opened up to me – as much as he could, anyway. He likened his recent mental state to the onset of Alzheimer's. He said it was like his mind was clouded, like he could only remember things in snippets, and because of that he couldn't connect his thoughts, couldn't put them together. But the thing was, he instinctively knew that he *should* be able to put them together, that there was a pattern there somewhere, but that it was being hidden from him in some way.'

'Memory loss is quite common in—' John began, but Lynn waved him to silence.

'Sorry, John, but let me finish. This is hard enough

to explain as it is. You see, *I'm* feeling it too.' She tapped her head. 'I'm *really* having to concentrate to hold this together. It's only because I've spoken to Dad, and because I've read his notes, over and over, that I'm able to override the . . . the conditioning, I suppose you'd call it. Because that's what this is. It's not *inside* us. It's being caused by an outside influence.'

Nick looked bewildered. 'I'm sorry – I don't follow.'

'What I mean is, we're being manipulated. All of us. We're being made to forget. They're doing it so that we can't fight them, so that it makes it easier for them.'

'Sorry, but who are "them"?' asked John.

'The Circus of Nights.'

There was a silence. Both men gaped at Lynn in bewilderment. But she could see that there was a suggestion of dawning awareness in their eyes, an indication that something might be breaking through.

Then the strain of trying to grasp what she had told them, of trying to retain it in his mind, clearly became too much for John. He clenched his teeth as though he had a migraine and rubbed a hand across his forehead.

'I'm sorry, Lynn,' he said, 'but you're going to have to run it by me again.'

She opened the plastic document wallet and took out what was inside.

'It would be easier to show you,' she said. 'My dad wrote it all down. Every time he had a stray thought or feeling, he wrote it in his notebook. That way he was able to look at the big picture, to put it all together.' She pushed the pad towards them, the one on which he had scrawled all that he could remember that afternoon.

'Unfortunately he lost the notebook at the circus. Had it stolen, he said. They didn't want him to remember, you see? They didn't want him to be a threat to them.'

'Sorry, but who are we talking about again?' asked Nick.

'The circus people. I think they meant to kill him. I think they meant to kill him in a way that would make it look like natural causes, because they're not ready to show their hand yet. But Dad's strong. Stronger than they expected him to be. He survived – and he *remembered*. Look.'

She indicated the notepad. Nick and John were still clearly confused, but Lynn sensed that they *wanted* to understand, that some kind of survival or protective instinct was driving them to try to make sense of what she was saying. They leaned forward over the notepad as she tore out the pages, one after another, and lined them up on the table in front of them.

'Read his words,' she said. 'Concentrate on them. Take them in. Eventually you'll see what you've been missing, and you'll understand what's been happening, why the Circus of Nights is here.'

She waited patiently, watching their faces, watching their eyes roam restlessly across the words and phrases in front of them. Putting events together – cause and effect – was a natural process, and she knew how disorientating it was to force yourself to relearn something that should have been obvious; something that subconsciously you had known all along.

Little by little she saw the confusion pass from their faces, to be replaced by a kind of stark wonder, a sense of . . . she struggled to think of the word and then suddenly it came to her – a sense of *awakening*.

'I see it,' John said. 'It's like . . . what are those optical illusions called where it seems like a meaningless jumble, but then, if you stare at them in the right way, three-dimensional shapes start to appear?'

'Magic Eye puzzles,' said Nick. 'Yes, you're right.' He suddenly sat back, a stunned expression on his face. 'My God, how could we have been so blind? So stupid?'

'You haven't been stupid,' said Lynn, and nodded at the Circus of Nights flyer stuck to the wooden support beam. '*They* did it to you. I don't know how – some kind of mass hypnotic command, I guess. But how that's even possible on such a massive scale, I have no idea.'

Nick glanced at where she had indicated and his face suddenly twisted with hatred. He jumped up from his seat, walked across to the flyer, ripped it from the beam and crumpled it in his fist. The few people around him who saw him do it stared at him with a kind of glazed shock. Nick glared back at them and resumed his seat.

'You have to *keep* reading the words,' Lynn said. 'You have to *keep* reminding yourselves, otherwise you'll forget again.' She handed them each a sheet of A4 paper. 'After I'd spoken to Dad I went back to the office and tried to put his notes into some kind of order, to establish a timeline, so that we can see more clearly what's happened, why the circus is here. Then I added a few notes of my own, things that I thought were relevant, typed it all up and did us a copy each. I suggest we keep rereading this, keep referring to it, in order to keep our minds focused.'

John and Nick read the sheet she had given them, the sheet which outlined, in bullet points, how Anna Miller and the child-killer Karl Mitterhaus had perished at their hands ten years ago; how Mitterhaus had cursed them with his dying breath; and how a spate of illness and bad dreams had culminated in the coming of the Circus of Nights.

'The barrier,' John said, pointing at one of the notes Lynn had added herself, an expression of wondrous realisation on his face. 'This is them too, isn't it? They've trapped us in here with them? In the lion's den, so to speak?'

'I think so,' said Lynn grimly.

'I'm sorry,' said Nick. 'What barrier?'

Quickly Lynn told him what PC Johns had told her about the 'sickness barrier' surrounding Shettle.

'I can confirm that the barrier is an unbroken circle,' said John. 'After Anthony's experience yesterday, he and I drove out this afternoon to see if we could find an exit route. But every single road out of Shettle affected us the same way. We even parked the car at the roadside a couple of times and tried to cut across fields and through the woods, but no dice. Poor old Anthony took the brunt of it, I'm afraid – though at his insistence, I might add. Sick as a dog, he was. He even passed out once when he pushed on a bit too far, and I had to wade in and drag him out by his feet. Nearly passed out myself.'

Nick was staring at him in horror. 'Is this for real?'

John grimaced. 'As real as . . .' Searching for an analogy, his gaze alighted on the chalked lunchtime menu on the blackboard beside the bar. 'As real as pies and mash.'

Nick's eyes were still wide behind his spectacles. 'But it's impossible!' he said. 'Who *are* these people?'

'I'm not sure they are even *people*,' muttered John.

Nick scowled. 'What's that supposed to mean?'

John's face was apologetic. 'I'm sorry, Nick, but we've all been avoiding this for too long. Perhaps we've just been too scared to admit it, or perhaps we just . . . just rejected what we couldn't fit into our modern, *rational* view of the world . . .' He took a deep breath, then said, 'But the thing is – and I can't believe I'm saying this – I think we're dealing with something . . . supernatural here.'

'Supernatural?' Nick didn't exactly scoff, but he spoke the word as if he was both afraid of it and found it impossible to accept.

John nodded grimly. 'How else do you explain the barrier and the . . . the mind control?'

Nick looked as though he *wanted* to answer, as though he wanted to dismiss it all as trickery – as 'smoke and mirrors', as Anthony had described some of the more outlandish illusions at the circus last night. But he couldn't. Couldn't bring himself to deny what he secretly knew.

Gently, John said, 'I'd forgotten it until now – been *made* to forget it, I mean – but for years I've been telling myself that Karl Mitterhaus was just a man. A man in peak physical condition, who had filed his teeth into points and had the strength of psychosis on his side.'

'That *is* all he was,' said Nick, albeit without much conviction.

'Really, Nick?' said John. 'Do you honestly believe that? Would a normal man have been able to influence Anna as he did?' Nick winced; John saw it, but chose not to acknowledge it. 'Would a normal man's body have decayed so rapidly after he was dead? Would a normal man – even one who was mad or high on drugs – really have been capable of such feats of superhuman strength? He held me up against the wall with one hand around my neck. He held me there as if I was a . . . a baby.'

'So what are you saying?' Nick growled, and finished his beer in one gulp. 'If he wasn't a man, what was he?'

John smiled bitterly, humourlessly. 'I feel daft even saying the word.'

'I'll say it, then, shall I?' said Lynn. The two men looked at her. She leaned forward.

'Vampire,' she said. 'Isn't that what you're thinking?'

Nick barked a laugh that sounded like a cry of pain and leaped to his feet. 'I'm getting another drink.'

As he stalked to the bar, Lynn said softly, 'Is that what we're up against, John? Vampires? Supernatural creatures that feed on human blood?'

His smile was ghastly, a hollow-eyed death mask. 'I don't know. Like I say, it sounds bloody daft.'

'But if it's true,' said Lynn, 'then they're here for revenge. They're here to kill your children. To kill *us* – me and Anthony and Kate and the rest. So the question is: how are we going to stop them?'

Fifteen

As dusk settled on the land, the softly glowing light within the big top seemed to increase in brightness, making the tent look like a vast domed lantern. Pete Blackstock stomped to the entrance, which was still sealed up tight, and kicked out at the dirty canvas.

'Oi!' he shouted. 'Anyone home?'

The only reply was the faint rustle of wind in the treetops at the edge of the field.

'I know you can fucking hear me,' he continued, 'so fucking come out unless you want me to cut my way in.'

Behind him, Darren, a pocket-sized version of his father, sniggered.

'Get down, you cunt,' said the cadaverous man standing next to Darren, his shaven head like suede in the encroaching gloom. He yanked back on the metal choke-chain wrapped around his hand, half-strangling the pit bull on the other end, which was rearing up on its stubby hind legs as if eager to enter the fray.

'Can I help you *gentlemen*?' The voice came from behind them. The pit bull spun, snarling, almost yanking the cadaverous man off his feet as it lunged at the white-faced dwarf who had seemingly appeared from nowhere. Although to the little man the dog must have seemed almost as big as he was, he didn't flinch. Indeed, he sneered with disdain as the dog reached the limit of its chain and was jerked off its feet forcefully enough that it flipped onto its back, its hindquarters coming down in the mud with an audible splat.

'You in charge here, shorty?' Pete Blackstock demanded, bunching his fists.

'I have authority enough to deal with the likes of you,' retorted the dwarf.

Pete stomped towards the little man. 'Don't get clever with me, you pint-sized fucker, or I'll get Brutus to rip your fucking head off.'

The dwarf rolled his eyes. 'Which one's Brutus?' he asked drily. 'The dog or the boy?'

Pete narrowed his eyes. 'You taking the piss?'

Clapping his hands, the dwarf said, 'Look, friend, do you think we could skip the whole testosterone bit and get to the point? Box office opens in an hour and I've got to make myself pretty for my audience.'

He grinned, revealing teeth that looked as brown as wood in his bone-white face.

'I want to talk to the organ grinder, not the fucking monkey,' Pete said, causing Darren to emit such a snort of laughter that snot shot out of his nose.

'Oh, now you're just being rude,' said the dwarf. 'In fact, I've a good mind to shoot you.'

So saying, he fanned out his stubby fingers in a magician's flourish, and a split second later a gun magically appeared in his right hand. He pointed it at the pit bull and then at Darren.

'Now which shall I shoot first, the mutt or the brat?'

The cadaverous man gave a bleat of distress, crouched down and wrapped a protective arm around the dog's neck. Darren took a step backwards, his face going almost as white as the dwarf's.

'Dad?' he said in a quavering falsetto.

Pete Blackstock's demeanour changed in an instant. He seemed to slump into himself, raising both hands, a cringing and obsequious expression on his face.

'Now come on,' he said. 'Let's not be daft about this.'

'You're trying my patience,' said the dwarf. 'Just tell me what you want.'

Pete attempted a companionable grin, but it emerged as a twitchy grimace. 'We want to get out of Shettle, that's all.'

The dwarf looked at him thoughtfully. 'Go on.'

'We came to . . . to *ask* you if you'd let us go. If you could show us a way out.'

The dwarf stared at him for a long time. Finally he lowered the gun and said, 'Wait here.'

He waddled away, disappearing around the back of the big top. Darren looked at Pete with wide eyes.

'D'you think he would've really shot me, Dad?'

Pete scowled at his son. '*I'll* shoot you if you don't fucking shut up.'

The cadaverous man, still crouched in the mud with his arms around his dog, swallowed, his prominent Adam's apple bobbing. 'Maybe we ought to just leg it, Pete,' he said. 'These fuckers are dangerous.'

Pete sneered contemptuously. 'Listen to you. Couple of fucking pussies. You just leave this to me, boys. *I'll* sort it.'

Before either Darren or the skinny man could respond, the dwarf was back, a figure drifting in his wake. As the figure got closer, Pete saw that it was a woman wearing long, rustling skirts, and he relaxed a little. He glanced at the dwarf, then nodded at the woman. 'Who's this, then? Your mother?'

Little could be seen of the woman except a tumble of russet curls from beneath the shawl she was clutching tightly around her head. Her cheeks beneath the dark glasses which concealed her eyes looked as white as the dwarf's, though smooth as alabaster. They contrasted with her lips, which were of such a deep red that they appeared swollen and bruised.

'What makes you think we can help you?' she asked, getting straight to the point.

With no sign of the gun, and only a woman to deal with, Pete had regained a little of his confidence. Hooking his thumbs into his jeans pockets and tilting his head to one side, he said, 'We know what you're up to.'

The woman's face and posture gave nothing away. 'Is that so?'

'Oh yeah. But your little mind tricks don't work on me. I'm not taken in by all this shit.' He wafted a hand at the big top looming above them.

'You must be very strong-willed,' said the woman drily.

'Oh, I am,' said Pete, nodding. 'I've got more about me than most of the fucking sheep who live here.'

The woman gave a contemptuous, unladylike snort. 'Don't flatter yourself, little man. You're nothing special. Your resistance to our "mind tricks", as you put it, is more accident than design. "Anomalous immunity", it's called. Which means that there are always one or two little sprats that slip through the net. It's of no consequence.'

Pete glanced at his companions. He looked less sure of himself now. Attempting to regain the initiative, he said, 'But you'll still help us get away, yeah? You'll show us a way out?'

'Why should we?' asked the dwarf.

'Well, we . . . we know about you, don't we? We could tell people.'

'And do you honestly think they would listen?' the woman said.

'They might,' replied Pete, trying to sound defiant. 'I'd *make* them listen.'

The woman gave a sudden bellowing laugh. 'And what would you tell them?'

'That . . . that you're up to no good. That you're here to fuck 'em up. Because it's true, isn't it? It don't take a fucking genius to work that one out.'

The woman said nothing for a moment. She simply stared at Pete, an amused smile on her face.

'What shall we do with 'em?' said the dwarf. 'Shall we kill 'em now?'

Pete blanched. Raising a defensive hand, he said, 'Oi, listen. Like I said there's no need—'

'Shut up, peasant,' snapped the woman. 'I'm thinking.'

Pete lapsed into silence. Like Darren and the skinny man, he stood motionless, waiting nervously for the woman's verdict. Finally she said, 'Show them the way out.'

The three of them gasped with relief, but the dwarf looked disappointed. 'Aw, do I have to?' he said petulantly. 'Can't we just kill them?'

'No,' said the woman, 'we can't.'

'Why not?'

'Because the box office opens in an hour and we don't want corpses strewn about the place. It gives the wrong impression.'

'We could feed them to the tiger,' suggested the dwarf. 'It hasn't had a square meal in weeks.'

The woman didn't move, but her voice hardened. 'I *said* no.'

'But it'll be dark soon,' whined the dwarf. 'I don't want to go tramping through the woods in the dark.'

'You're trying my patience, *jester*,' the woman hissed. 'How about I feed *you* to the tiger?'

The dwarf looked alarmed. Pete grinned, and then thought better of it, stifling the expression with a grimy hand. Nodding to the woman, he mumbled, 'Thanks.'

The woman stared at him from behind her dark glasses for a moment, but didn't acknowledge his gratitude. Then, without another word, she turned her back dismissively and glided away with a rustling of skirts. When she was out of earshot, the dwarf snarled, 'Turn out your pockets.'

'What for?' said Pete.

'Because if I'm going to show you the way out I want paying for it, that's what for. What do you think this is? A charity?'

'My dad doesn't have to pay *you*,' Darren bleated.

Suddenly, as if it had sprung out of his sleeve, the gun was back in the dwarf's hand. He pointed it at Darren's face. 'He does if he doesn't want a son with no head.'

Scowling, the two men and the boy turned out their pockets. The dwarf instructed Darren to bring the money to him. When Darren had placed it in his hand, the dwarf ran his eye over it and sniffed. 'Not exactly rolling in it, are you?' Raising his eyebrows, he pocketed the cash. 'Oh well, better than a poke in the eye with a sharp stick.' Pointing at Lee, the shaven-headed man, he gestured with his gun. 'You with the mutt, you go first. I want that bloody animal up ahead where I can see it.'

Lee glanced at Pete as if for permission. Pete gave a bad-tempered nod. 'Well, go on, then.'

Lee tugged on the dog's lead and took up his position at the head of the group.

'Now you,' said the dwarf to Pete, 'and the boy can walk behind you, in front of me.'

'Where we going?' Pete asked suspiciously.

The dwarf nodded towards the distant trees. 'Into the woods.'

'And we can definitely get out of Shettle through there, can we?'

'Either that or I could be taking you in there to blow your brains out,' the dwarf said, leering. 'But I guess that's a gamble you'll just have to take.'

Darren looked anxiously from the dwarf – who grinned nastily at him – to his father. 'Can't we just go home, Dad?' he said.

Pete looked as though he might have been wondering that himself, but at his son's words his face hardened. 'No, we fucking can't. Whatever these cunts have got planned for this place, I don't want to be here when it happens.'

'Very wise decision,' the dwarf said.

The weird little procession set off, trudging across the muddy field – tall, skinny Lee at the front and the dwarf in his grubby jester's outfit at the back. As they walked, Darren kept glancing nervously at the little man waddling along behind him, and was met each time with a sneering grin and a twitch of the gun barrel to encourage him to keep moving.

The sun had dipped below the horizon now, leaving a sky painted in broad slashes of denim blue and salmon pink. The land beneath looked black, the treetops of the woods they were heading for a mass of boiling darkness. As the light bled away, so the temperature dropped further, though Pete didn't know whether it was this or the waves of fear pulsing through him that made him clench his teeth to stop them from chattering. He wasn't used to being scared. He was used to scaring other people. It wasn't just the dwarf's gun that scared him, it was the atmosphere that hung around the circus like a bad smell. It was an atmosphere of *wrongness*. In fact, he didn't think it was exaggerating to say it was an atmosphere of *evil*. People in the past had described *him* as evil, but they didn't know what they were talking about. Compared to what he could sense here, his level of evil was like comparing a fart to a hurricane.

He had sensed it from the beginning, and hadn't been

able to understand why everyone else was so fucking blind, why they all thought the circus was so brilliant. Then he'd seen the look in their eyes when they talked about it, and had heard about the way people got sick when they tried to leave Shettle, and had put two and two together. That's when he'd decided to get out, and to take Daz and his cousin Lee with him. There was nobody else Pete cared about: his own parents were both dead, and the skanky bitch who'd given birth to Daz had fucked off with some greasy biker before their son was even out of nappies. He'd known it was risky going to the circus people for help, but he hadn't been able to think of any other way of getting out before whatever shit they'd got planned for Shettle hit the fan. So, despite being scared as fuck, he'd gone in the only way he knew how – all guns blazing. He'd figured, as he usually did, that attack was the best form of defence, and that if the circus people saw he meant business they might respect him for it and cut him some slack.

And his plan had worked – sort of. All right, so the little freak in the clown outfit was currently holding them at gunpoint, but at least the circus people had agreed to let them go. The dwarf might have joked about taking them into the woods and shooting them, but what benefit would his lot get from their deaths? It would only cause complications for them, especially if the three of them were found riddled with bullets. No, all in all Pete reckoned his gamble had paid off. He might have been forced to hand over the thirty-odd quid he'd had in his pocket, but at least the little fucker hadn't demanded his wallet. Once he, Lee and Daz had made it through the woods, they'd walk or hitch the few miles into Wenthorpe, find a cashpoint and within a couple of hours would be sitting in a warm pub with pints in their hands.

By the time they reached the bottom of the field and crossed the road to stand at the edge of the woods, the last of the day's light had bled completely away. The trees and foliage in front of them were a mass of black, glints of reddish light which limned the occasional tree trunk or branch providing only the barest suggestion of form and depth.

Lee came to a halt, a doubtful look on his face. Beside him the pit bull growled softly, its compact body a mass of tensed muscle, the hackles standing up on the back of its neck.

'Well, what are you waiting for?' the dwarf snapped.

'I can't see a fucking thing,' Lee said.

'So? Just walk forward in a straight line and I'll tell you when to turn left or right. It's not rocket science.'

Lee glanced down at the dog. 'Brutus don't like it.'

The dwarf's voice dripped with sarcasm. 'Oh, well, if *Brutus* doesn't like it you'd better all trot along home.'

Pete shouldered his way to the front. 'Oh, for fuck's sake, *I'll* go first.'

He ventured cautiously into the dark foliage, feeling his way ahead with his feet, arms held out before him.

'Careful, Dad,' called Darren.

'Never mind fucking careful,' growled Pete. 'Come on, you pair of wusses.'

They edged forward like blind men, Lee controlling the dog with difficulty. Brutus was spooked, whimpering and digging in his heels in an attempt to prevent himself being dragged further into the darkness.

Up ahead Pete muttered, 'Can't you control that fucking hound?'

'He's shitting it, Pete,' said Lee. 'There's something in these woods he seriously don't like.'

Pete snorted. 'Trust you to own the only fucking pit bull that's scared of the dark.'

'It's not the dark,' Lee said, shaking his head. 'He can smell something.'

'Yeah, your rank breath.'

From the back of the group, Darren said, 'Dad?'

The two men ignored him.

'Dad,' Darren said again, more insistently this time.

Pete turned irritably, but in the darkness he couldn't tell the difference between his son and numerous other black shapes. 'What the fuck is it?'

'It's that little guy – he's gone.'

'*What?*' said Pete, turning round and stomping back a couple of paces.

'He was right behind me, but he's not there any more,' Darren said. 'He's fucked off.'

Pete pushed past his son, narrowing his eyes as if that would enable him to penetrate the darkness. 'Oi!' he shouted. 'Little bloke!'

There was no reply.

'Fucking answer me, you little bastard, or I'll . . .' But there Pete's voice trailed off. He had no currency to haggle with. His bluster was nothing but empty threats.

For a moment they all stood motionless, Pete breathing heavily, Brutus whimpering as he tried to free himself from the choke chain, which jangled in the darkness like Marley's ghost.

Finally Lee said, 'What we gonna do now, Pete?'

Pete was at a loss. 'That fucker,' he muttered. 'That freaky little fucker . . .'

'Shall we just carry on, Dad?' suggested Darren. 'Try to find the way ourselves?'

Pete rounded on his son, his arm jerking forward in the darkness. As the back of his hand connected with the boy's face, making Darren cry out, Pete snarled, 'What's the fucking point? We don't know where we're s'posed to go, do we? We don't even know if there *is* a way out.'

'Way I see it, we've only got two choices,' said Lee. 'Go back to the circus or go home.'

Pete simmered, thinking hard. Then he said, 'There's a third choice. We set Brutus on the little bastard.'

'What?' said Lee.

'He can't have got far. Set fucking Brutus on him, get him to bring the cunt down.'

There was a faint but rapid movement in the darkness; Lee was shaking his head. 'No way. He'll get shot. That little fuck's got a gun.'

'Yeah, but he ain't got fucking night vision, has he? He'll never know what fucking hit him.'

'I dunno, Pete,' Lee said miserably.

'For fuck's sake!' Pete snarled. 'It's only a fucking dog! Would you rather just go home and get fucked over like the rest of the twats here? 'Cos believe me, something fucking bad is gonna happen soon. Something fucking *cataclysmic*. These circus cunts aren't messing about. They've got . . . well, I don't know what they've got – weird fucking juju powers or something. And they're here to seriously fuck this place up. Believe me, I know. I can *feel* it.'

There was a silence. Suddenly Pete got the creepy feeling that the woods were listening to his words, absorbing them, taking them in. He had never had much imagination, had never believed in anything beyond what he could see and hear and touch, but the idea was a hard one to shake all the same.

Then reluctantly Lee said, 'All right. I'll let him go. But he's so fucking freaked I can't promise he won't just run straight home.'

'If he does we're dead – and so is he. In fact, I'll personally strangle the fucker myself.'

The only response were Brutus's continuing struggles to twist his head out of the choke chain and Darren's quiet blubbing. The undergrowth rustled as Lee knelt down and started murmuring to Brutus. At first his voice was soft and calming, his words muffled, as if he had his mouth pressed into the dog's fur. Then in a louder, more urgent voice he said, 'Go on, then, Brutus. Go get him, boy.' There was a chink of metal as Lee released the chain and then they heard the dog streaking away, back in the direction from which they had come.

'He'd better—' Pete began, but no sooner had he started talking than they heard a brief, violent thrashing of undergrowth maybe ten metres away, as if something had leaped out of hiding. This was followed by a deep-throated snarl, and then a high-pitched howl of such agony that Darren screamed and Pete felt his body clench and ripple with goose bumps.

'Brutus!' Lee howled and stumbled forward into the darkness, only to immediately trip on something and go down with a soft, rustling thump.

As he clambered back to his feet, Darren began to hyperventilate, his breath coming in rapid, wheezy moans.

'Shut the fuck up, both of you!' spat Pete, waving his arms in a shushing gesture – not that they could see him in the dark.

When they eventually quietened, Pete listened for a moment, trying to pinpoint the location of whatever had attacked Brutus. But there was nothing – not the faintest rustle of undergrowth, nor the wind-soft sigh of breathing in the darkness. He could only hope that the animal had slunk off through the bushes to consume its kill in peace.

Licking his paper-dry lips, he whispered, 'Listen to me, both of you. If we just fucking keep our heads together we can still get out of this.'

'What was that thing?' Lee moaned, his voice thin and high with grief and terror. 'It got Brutus.'

'I don't know, and I don't want to know.' Pete's voice was a vicious whisper. 'And forget about Brutus. He's fucking gone.'

Darren was gulping and sniffing, trying desperately not to cry. Each word a lurching gasp, he asked, 'What do we . . . do, Dad?'

'We move slowly and quietly away from here. Then we get the fuck out.'

'Move where?' said Lee.

'Just away from that thing. We'll go deeper, then we'll double back. That way we might—'

At that moment something erupted from the undergrowth a couple of metres to his left. It passed so close to his face that he felt the breeze of it ruffle his hair and caught a strong whiff of its musky animal stench.

An instant later Lee was screeching in mortal pain and terror, the sounds so dreadful that for a moment Pete felt his legs crumpling beneath him as if his muscles had turned to soup. Then adrenalin flooded his system and he was up on his toes and running, hands flailing through the dark.

He didn't get far. Within seconds he hit something – a bush or a low branch – with such force that it went straight through the material of his jeans and the flesh beneath, puncturing the tender spot at the top of his thigh. The pain was unbelievable, like a bomb detonating inside him. He screamed and went down, hitting his head twice as he did so. As he lay on the ground, dazed, he became aware of a hot wet pumping sensation at the top of his leg. He put his hand there and was shocked to feel his own blood, a lot of it, wet and warm and slippery. It was *pouring* out of him, like water from a tap.

Somewhere, distantly, he heard Lee still screaming, and then all at once the screaming stopped. And even though Pete didn't think anything could be worse than Lee's screams, the silence *was* worse, because now he didn't know where the animal was. Unable to move, he lay there, blood pumping out of him and his heart crashing madly in his chest, hoping that the creature would be so gorged after killing and eating Lee that it would lose interest in him. Either that or it would go after Darren next and leave him alone.

'Please God,' he whispered, praying for the first time in his life, 'please God, please God, please God.'

He repeated the words over and over. He was still repeating them when he smelled that animal stench again and felt a gust of hot, meaty breath on his face.

Sixteen

As soon as the door opened, the question on John's lips was replaced by a different one entirely. Instead of asking whether Chris was in, he found himself saying, 'Caroline, whatever's the matter?'

It was almost impossible for someone as beautiful as Caroline Blaine to look haggard, but it was clear that not only had Chris's wife been crying but that she was still upset.

For perhaps two seconds Caroline stared at John with a fierceness that suggested she was doing her utmost to hold it together; then her chin dimpled, her lips trembled and she began to blub.

'Hey, hey, come here,' John said, stepping over the threshold and wrapping his arms around her. Caroline folded herself into him and began to sob harder, her shoulders shaking. Over her head John flashed Lynn an urgent and meaningful look, but his voice was its usual calm rumble. 'Lynn, would you mind putting the kettle on?'

Lynn slipped past John and Caroline into the house, which allowed room for Nick to step forward and pat

Caroline's back awkwardly. Still in his calm, best-bedside-manner voice, John said, 'Shall we go inside so you can tell us all about it?'

At first Caroline seemed not to have heard the question, and then she nodded against his chest.

'Come on, then,' said John, easing her gently back into the house. Over his shoulder he said, 'Nick, would you mind getting the door?'

Once they were in the sitting room and Lynn had handed round the mugs, John leaned forward from his position at the end of the settee. 'Now then,' he said, 'what's wrong?'

Caroline was perched on one of two identical midnight-blue armchairs flanking the fireplace. Her ankles and knees were pressed tightly together and her hands enfolded the mug in her lap. She had stopped crying, but her face – aside from her bloodshot eyes and puffy red eyelids – was pale.

'It's silly,' she said. 'Just a family thing.'

'It's not silly if it's upset you,' replied Lynn.

'And there's no "just" when it comes to family,' John added, taking a sip of his tea. His manner was relaxed, unhurried, but Lynn suspected he was as anxious as she was to find out where Chris was and to discover the reason behind the 'family crisis' that had reduced Caroline to tears and prevented Chris from meeting them in the pub.

Caroline stared down into her mug and said wearily, 'It's Sam.'

'She's all right, isn't she?' said Nick quickly, earning a glancing look from John, an unspoken warning not to jump in too soon.

Caroline nodded wryly. 'Oh, *she's* all right. It's the rest of us who're upset.' She paused and then said, with a hollow laugh, 'Would you believe she's in love?'

'In love,' prompted Lynn.

'Or so *she* says, anyway. Course, she's only known the boy two minutes, and already she's behaving like it's the greatest romance the world has ever known. She's become so blinkered she's like a different person. She doesn't seem to care who she upsets.' She shook her head. 'Sorry, I'm not making much sense, am I?'

'You're making more than you realise,' John said, though the only indication that her words had alarmed him was the fact that he was sitting a little straighter. 'If you don't mind me asking, who is this boy that Sam's supposedly fallen in love with?'

Caroline rolled her eyes and sniffed. 'His name's Emil. He's with the circus. He's one of the acrobats – the one who did the trick with the panther.'

Lynn's heart skipped a beat. She took a gulp of hot tea. It was the only thing she could think of to stop herself rushing over and shaking Caroline by the shoulders.

With admirable composure, John said, 'I see. And where's Sam now?'

'She's with him again. *Emil*. At least, we assume so.'

'Aren't you sure?' asked Nick.

'She came back at lunchtime, having been out all night and making us sick with worry. When she got back she and I had the most almighty row and she stomped upstairs and shut herself in her bedroom. Then Chris came back and *they* had a slanging match, which ended up with him grounding her until further notice. But when our backs were turned she just took off. That's what's so upsetting. She's never caused us trouble like this before. She's always been such a good girl. So mature. Like you, Lynn.'

Lynn tried to smile at the compliment, but it came out as a tight-lipped grimace.

John said, 'And I'm guessing that Chris has gone after Sam?'

Caroline nodded. 'He's gone to the circus to have it out with the two of them – with Sam and Emil, I mean.'

John took an apparently leisurely sip of his tea, then put his mug on the floor by his feet and stood up.

'Perhaps we'll catch up with him there, then. I know this is a family matter, but he might appreciate some moral support.'

Caroline looked surprised. 'You're going already?'

'We don't want to outstay our welcome when you've had such an upsetting day,' he replied smoothly. And then he added, 'Unless you'd *like* one of us to stay with you, that is?'

Lynn held her breath. She had an idea that if Caroline said yes, she would be the one who'd be assigned babysitting duties. But Caroline shook her head.

'Of course not. I'll be fine. I'm sure all this silliness will blow over in a day or two.'

John smiled warmly. 'I'm sure it will,' he said.

Seventeen

The Circus of Nights was preparing for the evening's business when Chris arrived. Thickset men in woolly hats and fingerless gloves (*roustabouts* was the word that popped into Chris's mind) were opening up the concession trailers that snaked up towards the big top. Soon these same men would be cooking up burgers and hot dogs, getting the popcorn and candyfloss machines running, and filling the night air with smells that somehow managed to be both nauseating and desirable in equal measure. For now, though, they were simply folding back shutters and clicking on rows of coloured light bulbs to conceal the drabness beneath, pausing only to watch him with silent, deadpan hostility as he passed by.

Chris was partly nervous, partly angry. In fact, mostly he was angry, which was an almost welcome feeling. Recently his mind had been filled with a thick fug, even on the days after a good night's sleep, and his current anger had cut through that like the zing of lemon through a bland dessert, giving him a focus, a purpose. The only problem was that he wasn't entirely sure who he was angry *at*. Sam, for sure – her behaviour was unacceptable, and so out of character. But was he angry at the circus people too? Or specifically at Emil, who Chris remembered as the enigmatic and charismatic 'panther guy' from the previous evening? Certainly Chris had been uneasy about the way Emil had targeted his daughter in the crowd and blown her a kiss, but he had later shrugged that off as nothing more than a touch of extravagant showmanship. But had there been more to it? Had the display been a blatant play for an impressionable and (Chris liked to think) still relatively innocent young girl? Or had Emil and Sam met even *before* Emil's gesture?

Whatever the answer, Chris was sure of one thing: the relationship was not one he wanted to encourage. In fact, for reasons he could barely articulate or understand – and it was far more than his natural parental fear of Emil taking advantage of Sam sexually, or even persuading her to give up everything and run away with him – the thought of Sam spending time around the circus, and around Emil, filled him with a profound, almost overwhelming sense of dread.

He stalked up to the entrance tunnel, which jutted from the big top like an elongated snout from a fat round head. Despite the activity around the concession trailers, there was no one around here. He hesitated a moment, then called out, 'Hello?' Receiving no response, he walked right in.

As he emerged from the tunnel and the big top opened out before him, he remembered the smells from last night, the enticing scents of food and sawdust and people. For a moment he felt drawn in, as excited as a child, and then his purposeful anger re-exerted itself and he shook himself free of the feeling – *literally* shook himself, like a man breaking free of a hypnotic trance. Now when he looked around he saw only empty rows of seats backed by gently billowing canvas walls, high-set spotlights focusing on the circus ring and thus deepening the shadows above. All at once he felt uneasy. When he walked forward he found himself taking slow, cautious steps, treading softly so as to stifle the thump of his boots.

Chris cleared his throat. The sound echoed up towards the shadowy ceiling, and for a moment seemed to be answered by a brief but rapid fluttering sound, as if a bird was trapped up there.

'Hello?' he shouted again, his voice booming up. 'Anyone about?'

Just as he was wondering what he would do if no one answered, a harsh, nasal voice said, 'We could have you prosecuted.'

Chris whirled round. Standing at the entrance tunnel, partly in shadow, was the dwarf in jester's costume.

'Coming in here without a ticket,' the dwarf continued. 'Don't you know you're trespassing?'

Chris waved a defensive hand towards the entrance, and then lowered it, clenching his fist, determined to hold on to his righteous indignation. 'There was no one about,' he said, 'and no one to stop me. I shouted, but there was no answer. So I walked in.'

The dwarf sneered. 'Is that what you do when you knock on people's doors and they don't answer? Just walk in?'

'Of course not. But doors are usually closed, locked, for a reason. This one wasn't. And this is a public place, isn't it?'

'Only if you've got a ticket,' said the dwarf. 'Only if you've paid.'

'I'm not here to see the show.'

The dwarf's eyes narrowed. 'So what *are* you here for?'

'I'm here for my daughter.'

Still narrow-eyed, the dwarf assessed him for a moment. 'There are no daughters here.'

It seemed an odd phrase, but Chris let it go. 'She came here to see Emil. Her name's Sam.' Voice hardening with conviction, he said, 'I know she's here, so don't try to tell me she isn't.'

The words were barely out of his mouth when, behind the dwarf, the tunnel entrance suddenly darkened. Chris stared, blinked, uncertain for a moment what he was seeing. He had the unsettling impression that the darkness was seeping from the dwarf, that the man's shadow, which currently stretched out before him, had somehow split and was elongating behind him now too. In fact, not only was it elongating, but it was spreading out like smoke, creeping up the canvas walls, slowly and subtly obliterating the light.

The peculiar illusion lasted for no more than a second or two, and then a hulking figure emerged from the tunnel entrance behind the dwarf. Despite the fact that it was the formidable figure of the strongman, Chris breathed a sigh of relief. Of course, it had been the man's sheer bulk blotting out the light at his back which had given the impression that the tunnel was filling with darkness. As the strongman stepped into the big top, the light that he had been blocking, blazing from the myriad bulbs strung along the fronts of the trailers outside, once again filled the spaces where the shadows had been. Without a word to Chris, the dwarf crooked his forefinger and the strongman bent over so that their heads were at the same level. Cupping his hand around the giant's ear the dwarf whispered something. The strongman glanced at Chris, nodded, then turned and lumbered back down the tunnel.

Putting aside the question of how the dwarf had actually summoned the strongman, Chris asked, 'What was all that about?'

'Enquiries are being made,' said the dwarf.

'How long will that take?'

The dwarf spread his hands. 'It will take as long as it takes.'

He stood serenely, staring at Chris. Chris stared back, refusing to be intimidated. The waiting and the silence stretched on, neither man inclined to make small talk. Finally, just when Chris was on the verge of demanding how much longer he would have to wait, he caught a flash of movement in his peripheral vision. Startled, he spun round. The panther-man, Emil, was standing at his shoulder, staring at him with eyes so dark that Chris assumed he was wearing black contact lenses.

Though he had refused to let the dwarf's silent scrutiny faze him, Chris found it more difficult not to be unsettled by Emil's presence. The panther-man was so still, his darkly handsome face so expressionless, that he seemed conversely to exude a coiled, latent power that made Chris instinctively want to step back from him, even raise his hands in a defensive stance.

Gathering his resources, trying once again to recapture his anger and indignation, he forced a question from his dry throat: 'Where's my daughter?'

Emil regarded him not exactly arrogantly, nor even as if he was a minor irritation, but more as if he was nothing at all, a speck of dust, a smear of dirt.

'That's no longer your concern.'

His voice was a slow drawl, and bore the hint of a foreign accent – Polish, perhaps, or Czechoslovakian?

Chris felt fear lance through him, but there was anger there too, which he seized on gratefully. 'Of *course* it's my concern. She's my daughter!'

'And now she is my companion.'

'Like fuck she is. She's seventeen. She's my responsibility. I'm her legal guardian.'

Emil looked as though he was growing bored of the conversation. He crooked a finger to someone behind him, and suddenly Sam stepped forward, as if she had been waiting in the shadows.

'Sam!' Chris blurted, so relieved that he momentarily forgot how angry he was.

She, however, didn't share his enthusiasm. Coldly she said, 'Why have you come?'

She looked healthy but pale. Someone – Emil, maybe – had given her a black diaphanous scarf, which she was wearing around her neck, tied in a loose knot at the front.

'I've come to take you home,' Chris said.

Sam shook her head. 'I'm not coming home.'

'Yes, you bloody are. You're not staying here with these people.'

'I'm staying with Emil. I love him.'

'How *can* you love him?' Chris scoffed. 'You've only just met him. Besides, you're seventeen.'

'So?'

'So I'm still responsible for you. I can *make* you come home.' He reached into his pocket, suddenly aware of how much his hands were shaking, and produced his mobile phone. 'I could call the police right now to make it happen. I'm perfectly within my rights.'

He *thought* that was true, but part of his mind was still such a fug that he wasn't entirely sure. He tried not to look at Emil, who was standing silently as Sam clung to his arm, still staring at him with that weirdly empty intensity of his.

'Do what you like,' Sam said. 'I'm not coming with you.'

Still clutching his phone, Chris stepped closer to his daughter. 'Sam, what's happened? What kind of grip have these people got over you?'

'I think it's time for you to go now,' barked the dwarf.

Chris half-turned to see the little man still standing by the tunnel entrance, his squat body almost in silhouette. Behind the dwarf the section of tunnel wall that he could see was a moving shadowplay, the shadows growing thicker and darker as their owners approached. Chris's spirits sank; clearly the little man had called for reinforcements.

Stepping away from Emil, he thumbed the '9' on the

keypad of his phone. 'Right,' he said, 'you leave me no alternative. I'm calling the police.'

He was about to press the second '9' when three figures emerged from the tunnel behind the dwarf and stepped into the big top. Chris was astonished to see that they weren't circus people, as he had expected and feared, but his friends Nick Miller and John Kersh, plus Alan Michael's teenage daughter Lynette.

'What are *you* doing here?' he asked.

Taking in the situation at a glance, John said mildly, 'Evening up the odds a bit, hopefully.'

The dwarf had spun round to face the newcomers. His face twisted in fury. 'You can't just walk in here.'

'I think we just did,' said Nick, looking tense and pale despite his defiant words.

Sensing movement on the other side of him, Chris turned to see that Emil had wrapped his hand around Sam's arm just above the elbow. The acrobat's hand, the back of which was covered in spiny black hairs, was so large that it encircled his daughter's arm completely. For a moment Chris assumed that he and Emil were about to become involved in a grotesque tug of war with Sam as the prize, but then Emil pushed her towards him.

'Go with him,' he said, as if he found the situation unutterably tiresome.

Sam twisted her head to look at Emil, her face beseeching. 'I don't want to,' she wailed. 'Please don't make me. I want to stay with you.'

Emil's expression didn't alter. Dismissively he said, 'Go now.' Then, with apparently little effort, and yet so forcefully that Sam stumbled and would have fallen if Chris hadn't stepped forward and caught her, he gave her a shove, before turning abruptly and striding away.

'Hey!' Chris called after him, delighted by the outcome of the encounter but outraged at his daughter's rough treatment.

Emil, however, didn't look back. He slipped into the shadows and was gone.

Eighteen

'Try calling again.'

PC Tim Johns rolled his eyes, but it was too dark in the woods for his shorter, younger colleague to catch the expression. PC Craig Neal couldn't fail to pick up on the sarcastic tone of his partner's response, though.

'Wow, what a great idea. I would *never* have thought of that.'

'All right, mardy arse,' Craig said. 'There's no need to have a go at *me* just because we're short-staffed. I'm stuck with a double-shift too, you know.'

'I'm not having a go because of that,' PC Johns retorted. 'I'm having a go because you have an annoying tendency to state the bleeding obvious.'

Craig Neal sighed and decided to button it for now. Tim Johns was one of those people who always had to have the last word in an argument. Craig got along with his colleague well enough, but his pig-headedness became a bit wearing sometimes. Walking forward a few paces, he shone his torch into the trees as his partner thumbed in the number of the mobile from which the emergency call had been made. They had tried it once, with no result, when they had first got out of the car, but they were maybe a quarter of a mile deeper into the woods now.

In the bone-white torchlight bushes seemed to jump and move, shadows to scuttle out of sight like dark, hunched figures. Trees were pale, thin revenants with crooked, grasping arms. Craig couldn't deny that the woods spooked him more than a little, though if he had admitted that to Tim he would never have heard the last of it. Tim had the misplaced notion that fear and caution (along with the likes of compassion and empathy) were weaknesses and therefore, somehow, 'gay'. He even thought that buying flowers for your girlfriend or taking her out for a meal, was 'gay'. Needless to say, Tim didn't have a girlfriend; Craig did.

'Okay, that's it,' Tim said, pressing the last number on his keypad. 'Now come to momma.'

The two men stood silently, listening. After a moment they heard a faint, tinny musical refrain drifting from the darkness somewhere ahead. It was something rappy, something dancey, and it made Craig's stomach tighten. He was all too aware that the fact they were hearing it automatically cranked the seriousness of the situation up a few notches.

Tim, however, appeared to have no such qualms. 'We are cooking with gas,' he said. 'Let us proceed with extreme prejudice.'

Craig scowled. 'This isn't a joke, Tim. Just remember what it said on the call log. The caller sounded like a kid so terrified he could barely speak. The fact that we can hear the phone suggests it wasn't a hoax.'

Tim snorted. 'So tell me something I don't know. I was only trying to lighten the situation.'

'It's not the time or place,' said Craig, and before Tim could retort, as Craig knew he would, he shouted, 'This is the police. Is anyone out there? Are you hurt?'

Aside from the phone, which was repeating the words 'motherfuckin' bitches' over and over, as if it had Tourette's, there was no response.

'If you can hear me, please answer. We need to pinpoint your location.'

No reply.

Sweeping their torches in slow arcs in front of them, Tim and Craig moved deeper into the wood. Each time the ringtone cut out, Tim thumbed in the number again. After five minutes of slow but steady progression, they knew they were getting close.

'It's somewhere round here,' Craig said, his torch beam bleaching the long grass and tangled foliage. 'We're virtually on top of it.'

Twenty seconds later Tim shouted, 'Found it!' The triumph in his voice suggested he considered himself the winner of some kind of game.

Craig was half a dozen metres to the right of where the still-bleating mobile lay in the long grass. 'Don't touch it,' he said, but he sounded distracted.

Tim glanced across at him. 'You all right?'

'Not really.'

'Why? What's up?'

Craig swallowed. 'Come and have a look at this. But mind where you put your feet.'

Tim snapped off the thin end of an overhanging

branch and jammed it into the ground next to the mobile. Then he trudged over to join his colleague.

'What you fou— Oh, shit.'

In the light of Craig's torch the blood spattered up the tree and across the leaves of the bush beside it looked black. At the base of the bush, tangled in its lower branches, was a length of what looked like twisted, bloodstained cloth – or maybe cloth and something else. There was so much foliage and so many shadows it was difficult to tell.

'Tread carefully,' said Craig, and began to move forward with excruciating slowness, as if he was afraid not of disturbing evidence but of waking something dangerous from its sleep. When he was close enough to the tree, he stood on tiptoe and shone his torch over the bush into the dark hollow beyond.

'Oh God,' he breathed.

'What?' said Tim, a couple of paces behind him, but Craig didn't answer. A moment later Tim was standing shoulder to shoulder with Craig. He too pointed his torch into the hollow, doubling the brightness of the light.

Even though the body had been ripped apart, it was still possible to tell that it had once belonged to a young boy. Pieces of the boy, some of them clad in torn fragments of bloodstained cloth and denim, were scattered over a wide area. The largest piece, which lay on the ground less than three metres away, was the torso, with the head and one leg still attached. The stomach and chest was an empty red cavity from which splintered ribs protruded like bony grasping fingers.

The head, clinging to the torso on a gristly thread of neck, had been savaged so thoroughly that it was little more than a ball of gnawed meat. Most horrifying because it was most recognisable, though, was the arm, which had been severed – or more accurately twisted or chewed off – at the elbow. Although the arm was punctured with what appeared to be teeth marks, the hand was perfectly intact, its fingers curled inwards like the legs of a dead spider. There was even a watch on the wrist.

Shaking all over and cold with shock, Craig was reaching to turn on the radio attached to his breast pocket when he heard a groan and a thump beside him. He looked down to see his partner lying in a crumpled heap at his feet, splintered shards of light from his dropped torch illuminating his boots. PC Tim Johns had fainted.

Nineteen

John had thought that he and Nick might be considered *persona non grata* after their earlier intervention, but no one – not even the dwarf, who was once again conducting his gravelly-voiced spiel outside the 'Mirror of Life' – raised an objection to their purchasing tickets and taking their places inside the big top. As they sat down, Nick leaned towards John and murmured, 'Ever get the feeling you've just walked into a trap?'

John was feeling, in fact, like one of a shoal of fish being circled by sharks, but he tried to sound reassuring. 'Don't worry, they won't try anything here. As long as we don't wander off by ourselves we'll be fine.'

He and Nick had attended the second evening's performance of the Circus of Nights in order to (as John had told Lynn) 'keep an eye on things'. After their successful rescue mission earlier – their success, John suspected, more to do with Emil's tactical, and almost certainly temporary, withdrawal than anything else – Lynn had headed back with Chris and a strangely docile and subdued Sam in order to give them the benefit of her own particular de-brainwashing technique. John had phoned Lis to tell her that on no account were she and Anthony to attend the circus that night (like almost everyone else in Shettle, she had fallen under the circus's spell, and at first had argued with her husband, but at his absolute insistence had eventually, reluctantly, complied) and Nick, unable to reach Kate, had sent her a text telling her the same thing. John had the uncomfortable feeling that at present he and his friends were floundering, doing little more than keeping their heads above water, and that at some stage they would have to become proactive if they were going to have any chance of stopping the circus people from doing what they had come here to do. But on the other hand, at least they were now *aware* of the danger. Their de-brainwashing in the pub coupled with their mutual support for one another and a systematic rereading of Lynn's notes every half-hour or so had resulted in John's mind feeling clearer than it had in weeks.

As a consequence, John had spent the evening not falling under the spell of what was happening in the ring (though averting his eyes from the tiger-lady had been a struggle), but instead watching the crowd. What he had seen had worried, even horrified, him. The faces of the audience, even those of the children, were avid, but not in a lively and excited way. Although they made the right noises and gave the right responses, and occasionally, briefly, seemed to snap out of their trances and look around with something like bewilderment, for the most part they appeared slack-jawed and sleepy-eyed, as if under the influence of strong sedatives. They looked, in short, like particularly susceptible volunteers at a hypnotist's show, and John couldn't help but think that the Circus of Nights had manipulated them almost to the point of incapacity by setting itself up as both a sickness and a cure. His theory was that somehow, before its arrival, the circus had sent forth some kind of low-grade hypnotic suggestion, something which had made a large proportion of Shettle's inhabitants so anxious that as a result they had suffered a variety of ailments, both mental and physical. Then, when the community had reached the point where it was crying out for something to take its mind off its woes, the circus had come to town to captivate and enchant a desperate and malleable population. As Lynn had already suggested, it seemed clear to John that these tactics had been employed so that the circus people (it still seemed ludicrous to describe them as 'vampires') could go about their murderous business without fear of resistance. But whereas this – and the 'sickness barrier' – suggested that they possessed powers both terrifying and formidable, it also, conversely, gave him a grain of hope. Because if the circus people felt a *need* to subjugate the population, then didn't that suggest they would be vulnerable if that mental conditioning could be broken? And hadn't Lynn showed Nick and himself that it *could* indeed be broken, that the powers employed against the people of Shettle, impressive though they were, were not absolute?

How to break that conditioning, though? Some kind of community meeting, perhaps? Of course, not everyone would attend, but if they could convince *enough* people of the Circus of Night's true intentions, then maybe they would have a chance of stopping them.

John had a sudden image of thirty or forty townsfolk riding into battle on horseback with holstered six-shooters slung around their waists, or marching on the big top brandishing flaming torches like in an old Frankenstein movie, and he almost smiled. Almost, but not quite. Because, to all intents and purposes, that was probably how it *would* be. The Circus of Nights had cut Shettle off from outside help and was effectively laying siege to the community, and the only way the inhabitants were going to stop them—

Your children will die. Your community will die.

—would be by fighting – *literally* fighting – back.

The thoughts were still bubbling in John's head when the police arrived. It was halfway through the act with the clowns and the chimpanzee, and at first when a number of dark-uniformed figures marched out of the entrance tunnel, he thought it was a new part of the act. But then John saw that one of those dark-uniformed figures was Superintendent Alex Benson, who he had encountered in a professional capacity on many occasions. Capable but somewhat inflexible, Benson was a portly, straight-backed man, his peaked cap perched on a head of prematurely silver hair that made him look distinguished rather than old.

As Benson and the ringmistress marched into the ring, the big top fell silent. The clowns stopped their capering and pratfalling, and even the chimpanzee ceased its hat-stealing antics. There was a brief pause as the last of the hubbub died down and then the ringmistress said,

'Ladies and gentlemen, we apologise for the interruption to this evening's performance, but Superintendent Benson here, who I'm sure many of you know, has an important announcement to make.' She turned to Benson and offered him the floor. 'Superintendent.'

Benson nodded his thanks and stepped forward. Looking up at the audience he said, 'Ladies and gentlemen, due to a serious incident in Shettle Woods this evening I am afraid that tonight's performance of the Circus of Nights will no longer be able to continue. I would like to express my apologies to you all, and also my official gratitude to the proprietors of the Circus of Nights for their cooperation in conceding to my request to curtail the show in order to allow urgent police inquiries to proceed without delay. If you would all make your way in a calm and orderly manner to the main exit, and vacate the immediate vicinity as speedily as possible I would be most grateful. I'm afraid I can't provide any further information at this present time, but as soon as I am able to do so I will. Your coopera-tion is much appreciated.'

As soon as he had finished speaking he marched out of the circus ring with the ringmistress in tow. In his wake rose a swell of speculative chatter. There was shock in the voices and on the faces of many of the audience, but there was also a fair bit of anger too at the suspension of the night's entertainment, even a scattering of heartfelt boos which followed Benson down the exit tunnel.

As people stood up and began to shuffle towards the exit, Nick said, 'What do you make of that?'

John was dry-mouthed. 'I think someone's died and I intend to find out who. It's the only way it'll stop me imagining the worst.'

Though his instinct was to force his way through the crush of people as swiftly as possible, John tried to remain patient as he and Nick trickled along towards the exit with the rest of the audience. There were a few muttered demands from people for their money back, but not that many; most people seemed merely disappointed that they hadn't had their full fix of the circus for that night. Five minutes ago Benson's announcement had temporarily jerked Shettle's bewitched inhabitants out of their collective stupor, but now the talk was not of what might have happened in the woods, but of how they could possibly survive the next twenty-four hours without having seen Michael and Helga's trapeze act, or Emil the panther-man's acrobatics.

As soon as he was outside in the open air, John broke free from the straggling line of people heading towards the gate leading out of Hobbes' Meadow and headed towards the nearest police officer. The PC, who looked slighter and younger than a policeman *ought* to look, in John's opinion, raised a hand.

'If you could keep to the designated route, sir.'

John raised himself to his full height and adopted his most authoritative voice. 'I am Dr John Kersh. I am known to Superintendent Benson, having assisted both Shettle and Wenthorpe police on several occasions in the past. Given the current dearth of medical personnel in Shettle, I'm here to offer my professional services to this inquiry.'

Cowed, the young police officer said, 'Er . . . if you could just wait here a moment in that case, sir?'

He scuttled away. Nick, who had been hovering behind John, said, 'They might let *you* through the cordon, John, but I doubt they'll need a schoolteacher's help, so I think I'll head home.' He held up his mobile. 'I'm a bit worried about Kate. She isn't answering her phone and she hasn't replied to my text.'

John nodded, and the two men said their goodbyes, John promising to keep Nick up to date on what was happening. As Nick stepped back into the crowd, John heard squelching footsteps approaching from his left. He turned to see the young officer returning.

'If you could follow me, Dr Kersh?'

The officer led John around the back of the big top, towards a cluster of caravans and cages further up the hill. The caravans were arranged in a tight circle, reminding John of an old Wild West wagon train. Back then the pioneers had parked their wagons in a circle as protection from bandits and predators. Ironic, thought John, that on this occasion the outsiders themselves were the predators. It was the people of Shettle who needed protection from *them*.

A small group were standing beside the biggest, most brightly coloured caravan, talking. As John approached he recognised Superintendent Benson, the ringmistress, now wearing a thick red cloak over her costume, and the two young trapeze artists, Michael and Helga. There was another man too, in a grey suit and light brown overcoat, who had a pockmarked face and thinning hair dyed an unconvincing shade of chestnut brown. John's guess that he was a plain-clothes officer was confirmed when he was introduced as Detective Sergeant Barry Styles.

'Thanks for offering to help, John. It's much appreciated,' Benson said.

'Least I could do,' John replied. Directing his question pointedly at the ringmistress he said, 'So what's happened?'

She appraised him coolly. If she was aware of his identity or his part in the incident involving Emil and the Blaines earlier she didn't let on.

'Three bodies have been found,' Styles said bluntly. 'Two adult males estimated to be in their late twenties to mid-thirties, and one infant male aged somewhere between eight and twelve.'

John winced inwardly, but remained composed. 'Have they been identified?'

'Not officially, but from evidence found at the scene the adult males are thought to be Peter Blackstock and Lee MacMillan, both from Shettle, and the child is thought to be Peter Blackstock's son Darren.'

John nodded. 'I know the Blackstock family. How did they die?'

'They were attacked,' said Benson.

'Murdered, you mean?'

The superintendent shook his head. 'They were attacked by an animal. A large predator.'

'A big cat?'

Benson shrugged. 'It's too early to say, but it's a reasonable assumption.'

'It wasn't one of ours,' said Helga.

John was surprised by her voice, but tried not to show it. She was what his mother would have called 'a slip of a thing', but her voice was deep and husky, sultry even. Benson and Styles were experienced and professional police officers, and yet the effect she had on them was extraordinary. As soon as Helga began to speak their eyes snapped in her direction, adopting a dreamy, somehow glossy lustre. Benson licked his lips and a lascivious smile appeared on Styles's face.

Clearing his throat to break the moment, John said, 'Can you prove that?'

Helga turned her gaze on him. It felt to John like something crawling over his skin – and not something wholly unpleasant, either. In the gloom her eyes looked a deep lilac. She smiled.

'Follow me.'

She turned and walked away, moving like a ballet dancer, her feet hardly seeming to touch the floor. She was still wearing the thin silky leotard in which she performed her trapeze act. John noticed both Benson and Styles gazing at the muscles rippling in her tiny back and buttocks.

She halted beside a cage concealed beneath a shaggy, threadbare cloth that looked to have been stitched together from animal skins. With a flick of the wrist she flipped the cloth up and onto the roof of the cage. Inside, leaning against the bars and peering at them, was a tiger.

'This is Camilla,' said the ringmistress. 'As you can see, she's all present and correct.'

Benson and Styles walked around the cage, examining the locks.

'Who has the key to these padlocks?' Benson asked.

'Only me,' said the ringmistress. 'And I have them on my person at all times, apart from when I'm performing.'

'Hmm.' Benson rubbed his chin. 'All of this will have to be corroborated. And the tiger will have to be examined.'

The ringmistress flipped a hand as if it was of no consequence, and glanced meaningfully at John. 'I have no objections. We have nothing to hide here.'

The male trapeze artist, Michael, had moved to a second cage, this one too draped with an animal-skin cloth. Flipping it aside, he said, 'And this is Emil.'

Inside the cage, reclining on a bed of straw, was a black panther. John looked at Michael sharply. 'Emil? Isn't that the name of your acrobat?'

Michael smiled. 'They perform together, so they share the same name. It amuses us.'

Again the two officers examined the locks. Apparently satisfied, Benson asked, 'You're sure there's no way one of your animals could have escaped, or been temporarily released to roam the countryside, within the past twelve hours?'

The ringmistress's mane of russet curls swished from side to side as she shook her head. 'Quite sure.'

'And yet there's no other alternative, is there?' said John pointedly. 'It's far too much of a coincidence to assume that there's *another* wild animal roaming the woods.'

Helga padded towards him. She was not unlike a cat herself. Fixing him with her lilac eyes, she purred, 'Our animals wouldn't hurt a fly, Dr Kersh. Look.'

So saying, she stepped forward and thrust her child-like arm through the bars of the tiger's cage. With a roar the tiger pounced, and before anyone could react it had clamped its huge jaws around her tiny limb. As the animal shook and gnawed at her arm, Helga simply stood, smiling at the horrified men. Finally, she turned and murmured, 'Let go, Camilla.'

Immediately the tiger released her and backed away to the far side of the cage. Helga pulled her arm back through the bars and showed it to the men. It was intact.

'You see,' she said. 'Camilla's nothing but a big pussy cat.' She glanced across at the panther, a teasing smile playing around her lips. 'And so's Emil.'

Twenty

A thin drizzle sifted through the crooked trees surrounding the gaping ruin of Mitre House. There was little left of the building but a pit full of charred wood and brick, and a few thin jagged outcrops of soot-blackened outer wall. The locals never came here – not even junkies looking for somewhere quiet to shoot up, or ghost-hunting children on a dare. Mitre House was a cursed place, a shunned place. It was said that even birds avoided flying over it.

There was movement among the ruins tonight, though. The moonlight lit up the rain like falling silver needles and provided enough cold luminescence for two of the three visitors to be able to pick their way through the debris without twisting an ankle. The third of the trio needed no such help to light his way. Emil's vision was as sharp in the dark as it was in the daylight – sharper, perhaps.

The strongman, who had no name that the ring-mistress was aware of, remained as stoic and silent as ever, despite the fact that his bearskin was sodden and dripping and the bone-chilling rain ran down his naked arms and legs. The ringmistress herself, who had once had a name in a different life many years ago, but was now known simply as Madame Serena, stood and shivered despite her thick layers of clothing, clutching her shawl around her head as she watched Emil moving slowly along the wall of what had once been the vast cellar, touching and probing with his fingers, his black-maned head thrown back as though sniffing the air.

She wanted to tell him to hurry up. She wanted to ask him how much longer. But she knew it was pointless. Emil was Emil; he answered to no one. And Karl had been his brother. Which meant that in this matter, above all others, he was relentless and unswayable.

Finally he stopped and touched a section of the northwest-facing wall a little above his head.

'Here?' he said, glancing at Serena.

She shrugged. 'I don't remember. Karl was in my mind. He still is, but he sleeps there now.'

Emil's black gaze lingered on her for a moment and then he nodded at the strongman, who lumbered forward.

Despite the strongman's size and prodigious strength, Emil could have torn him apart in an instant. However, such menial tasks as the one he had called the giant forward to perform were beneath him; he was a nobleman of Wallachia, after all, and a descendant of one of the ancient families. The strongman placed his hand where Emil had indicated and pushed until his teeth were clenched and the muscles stood out on his massive arm.

'Perhaps the mechanism's fused, or was damaged in the fire,' suggested the ringmistress.

Emil ignored her. 'Again,' he hissed at the strongman.

The strongman pushed again, his lips curling back in a snarl, beads of sweat springing out on his forehead to blend with the rain. He pushed until his entire body was shaking with effort – and then suddenly the stone tilted back as if on a pivot, and with a grinding sound an entire section of wall opened like a sliding door, revealing a gaping black hole.

There was no expression of triumph on Emil's face. His features remained as fixed and haughty as ever. The ringmistress picked her way through the debris towards the two men, producing a torch from the voluminous folds of her skirts. She switched it on and shone it into the hole, revealing a dank, narrow passage with an uneven floor and dripping walls.

Without a word she stepped into the passage, the torchlight slithering ahead of her. Emil followed, but the strongman stayed out in the rain, arms folded, like a nightclub doorman.

The air in the passage was fetid, not only because the place had been closed up for a long time but because it was ripe with the stench of decay. The ringmistress pursed her lips and attempted to breathe as shallowly as possible, but Emil seemed unaffected by the stench.

After thirty or forty metres the passage opened out into a larger area, a natural rock-walled dungeon. Skeletal corpses, many of them children, hung from rusted iron manacles attached to the walls. In the centre of the floor stood an exquisitely fashioned silk-lined coffin on a stone podium or altar. Inside the coffin was the body of an old man, his skin grey and withered, though not decayed. A splintered spar of wood still jutted from his chest, surrounded by a shallow well of blackened and congealed blood.

For the first time Emil showed some emotion. His black eyes flashed and he hissed like a snake, his lips curling back and curved, pointed canine teeth springing forward from his gums like retractable blades.

'My brother,' he said thickly. 'Soon you will live again. The sins of the fathers shall be visited on the children, and on the parents too.'

The ringmistress glanced at him and nervously licked her lips. In a hesitant voice she asked, 'Must they all die?'

Emil glared at her. His eyes were pools of utter darkness.

'All,' he said.

Twenty-One

Kieron tossed his PS3 controller aside and flopped back on his bed as if he'd been shot. On the screen his car veered off the track and exploded in a ball of flame. Matt glanced at his brother in astonishment.

'What are you doing?'

'I'm bored,' Kieron announced. 'Bored, bored, bored, bored, bored.'

It was late morning on Friday, 14 October. Rain fell from a sky the colour of slate, but that wasn't why the boys had been confined to the house. They'd been grounded because . . . well, just because Mum and Dad said so. The closest they'd got to a reason had been when Dad had told them, 'Sorry, boys, you've done nothing wrong. You'll just have to trust me that it's for your own good.'

Kieron didn't know *exactly* what was going on, but he knew it was something to do with Sam. She'd gone off somewhere, spent the night sleeping over at someone's house without telling Mum and Dad where she was, and now she was totally grounded, virtually locked in her room and not allowed out. He didn't know why that meant that he and Matt had to suffer, though. They hadn't even been allowed to go to the circus last night and he'd *really* wanted to. Even though he and the rest of the family had gone the night before, he'd been looking forward to going again. In fact, he couldn't remember when he'd ever looked forward to something so much.

At least the disappointment had been tempered a little by Dad telling them this morning that they had another day off school. It was something to do with the bus not being able to get through, though why that meant Dad couldn't drive them to Wenthorpe Kieron had no idea. Not that he was going to ask. He didn't want to put ideas into Dad's head. He'd just smile and take the extra-long weekend, thank you very much. Chances like this didn't come up all that often.

Now, though, he was restless. He'd told Matt he was bored, but that wasn't quite it. Normally he'd be happy chilling at home, playing computer games and watching TV, but today it wasn't enough. Today he needed to do something else, *be* somewhere else. He needed to . . .

'Let's go to the circus.'

The words popped out of his mouth as if they'd bypassed his brain completely. As soon as they *were* out, though, he realised that, yes, *that* was what they should do. That was what they *must* do.

Matt, on his last lap and determined to win the race, even though he had no competition now, said, 'Tonight, you mean?'

'No.' Kieron felt the idea grabbing hold of him and refusing to let go. 'Let's go *now*. Just me and you.'

Matt gave himself a little cheer as he won the game, then put the controller aside. He looked at his brother quizzically. 'But it won't be open.'

'That doesn't matter. The circus people will still be there. We can talk to them. Maybe they'll give us a guided tour. It'll be cool.'

Matt shook his head. 'Mum and Dad won't let us. We're not allowed out, remember.'

Kieron scowled. '*Fuck* Mum and Dad,' he said, only mildly surprised at the sudden depth of his hatred.

Matt was shocked. 'You can't say that.'

'I just did. So are you coming or not?'

Kieron jumped to his feet, as if he intended going to the circus with or without his brother. But a little voice in his head told him that his brother should come too, that it would only be fun if they went together.

'I don't know,' Matt said.

'Yes, you do. You want to, don't you? I can see it in your eyes.'

Matt looked at his brother curiously. Instead of denying it he said, 'How will we get out?'

It turned out that escape was much easier than either of them had anticipated. Kieron suggested they sneak downstairs on the pretence of getting a drink to see how the land lay and simply take it from there. As it turned out, Dad was in his office off the kitchen, doing something on his computer, and Mum was in the laundry folding clothes, so they simply grabbed their cagoules from under the stairs and let themselves quietly out the front door. Twenty minutes later they were standing at the gate leading into Hobbes' Meadow.

Their coats seal-shiny with rain, they stood for a few moments looking across at the big top maybe two hundred metres away. Perched in the middle of a muddy field beneath a louring sky, it resembled a vast wet toadstool. The track up to it was a dark thread, the grass crushed into the mud by the passage of many feet. The boys looked at one another, as if momentarily doubting their decision, and then Kieron said, 'Come on.'

They didn't speak again until they were standing beside the slimy canvas wall. Reaching out to touch it, Matt whispered, 'Where is everybody?'

'They're probably inside, out of the rain,' replied Kieron.

'Inside the big top, you mean?'

Kieron shrugged. 'Some of them, maybe. Practising for tonight.'

'I wish we could see,' Matt said wistfully.

Kieron glanced down to where the canvas met the ground. 'Maybe if we walk all the way round we'll find a loose bit where we can sneak inside.'

Lowering his voice still further, Matt said, 'Do you think they can hear us?'

'Some of us can.'

The voice, a rasping bark, came from behind them. The boys whirled round to see the white-faced dwarf in his jester costume leaning against one of the trailers with his arms folded. The dwarf was grinning, his brown teeth standing out like a double row of tiny tombstones.

Stepping back from the big top, Kieron raised his hands. 'We're not doing anything, honest.'

'I never said you were. Come for a look round, have you?'

The boys nodded dumbly. Flipping a thumb behind him, the dwarf said, 'Here would be a good place to start.'

He was pointing at a trailer with a red and gold sign above it which read 'Mirror Of Life'. Below the sign was a pair of red velvet curtains.

'What's in there?' asked Kieron nervously.

The dwarf's grin widened. 'Why not find out for yourselves?'

'We haven't got any money,' said Matt.

The dwarf spread his hands. 'Ah, well. For two brave boys I'm sure I can make an exception.'

Kieron and Matt looked at one another, and then Kieron nodded. 'Okay.'

As they moved forward, the dwarf pulled one of the curtains aside for them – not by much, just enough for them to see a thin black triangle beyond. 'Step inside and keep walking. It'll be dark, but don't worry. You'll be quite safe.'

It had been some years since Matt had held his brother's hand, but he reached for it now. He was surprised not only that Kieron didn't pull away, but that he actually gripped the proffered hand and squeezed it. Together the brothers slipped through the gap between the curtains and into instant and profound blackness. They came to an abrupt halt. Matt whispered, 'Kieron?'

'What?'

'Nothing. Just checking you're there.'

Kieron snorted, though it was not the casually

contemptuous snort Matt was used to; instead it sounded half-hearted, uncertain. 'Course I'm still here. You can feel my hand, can't you?'

'Yes, but . . . don't let go,' said Matt.

'I won't.'

After a brief silence Kieron said, 'The little man said to keep walking. So come on. Let's take it slowly.'

The boys crept forward, feeling with their feet as (unbeknownst to them) Alan Michaels had done before them. They had taken maybe fifteen steps when Matt whispered, 'I don't like this.'

'Come on,' said Kieron again, trying to sound braver than he felt. 'Just a bit further. We'll go five more steps and if we still haven't found anything we'll go back. How's that?'

'Okay,' said Matt.

The boys shuffled forward again, but had taken no more than a couple of steps when they both cried out. They had walked into something soft and furry. Though they had no way of knowing the other was doing it in the darkness, they both clamped their spare hands over their mouths to try to stifle cries that had already escaped.

Kieron was the first to recover. Peeling his hand from his mouth he reached out tentatively.

'It's okay,' he said. 'I think it's just another curtain.' He gave it an experimental shove. It billowed, revealing a sliver of light to his right. 'Yeah, look, it's two curtains, one on top of the other. If we go between them there's light at the end. Come on, I'll go first.'

Less than a minute later the boys were blinking and

shading their eyes against the sudden glare of golden light. This time Matt was the first to recover.

'We're in a corridor,' he said, squinting. 'Wow, Kieron, look at all these mirrors.'

Kieron rubbed his eyes and blinked. Then he started laughing. He and Matt were standing in front of a mirror that made them look tall and thin with fat little heads. He bent his knees and his head stretched like toffee.

'That's so cool,' he said.

Matt moved to his left and stood in front of the next mirror. 'Hey, look at this one.'

Kieron guffawed. 'You look like a frog!'

'Ribbet,' said Matt. 'Ribbet, ribbet.' He turned to look at his reflection in the mirror behind him. 'Hey.'

Kieron glanced at him. 'What?'

'Where's the curtain gone? The one we came through?'

Kieron turned too. Behind them was now only a solid wall with another of the distorting mirrors hanging from it. He looked at his brother with wide eyes – not quite scared, but certainly alarmed – and stepped forward to run his fingers around the edge of the mirror. He had been half-expecting it to be loose, for there to be an opening behind it, or a hidden door, but the mirror was stuck fast to the wall.

'Must be a trick,' he said. 'Like in a funhouse. One of those false walls that slides into place when you're not looking.'

Matt looked up the length of the corridor. When he spoke there was the faintest edge of panic in his voice. 'There's no other way out. We're trapped in here.'

'Course we're not,' said Kieron soothingly. 'There's bound to be a way out. We just haven't found it yet.'

The boys moved tentatively down the corridor, glancing at their reflections in the mirrors on either side. The mirrors made them look fat or thin, or pulled their bodies grotesquely out of shape, but neither of them was laughing now. They had almost reached the end of the corridor when Kieron halted.

'That's weird.'

'What is?'

Kieron had turned to face the mirror on the right-hand wall at the end of the corridor. 'Look at this one.'

Matt stood beside his brother. The mirror they were looking into was taller and wider than the others. He shrugged.

'So? It's just a normal mirror.'

'Exactly,' said Kieron. 'It's *normal*. That's what's weird. What's the point of having a normal mirror in a place like this?'

Matt shrugged again. 'Maybe . . . maybe it's just to remind you what you *really* look like.'

Kieron gave him a pitying look. 'That's so lame.'

'Well, *I* don't know,' Matt said, frowning. 'Why does it matter anyway? I just want to get out.'

'Yeah, but maybe this *is* a way out,' said Kieron. 'Maybe that's why it's normal. It could be a clue.'

'What kind of clue?'

'I don't know. Maybe . . .'

Instead of elaborating, Kieron stepped forward and touched the surface of the mirror. Immediately there was an odd but subtle rippling effect, as if he had touched not glass but water. Next moment Matt gasped. The brothers were no longer alone. Standing behind them were the two trapeze artists from the circus – Michael and Helga.

The boys whirled round. There was no one there.

'What's going on?' said Matt. 'I don't—'

And then a husky, flirtatious voice spoke from behind them. 'Look again.'

Once more, the boys spun round. Michael and Helga were back, or rather their reflections were. But this time *only* the trapeze artists could be seen in the mirror. Although it seemed impossible, the boys' reflections had disappeared. Fearfully Kieron reached out and touched the mirror's surface, immediately snatching his hand back as if stung. 'I don't get it,' he said, his voice small, hollow. 'It's just glass.'

'Want to know how it's done?' asked Helga teasingly, her voice echoing around them.

'Is it a trick?' Matt asked.

She smiled. 'Oh yes. It's a trick. Close your eyes and reach out your hands.'

The boys hesitated a moment, but there was something about her voice that demanded obeisance. They stretched out their hands, closed their eyes . . .

. . . and felt themselves grabbed and tugged forward through what felt like a blast of freezing cold air.

It was like stepping from a warm hallway into a cold winter's night. Matt's eyes popped open, and for a moment he felt completely disorientated. He was no longer in the golden corridor of mirrors but somewhere dank and dark, with rocky walls. Water dripped from the ceiling and there was a terrible smell that made him feel sick.

Then his eyes flickered to the left and fear clawed its way into his throat. There was a skeleton hanging from the wall. A skeleton to which scraps of rotting cloth and leathery skin still clung. Where were they? In the haunted house? Did the circus even *have* a haunted house? He felt strong hands on his shoulders turning him around. As he turned he saw something else – an old man in a coffin with a piece of wood sticking out of his chest. Then Helga was smiling at him.

'Where are we?' he asked. To his right he was aware that Michael had his hands on Kieron's shoulders just as Helga had her hands on his.

'In the last place you'll ever be,' Helga purred.

Then she opened her mouth wider, showing him her teeth.

Matt screamed.

Twenty-Two

John reached the junction with Hobbes' Lane just as a police car appeared in his rear-view mirror. By the time he had bumped down the lane and parked just shy of the gate into Hobbes' Meadow the car was only fifty metres behind him. Beyond the gate, parked slightly askew with twin curling snakes of tyre tracks behind it, was Chris Blaine's silver Mazda.

As he cut the engine, John had a sudden flashback to ten years before when he'd last pulled up behind Chris's car on a country road. He'd had a Cavalier back then, hadn't he? Dark blue or black. Weird how his mind, now that it had shaken off the fog of the past few weeks, had started to throw up sharp but random details.

Sitting beside him in the passenger seat, Nick pointed. 'There he is.'

John twisted round to look. Chris was all but running up the hill towards the big top, his boots slipping in the mud.

Feeling slow and clumsy, John shrugged off his seat belt and unfolded his tall, broad-shouldered frame from the car. Standing up he shouted across the car's roof, expelling a jet of steamy breath from his mouth. 'Chris! Wait!'

The police car, packed with dark-uniformed figures, pulled in behind his own car with a wet crunch of gravel. Superintendent Benson was the first to get out. 'What's this all about, John?'

Kersh paused, torn between explaining to Benson why he had called him and going after his friend. Making a snap decision he pointed at Chris and said, 'That man is Chris Blaine. He's a friend of mine. About twenty minutes ago he discovered his two sons had gone missing. He has reason to believe they came here, and that the circus people mean them harm. I think so, too. In light of that, and after what happened yesterday, I thought it best to call you, if only to stop things turning ugly . . .'

In fact, ever since he had called the police fifteen minutes ago, John had been wondering whether he had made the right decision. He knew that the influence the circus people had exerted over the town had been designed to muddy the thinking of the populace (the police included) and deflect suspicion and attention away from them (more than that, it was designed to make the Circus of Nights seem like the one saving grace in an otherwise dour and onerous world), and so had been worried that while Chris was heading towards yet another showdown in the big top, Benson would delay him with questions, or, worse still, simply refuse to believe that the Circus of Nights could do any wrong.

To his credit, however, Benson was made of sterner

stuff. He took in what John told him with a frown, and then – his ability to assess a situation kicking in ahead of the Circus of Nights' conditioning – gave a brief nod and said, 'All right, then. Let's find out, shall we?'

The six of them – himself, Nick, Benson and three uniformed constables – trooped across the field in Chris's wake.

'How old are the boys?' Benson asked.

'Twelve and fourteen,' said John.

'And what makes Mr Blaine think they came here?'

John paused. Despite Benson's willingness to go along with him this far, he wasn't sure how much he should push it with his negative comments about the Circus of Nights. Perhaps if he pushed *too* hard some kind of mental defence mechanism would kick in. If he told Benson that the Circus of Nights was here to destroy Shettle without Lynn's evidence to back it up, might Benson think he was crazy, or wasting police time, or worse? He, Nick (who had been relieved to discover that Kate had been with Anthony last night and had not answered her phone simply because it was out of battery), Chris and Lynn had been discussing the situation all morning on email, with particular regard to how best to rip aside the Circus of Nights' veils of grand-scale deceit. Their best option – not least because they were running out of time – still seemed to be a meeting of as many of the community as they could muster, preferably involving a big-screen presentation and information handouts. As Nick had pointed out with grim humour, it seemed 'a ridiculously parochial way to combat evil' but, short of hiring a crack team of kick-ass, demon-hunting ninjas, it was pretty much all they had.

Aware that he had not yet answered Benson's question and that the superintendent was looking at him quizzically, John said, 'It's a bit of a long story, but he thinks the boys were enticed here.'

'Enticed why?'

Taking a deep breath, John said, 'Chris's daughter has been carrying on with one of the circus people, seeing him behind Chris's back, even stopping out all night. Naturally Chris isn't happy about that. It's led to some very bad feeling.'

Even as he spoke the words, he was aware of how flimsy they sounded. Luckily, however, they had almost reached the big top now, and could already hear Chris around the other side of it, shouting, his voice raw and desperate.

'Where are they?' he was yelling. 'Where are they, you fuckers?' Then they heard him bashing on the doors and walls of caravans and trailers, hard enough to suggest that he was trying to punch his way in.

Until now John, Nick and the four police officers had been walking briskly, but now John broke into a run. He led the way round the side of the big top, his long legs enabling him to draw ahead, his feet squelching on the boggy ground. When he reached the other side he saw Chris flailing at the door of a caravan, almost sobbing as he shouted, 'Come out! Come out and face me, you fuckers!'

John ran towards his friend. Sensing movement in his peripheral vision, Chris spun round, fists raised. His eyes were wild, his face wet with snot and tears. As soon as he saw John, however, he lowered his fists and took several staggering steps towards him, almost slipping in the mud.

'They've got them, John,' he sobbed. 'They've got Kieron and Matt.'

'If they have we'll find them,' John promised. He reached Chris and patted him on the shoulder. Indicating Benson, who was already striding towards the ringmistress's door, he said, 'I've brought help, don't worry.'

'What makes you think your sons are here, sir?' one of the constables asked, approaching Chris as if he was a dangerous animal.

Chris shot him a dismissive, almost contemptuous look. 'I just know they are. The circus people made them come.'

'*Made* them?' The constable frowned. 'How do you mean?'

Before Chris could reply, John said quickly, 'Let's just see what they've got to say for themselves, shall we?'

'Madame Serena,' Benson called, knocking on the door of the ringmistress's brightly painted caravan, 'this is Superintendent Benson. Would you open up, please?'

There was a pause, then the click of several bolts and the sound of a key being turned. The door opened a crack and the ringmistress, wearing a headscarf and dark glasses, peeked out timidly.

'Is it safe?' she asked. 'There was such a racket going on I thought we were under attack. What on earth's happening?'

Beside him, John felt Chris grow tense. He draped a

friendly but restraining arm around the smaller man's shoulders.

'You know exactly what's happening,' Chris shouted. 'Where are my boys, you poisonous bitch?'

As the ringmistress peered at him in apparent bewilderment, John gave his shoulder a warning squeeze. Nick, who was standing on Chris's other side, murmured, 'Take it easy, mate.'

Benson looked across at Chris with a pained expression. 'Please allow *me* to conduct this inquiry, Mr Blaine. I understand how anxious you are, but we'll get along much quicker if you don't shout out insults and unfounded accusations.'

'Is this about the murder in the woods, superintendent?' asked the ringmistress, her voice and body language suggesting she was flustered, confused.

'You know it fucking isn't!' Chris shouted.

This time Benson all but pirouetted. '*Mr Blaine!* If you don't stay silent, I will have you removed.'

'They're my *sons!*' Chris wailed.

'I appreciate that. But you're doing them no good at all with your continual accusations.'

One of the constables moved forward, but John waved him away irritably. 'The superintendent's right, Chris,' he murmured. 'I know it's hard, but let him do his job, eh?'

'They're here, John, I know they're here,' Chris muttered, his voice shaking, his face threatening to crumble. 'They should be looking for them. They should be ripping this place apart.'

'And they will,' said John soothingly. 'You just have to be a little bit patient, okay?'

Chris's face creased in anguish, but he nodded. John felt him slump and tried to hold him up.

'I have to sit down,' Chris said. 'Let me sit down.'

As John and Nick lowered Chris gently to the muddy ground, Benson turned back to the ringmistress.

'I'm afraid this gentleman's two sons have gone missing,' Benson said. 'He believes they may have come here.'

The ringmistress put a hand to her mouth to stifle a gasp of shock. It was a gesture so theatrical that it was almost mocking – or so it seemed to both John and Nick, who glanced at each other over Chris's head.

'How terrible!' she said. 'But I assure you, superintendent, that the boys have not been here. We haven't seen anyone from the village since you and your men left this morning.'

'There are suggestions that some of your people may have threatened the boys in some way. Would you know anything about that?'

'Threatened?' The ringmistress spoke the word as if it was foreign to her, and then gave a silvery laugh. 'Oh, I can't believe that. I really can't. We're simply here to delight and entertain. That's our job. Our *purpose*. As you know yourself, superintendent—' and here, although he couldn't see her eyes, John had the impression that she had tilted her head to look pointedly at himself and his friends '—your men found no evidence, no evidence *at all*, that we were in any way involved in those terrible murders yesterday.'

John stared back at her, refusing to allow her the satisfaction of seeing him drop his gaze. He had spoken to Benson this morning and already knew that what she had said was true. It was also true that the big cats had been thoroughly examined and that no physical evidence had been discovered to link them to the killings. And now, with an awful sinking feeling in his stomach, he knew exactly what the ringmistress was telling him. She was saying that, despite what John had promised to Chris, the missing boys would not be found – not here, at any rate. She was saying that there would be nothing to link their disappearance (or worse) with the circus, at least not until it was too late to matter any more.

'I realise it's a terrible imposition once more, Madame Serena,' Benson was saying, 'but I'm afraid that in light of the current circumstances I am going to have to organise a thorough and immediate search of the site. We are also going to have to question your entire troupe once again. I trust you have no objections.'

Still looking at John, Nick and Chris, the ringmistress slowly and theatrically spread her hands.

'No objections at all.'

Twenty-Three

W as he dreaming or awake? It didn't seem to matter, because whenever he opened his eyes or closed them *they* were there. Mocking him. Laughing at him. The white-faced dwarf. The woman with the red curls and the top hat. And *him*, of course.

Mitterhaus.

Time and again Alan saw Mitterhaus standing there, lips curling back to reveal long needle-sharp teeth. He cried out, tried to defend himself, but it was no use; he couldn't move.

Your children will die. Your community will die . . . to give me back my life.

'No,' Alan cried. 'No . . . no . . .' He raised the gun to shoot Mitterhaus, to protect his daughter. But the gun wasn't there. His hand was empty. He was surrounded by mirrors, and in each one was Mitterhaus's face, laughing and laughing . . .

Sometimes Lynn was there, sitting beside him, holding his hand. And that was comforting. But then he would see darkness forming behind her, and out of that darkness would come Mitterhaus, hands reaching out, unsheathing teeth that would tear and destroy. Teeth that would bring death, and worse than death. Eternal darkness. Eternal fear.

'Shh, Mr Michaels. It's all right. You're just having a nightmare.' Sometimes Nurse Collins would be there, tending to him in her gentle, unfussy way.

'Is this real?' Alan would ask her, and she would smile.

'Of course it's real.'

'Are *you* real?'

A tinkling laugh. 'I should jolly well hope so.'

'But they're real too, aren't they? They're real and I need to stop them.'

And at this she would pat him and shush him as if he were a frightened child in the night. 'You don't need to stop anybody, Mr Michaels. You just need to rest. Now come on, get some sleep and we'll soon have you on the mend.'

But he knew. He knew he had to stop them. If he didn't stop them—

Your children will die. Your community will die.

—they would take everything.

He knew he had to stop them and he knew what to do. When Nurse Collins was gone, when he knew he was alone, Alan got out of bed, crossed to his jacket hanging on the back of the door, and reached into the inside pocket for his mobile phone.

For a moment he saw the dwarf laughing at him, his white face looming and cracked, saliva frothing from between his brown tombstone teeth. The dwarf was holding his phone, waggling it in his little stubby hand, taunting him with it. Alan squeezed his eyes tight shut. 'No,' he whispered, 'no.' And then, as though he had willed it, he felt the phone in his hand, hard and cool and reassuring, like a tiny, smooth-edged brick.

He had been thinking hard. Somewhere, among the dreams and the memories and the drifting thoughts, he had been formulating a plan. He knew there was no time to ask his friend from Cardiff this time, so he would have to try closer to home. But he had contacts. People who might help – who *would* help for the right price. And he would pay whatever it took. To save Lynn. To save Shettle.

Pulling the covers over his head, like a child protecting itself from the monsters that lived in the dark, he switched on his phone and selected the 'Phone Book' option. He had to concentrate as hard as he had ever concentrated on anything before in order to stay focused.

'Dougie,' he whispered. 'Dougie, Dougie, Dougie.' He kept repeating the name until he found it and then he pressed 'Option' and 'Dial'. The trilling of the phone sounded immeasurably distant. He closed his eyes and imagined himself drifting through space, imagined himself as the signal, bouncing off satellites, shooting back down to Earth.

'Yeah?'

The voice was suspicious, unwelcoming. Alan felt as though this conversation was a tightrope through the blackness, and that to maintain his balance he would have to stay focused.

'Dougie?'

'Who wants him?'

'Dougie, it's . . . it's Alan Michaels. From the newspaper.'

'Mr Michaels.' The voice lightened only a little. 'Thought I might be hearing from you. These murders, is it?'

Murders? What murders? Alan felt his mind—

Your children will die. Your community will die.

—veering off course. He clenched his teeth, spoke quickly before Dougie could shatter his concentration.

'No,' he said, 'it's not information I want. I need you to get something for me.'

'Oh yeah?' Now Dougie sounded wary. 'And what might that be?'

'I'll pay whatever you want,' Alan said. 'But I need it today. Now.'

There was a pause of two seconds, maybe three. And then Dougie said, 'Go on.'

Twenty-Four

The meeting went far better than any of them could have anticipated. They held it in the community hall at three p.m. – the same community hall that John and his wife Lis had hired for a Halloween fancy-dress party two years before. It – the meeting, not the party – had been organised and advertised with indecent haste, but that couldn't be helped; time was of the essence. This was 14 October, the tenth anniversary of Karl Mitterhaus's death, and, as Nick had pointed out, if ever there was a time when the Circus of Nights would play out its final act then today was the day.

They had got the ball rolling almost as soon as Benson had called in what limited resources he could muster to organise a search for the missing boys. As police officers scoured the area, concentrating on the circus itself and the woods where the bodies of Pete and Darren Blackstock and Lee MacMillan had been found, John and Nick, together with Lynn, had worked their magic on Benson. It hadn't taken long for the scales to fall from his eyes. He was a strong-willed man and it turned out that subconsciously he had been fighting the circus's conditioning from the start.

'I knew there was something wrong,' he said. 'I knew there was something I wasn't seeing. I just couldn't put my finger on what it was.'

With Benson on their side, the rest had been . . . if not easy, then certainly less of an uphill struggle. With both the Superintendent's blessing and the Blaines' permission (Chris had gone home to be with Caroline and Sam while they waited for news of the boys), they had advertised the meeting as an appeal for ideas and information which would, with luck, lead to Kieron and Matt's safe return. Lynn hadn't felt entirely comfortable exploiting the boys' disappearance (*you'll never work for one of the tabloids with that attitude, girl*, she told herself wryly), but she knew it was the only way to create maximum impact and therefore hopefully draw more people to the meeting.

And so it had proved. Thanks to the eye-catching posters and flyers which she had designed in double-quick time – 'MISSING BOYS' along the top in black, family photos of Kieron and Matt Blaine grinning into the camera directly underneath, and information about the meeting, with the pertinent details capitalised in red, beneath that – the hastily arranged meeting attracted at least a hundred, and possibly closer to a hundred and twenty, concerned citizens.

Benson had spoken first, explaining where and when the boys had last been seen, providing details of the current police efforts to find them, and appealing for any information that the people of Shettle might be willing to offer. Then Nick, John and Lynn had stepped forward for the trickier business of trying to explain to the assembled crowd how the Circus of Nights had duped them and why Madame Serena and her troupe were *really* in Shettle.

They used Lynn's notes projected onto a large screen to drum their message home. They handed out copies of the notes to everyone at the meeting and urged them to study them closely, to reread them over and over in an effort to lock the connections between events into their heads.

There was resistance at first; there was confusion; there was anger. But eventually (after much debate, and even one or two walkouts) there was a gradual and general awakening that for Nick, John and Lynn was heartening to see.

After that came the more practical business – a discussion of what to *do* about the Circus of Nights.

'Sling 'em out!' someone shouted.

'Arrest the lot of 'em!' suggested another.

As the volume rose, John and Benson simultaneously raised their hands for silence. They glanced at one another and then John made an 'after-you' gesture, stepping back to allow the superintendent to speak first.

'Whilst I appreciate your enthusiasm and community spirit, and whilst I now regard the Circus of Nights as a potential threat *to* that community spirit,' Benson said, 'I feel I ought to point out that, to date, there is no evidence to suggest that these visitors to our community have actually broken the law. I would, therefore, like to emphasise that although your support, diligence and eagerness to help is both welcome and encouraging, speaking as a representative and upholder *of* the law I cannot condone any behaviour that may be construed as coercion, intimidation or vigilante justice. And neither can I condone violence of any kind. Is everyone clear on that?'

There were grumbles and mumbles of both assent and resentment. After a moment Benson added, 'You can regard that as the *official* police stance on this matter.' He paused to allow the implication of his words to sink in. Then he said, 'And now I'll hand you back to my friend and colleague, Dr John Kersh.'

John talked about how dangerous the Circus of Nights was, and of how careful the people of Shettle needed to be. Although he fell short of suggesting that there was anything *supernatural* about the circus troupe, he did remind his audience how easily not just they but the entire community had been manipulated and of how the inhabitants of Shettle had been imprisoned within what had become known as the 'sickness barrier'.

'We don't know what these abilities are or where they come from,' he concluded, 'but we can't deny their existence. All I can tell you for sure is that the circus people have powers that are currently beyond our understanding, as a consequence of which I suspect they won't be shifted easily. Public pressure alone won't do it, but while I don't profess to have all the answers what I *do* know is that a large part of the battle is getting the people of Shettle to understand the danger they're in, and we've gone an awful long way towards achieving that objective this afternoon. The important thing to remember is that the

Circus of Nights went out of their way to hoodwink us, which must mean that they *fear* us, that they're *vulnerable* in some way. Our ultimate task is to find and exploit that vulnerability. But your *immediate* task is to pass on what you've learned this afternoon to your family and friends, to spread the word as widely as you can. Keep reading the notes – and not just that but *photocopy* the notes, pass them on to whoever you come into contact with.' He paused to allow his words to sink in and then raised his hands. 'That's all I have to say. Thank you for listening.'

Back in John's car, once the meeting was over, Nick leaned back in the passenger seat with an almighty sigh.

'You all right, buddy?' John asked.

'Yeah, it's just . . .' Nick began, then thought better of it. 'Naw, it's fine.'

'You sure?' said John. 'Nothing you want to share with the group?'

Lynn, sitting in the back, said, 'I can cover my ears if you'd prefer.'

Nick smiled at that, albeit faintly, and then he said, 'It's just today. 14 October. Like I said, it's the tenth anniversary of Karl Mitterhaus's death. But it's also . . .' He tailed off.

John's eyes widened. 'Of course! Oh, Nick, I'm so sorry.'

'What?' said Lynn, leaning forward between the two front seats.

John glanced at Nick, wondering whether he should speak on his behalf, but then Nick said almost matter-of-factly, 'Today is also the tenth anniversary of Anna's death. My wife.'

Lynn reached through the gap and placed a hand awkwardly on his shoulder. 'Sorry,' she said. 'I should have realised. I mean . . . I was there that day too, kind of. It was also the day my friend Jenny died. I only knew her a few weeks, but I still think about her.'

There was a sombre silence in the car for a few seconds, and then John said, 'I think we all deserve a drink. Raise a glass to absent friends.'

Nick was about to agree when Lynn's mobile rang. Mouthing an apology she said, 'Hello?'

She listened a moment, then said, 'What? Oh my God, when? . . . Thanks.'

John glanced at her face in the rear-view mirror. 'What is it?'

'It's Dad. He's left the medical centre.'

'*What?*' John was appalled. 'But he needs constant monitoring, at least for the next few days. Who the hell has been stupid enough to discharge him?'

Lynn shook her head. 'No, no one's discharged him. What I mean is, he's disappeared. When no one was watching he unplugged himself from all the machines and just . . . left.'

Twenty-Five

As soon as the coast was clear, Alan rose from behind the drystone wall against which he had been crouching. Feeling dizzy and a little faint, he stood for a moment, blinking away the firework flashes behind his eyelids and waiting for the world to come back into focus. If he was spotted now the game would be up, but there wasn't much he could do about that. He was in the hands of Fate and, if there was any balance and justice in the universe, then Fate would be on his side.

His luck had held so far and, given his present state and the odds he was up against, it was comforting to think that a greater power might be working through him. Not God. The idea of a benign deity up there in the sky, overseeing creation as if it was the world's biggest soap opera, had always struck him as a fairy tale for people terrified of their own mortality. But it was comforting to think in terms of cosmic balance, of good and evil vying for supremacy and eventually cancelling each other out. He knew the theory didn't bear close scrutiny, but he wasn't in the right frame of mind for close-scrutiny thinking right now. This was tunnel-vision thinking, and he knew it. This was focusing-on-the-tiny-chink-of-light-in-the-darkness-and-heading-straight-for-it thinking.

Dougie, an ex-gang member whom he had met in a pub six years ago while working on a story about how gang warfare had come to Shettle, and who had been providing him with sneaky snippets of information ever since (for hefty financial recompense, naturally), had come good. He had provided exactly what Alan had asked him for in double-quick time, albeit in return for a ludicrously inflated sum. Moreover he had picked Alan up from the car park of the Imperial Dragon Chinese restaurant, as requested, and had driven him first to the bank to get the cash and then to the top of Hobbes' Lane. As Alan had stepped from the car into a murky rain-streaked afternoon and opened the back door to retrieve the sawn-off shotgun from the rear footwell, Dougie had even leaned across and muttered, 'Stay lucky, mate.'

Further down the lane, in a line close to the gate, had been four police cars. There had been another police car down by the woods, parked next to a bedraggled line of yellow and black incident tape looped around several trees. Knowing that if he was spotted with the shotgun he'd be stopped and questioned immediately – probably arrested, in fact: there were few legitimate reasons why someone should be carrying a sawn-off shotgun – Alan had raised a brief hand to Dougie and then slipped into the trees by the side of the road even before the car which had brought him here had driven away.

The clump of dripping trees and bushes at the north end of Hobbes' Lane, which butted up against the top right-hand corner of Hobbes' Meadow, was dense but no more than six or eight trunks deep. It had taken Alan less than thirty seconds to squelch his way through them, beyond which, over the drystone wall which stretched all the way to the far end of Hobbes' Lane, was a panoramic view of the encampment huddled in the shelter of the big top. Here he had seen several dark-uniformed police officers milling about and had ducked down behind the wall, out of sight. After watching the officers for a while, it had become obvious that they were conducting a systematic search of the caravans and trailers behind the big top. As far as Alan could see, there had been no objections from the circus people, who stood patiently in the rain while their homes were searched.

In some ways Alan was glad of the delay, of the chance to recoup a little of his already meagre energy. Getting up out of bed, getting dressed and walking the few hundred metres from the medical centre to the car park of the Imperial Dragon had exhausted him. By the time Dougie had arrived to pick him up, Alan had been sitting on a low wall, wheezing and gasping, sweat pouring down his face. His chest had felt tight and his head had been so heavy that he had barely been able to lift it when Dougie's black Subaru had pulled up beside him.

'Jesus, man, you look ill,' Dougie had said. The cashier at the bank had regarded Alan with alarm too, as if she fully expected him to expire on the spot. Sitting in Dougie's car with the air conditioning cooling the sweat on his face, he had recovered a little during the ten-minute drive from the bank to Hobbes' Lane. But pushing his way through the sodden trees, even though it had taken less than thirty seconds, had drained his resources again, to the extent that by the time he reached the wall on the far side he was once more weak as a kitten.

Now, almost thirty minutes later, he was as good to go as he was ever likely to be. He had watched the police conclude their search, with no apparent result, and slowly filter away. A few minutes later he had heard three of the four police cars start up, one after the other. The growl of their engines had grown increasingly louder as they had driven up the lane and passed the clump of trees shielding him from view, and then each of them had idled for a moment at the junction, before turning right onto the road that would take them back into Shettle.

He had waited for the sound of their engines to fade completely before standing up. Although one of the police cars was still parked in the lane, which presumably meant that a small police presence had remained on site, Alan could not see a soul now in the encampment beyond the wall. The only signs of life came from the animals in their cages – the chimpanzee, the tiger, the prowling panther. Leaning over the wall, he carefully dropped the shotgun into the long grass on the other side. Then he took a deep breath and clambered up and over.

Even the minimal amount of effort that this required

set his heart whacking erratically. Uncomfortably aware that he was now in full view should anyone happen to glance up from the encampment below, he paused a moment, hand pressed to his breastbone, as sparks twinkled and flashed before his eyes. Then he reached down carefully, picked up the shotgun and, after another deep, shuddering breath – one that caused his heart to spasm with pain – he curled his right forefinger around the trigger, slipped his left hand under the stubby barrel and began to trudge down the hill.

His plan was simple: to take out as many of them as he could. It was a tunnel-vision plan. The plan of a sick, scared man desperate to protect the only things that mattered to him. If he had to go down – and he suspected that he might – he would go down fighting.

Alan killed the chimpanzee first. Not because he had anything against the creature; just because he thought that if he started with the animals it would bring the real targets running. In the split second before it died, the ape seemed to realise what his intentions were. It began to screech in terror, throwing itself against the bars of its cage in a desperate attempt to break free. Then the gun roared and the animal was thrown back against the bars on the other side of the cage, its head all but ripped from its shoulders.

He moved on. The tiger lay in its bed of straw, gazing at him with mild disapproval as he took aim and fired. A hole erupted in its side, blood, meat and fur flying everywhere. The tiger flopped to the side, its huge, velvety paws shuddering for a moment before becoming still. A spatter of blood hit Alan's cheek, but he ignored it. Calmly he reloaded and moved on to the next cage, looking up as he snapped the breech of the shotgun back into position.

The panther was gone.

The cage door was swinging open, as if the damned thing had reached through and opened it itself. Wildly, rain flying from his hair and his breath rasping in his throat, Alan swung round, half-expecting to see the creature leaping for him, claws unsheathed. Instead, what he *did* see was the acrobat, Emil, standing three metres away, his face expressionless, his arms hanging loosely by his sides. Emil was staring at him with his depthless black eyes. And then his lips curled back, revealing long sharp teeth – panther teeth.

What the fuck are *you?* Alan thought, an instant before he jerked up the gun and fired.

He saw a hole appear in Emil's chest – and then he saw it close up again. It was like firing into oil, the surface giving way as the shotgun pellets hit it before rippling back into place in their wake.

Sweat sprang out on Alan's brow to mingle with the rain. Once more his chest tightened, as if his heart and lungs were caught in a vice. 'No,' he muttered. 'No.' He pulled the trigger again. Emil didn't flinch. The second blast ripped into him, and then, like the first, was absorbed. The front of Emil's black shirt hung in smoking tatters, but the flesh beneath was intact.

Emil took a step towards Alan. Fumbling, shaking, Alan tried to reload the shotgun. He broke open the breech, groped in his pockets for cartridges. And then, with shocking suddenness, the vice in his chest became a massive, unbearable weight, crushing down on him.

His arms and legs turned to cold rubber. The gun and ammunition dropped from his nerveless hands. Alan couldn't even raise his arms to break his fall as the ground tilted up to meet him. He had never known such crushing, debilitating pain. He couldn't move, couldn't speak, couldn't breathe. The last things he saw, as his senses closed down, were Emil's black eyes, swallowing him whole.

Twenty-Six

As they approached the junction an ambulance appeared behind them, siren blaring, strobing blue lights reflecting off their wing mirrors. John pulled over to let it pass and the ambulance turned left into Hobbes' Lane, slowing only a little as it lurched through the ruts in the uneven road.

'Oh God,' Lynn said from the back seat. 'That's for Dad. I know it is.'

'Try not to jump to conclusions,' John said. 'It could be here for any one of numerous reasons.'

'None of them good, though,' replied Lynn, voicing what they were all thinking. She leaned forward, hands gripping the backs of the two front seats, as John followed the ambulance down Hobbes' Lane.

Away from the lights of Shettle, the late-afternoon dusk seemed deeper, more oppressive. It softened and blurred and darkened the land like the onset of blindness, replacing light and colour with gritty purple-grey shadows. The blue lights of the ambulance reflected in icy flashes off the rain-darkened stone of the flanking walls. They reminded Lynn of the stuttering blips on her dad's heart monitor in the medical centre.

The blue lights stayed on even when the ambulance halted and two paramedics jumped out. Hurrying round to the back, they opened the double doors. Lynn saw one of them grab a blue bag with a shoulder strap and what looked like a scuba diver's breathing apparatus. The other picked up a medical kit the size of a small suitcase and a portable rolled-up stretcher.

'What's that equipment?' she asked, pointing at the blue bag, which the paramedic was now swinging onto his shoulder.

Almost reluctantly John said, 'It looks like a cardiac monitor and defibrillator.'

'And that other thing? The tank and mask? Is that oxygen?'

'Yes.'

'Oh God,' she said, 'oh God, oh God, oh God.'

Nick half-turned, gently placing a hand over the one gripping the back of his chair for dear life. 'Take it easy, Lynn,' he said. 'We don't know anything yet.'

Without a glance at the car pulling in behind them, the paramedics closed the ambulance doors, jogged through the gate and started up the hill towards the big top.

'Quick,' said Lynn. 'We need to catch up with them.'

'And do what?' asked John reasonably. 'Stop them? Ask them why they're here? Prevent them from doing their job?'

'That's my dad up there,' Lynn said, her voice cracking. 'I know it is.'

John's reply was characteristically calm. 'If so, then that would be all the more reason to let them get on with what they need to do. If there's a life to save, let them try to save it.'

Despite his words, as soon as John cut the engine Lynn was out of the car and running up the lane towards the gate. Just as she reached it, her foot came down in a muddy puddle and shot from under her. Nick rushed forward, but was unable to prevent her going down on to one knee. When he looped his forearms under her armpits and hauled her back to her feet, she was crying.

'Are you hurt?' he asked.

She sniffed. 'Not really. It's just . . . this is all a bit much for me. Oh Nick, what if it *is* Dad up there? What if . . .'

She choked on the rest of the sentence. Nick turned her round and wrapped his arms around her. Lynn pressed herself into him, sobbing against his chest.

'Hey,' he said gently, stroking her hair. 'Hey.'

John had reached them now. 'I'll go on ahead,' he said, 'see what's happening. It might be best if you were to hang back a bit.'

Nick nodded. John squeezed his shoulder, then went on alone. He knew that the others relied on him, saw him as a reassuring presence, but the truth was that for all his calm words and his practical, measured approach, he was just as clueless, just as much out of his depth, as the rest of them. He'd felt . . . not exactly good at the meeting, but *purposeful*. Proactive. But he'd been aware too that time was running out, that events were over-taking them, and had suspected that instead of getting the chance to consider their options and formulate a plan they would simply end up reacting to the escalating circumstances like a bunch of headless chickens.

And so it was proving. It was almost as if the phone call to Lynn had been designed to faze them. Because here they all were, back at the circus again, with no strategy and no means of defending themselves should things turn ugly.

He was halfway across Hobbes' Meadow when he saw the two paramedics reach the big top and hurry around the side of it. He trudged doggedly after them, and came upon a scene so chaotic that at first – due in part to the encroaching dusk and the relentless drizzle – it was hard to take everything in. At centre stage, lying on the wet grass, was a dark figure over which the paramedics were crouching. From their lack of urgency it seemed clear to John that the poor soul was beyond help.

A few metres behind the paramedics were three animal cages, one of which was empty, the door hanging open. The others contained animals – a chimpanzee and a tiger – which had clearly died violently. To the left, sitting on the steps of her caravan, was the ringmistress, wrapped in thick layers of shawls and skirts, sobbing into her hands. (Crocodile tears or real ones?) The white-faced dwarf in his jester's costume was perched on the step beside her, legs dangling, like a grotesque doll.

Aside from this, plenty of other people were milling around too. There was a quartet of dark-uniformed police officers, some costumed circus performers, and a few labourers (stagehands? carnies? John had no idea what the correct term for them was) who were standing about with their collars turned up, muttering and smoking.

One of the officers, his hands eerily white because of the latex gloves he was wearing, was holding a stubby-barrelled shotgun. Another was speaking urgently into the radio attached to his breast pocket. A little knot of performers – Emil, Michael, Helga and the strongman – was standing apart from the others, silent and still. Their faces were expressionless and John got the sense that they were like impartial onlookers at a scientific experiment – vaguely interested in the outcome, but emotionally uninvolved.

He trudged across the muddy wet grass towards the paramedics. Even though neither their positions nor their facial expressions changed in the slightest, he felt the eyes of Emil and his group tracking him every step of the way. One of the paramedics looked up at his approach and nodded a greeting. 'Dr Kersh.'

John nodded back. He recognised the man, but couldn't remember his name. All his attention was focused on the figure on the ground.

As he had feared, it was Alan Michaels. John didn't need to examine him to know that he was dead. His face was blue and mottled, eyes and mouth open, despite the rain that was falling into them. He pictured Lynn sobbing into Nick's chest, and his stomach clenched with pity at the thought of the anguish and grief that she would imminently be facing. 'What was the cause of death?' he asked bleakly.

'Massive myocardial infarction,' said the man whose

name John couldn't remember, raising his shoulders in a sad little shrug.

'You're sure?' Glancing across at Emil, John instinctively lowered his voice. 'There were no . . . unusual marks on the body? Nothing to suggest there might have been a contributory factor?'

The paramedic frowned. 'Well, we won't know for sure until the post-mortem, of course, but it looks like a classic coronary to me.' He glanced at his colleague for corroboration, who nodded, and then peered curiously at John. 'Why do you ask?'

John gestured with his eyes towards the dead animals in their cages and then nodded across at the policeman holding the shotgun. 'I'm guessing Mr Michaels here killed the animals before collapsing?'

The paramedic nodded. 'Looks that way. Nobody seems to know why.'

'Oh, believe me, they know a lot more than they're letting on,' John muttered.

'What makes you say that?'

Before he could reply, there was a shriek from behind him that made him jump.

'*Dad!* Oh no! Oh please . . . Dad . . .'

He turned to see Lynn running towards him, Nick hurrying after her. He stood up so quickly that his knees cracked, and he stepped forward, spreading his arms like a farmer trying to calm a skittish animal. Lynn faltered, as if considering which way to go in order to dodge him, and then she stumbled to a halt, peering over his shoulder. John put his arms loosely around her, trying to usher her away from her father's corpse.

'It's best if you don't look,' he said.

'Oh God.' She was weeping now. She looked wildly around and her voice rose shrilly. 'What did they do to him? What did *these bastards do to him?*'

'He had a heart attack, that's all,' John said soothingly. 'He wouldn't have known anything about it.'

'*They* caused it, though,' she said, pulling away and pointing accusingly around at the circus people. '*They* killed my dad, just like they killed the people in the woods and probably the missing Blaine boys too.' As the workers began to mumble resentfully and Emil and his group stared back at her impassively, she shouted, 'And they won't stop there. They won't stop until they've killed us all.'

She looked at the nearest police officer, the one who had been talking into his pocket radio. He looked back at her as if he wasn't sure whether to urge her to calm down or merely slap on the cuffs and haul her away.

'Why don't you arrest them?' she demanded, her eyes wild and reckless. 'Why don't you arrest the murdering bastards?'

The officer raised his hands in the same way that John had raised his a minute or two before. 'I think you need to calm down, miss,' he said.

Lynn looked outraged. 'That's my dad!' she yelled, pointing. 'That's my dad lying there *dead!* And *they* murdered him!'

John and Nick closed in on her. 'Lynn, this isn't doing any good,' Nick muttered.

'I appreciate that you're upset,' the police officer was saying, 'but nobody's murdered anyone here.'

'Yes, they have!' The ringmistress's head snapped up. Her face was tear-stained, furious. Now it was her turn to point accusingly – at Alan's body on the ground. '*He* murdered my animals. Killed them in cold blood.'

At her unexpected outburst Nick went white, as if he had seen a ghost. John was so distracted by both the ringmistress's words and Nick's peculiar reaction that he took his eye off Lynn for a moment. By the time he realised she was stomping across the grass towards the ringmistress it was too late to stop her.

'*Fuck your animals!*' Lynn screamed. '*And fuck you!*'

With a plunging heart John expected her to fly at the ringmistress, to physically attack her – he shuddered to think what would happen if she did. But she came to a halt a few metres away, shaking from head to foot.

'Why don't you leave us alone?' Lynn shouted, her fury turning to grief now, her voice cracking. 'Haven't you done enough?'

John reached Lynn and put his hands on her shoulders, just in time to hear Madame Serena's reply. Her voice was so low that he and Lynn were the only ones to hear it.

'No,' she said.

Twenty-Seven

When the doorbell rang Caroline went rigid and Chris leaped off the settee. Sam, however, barely reacted at all. She remained perched on the armchair against the far wall, knees drawn up to her chin, staring straight ahead. Her eyes were wide and vacant, as if her thoughts were elsewhere.

Before Chris could cross the room, Sue Penney, the Family Liaison Officer who had been assigned to them, rose from the chair beside the door and raised a hand.

'It's okay, Chris – I'll get it.'

'It could be news,' Chris said.

'It could be. Or it could be the press, or a nosy neighbour, or even the Jehovah's Witnesses. In which case, I'll send them packing.' Sue smiled as if she was relishing the prospect and slipped from the room.

Chris sat down again, lowering himself slowly and reluctantly, like a man doing leg exercises. He perched on the edge of the settee, hands clasped between his knees, his face both expectant and full of dread. He heard Sue's footsteps cross the hall, the door open, the murmur of voices, the rustle of someone wearing a thick waterproof garment entering the house. He rose again as feet scraped on the doormat and then approached at a measured pace across the wooden hallway floor, echoed by Sue's lighter steps. By the time the door opened, admitting the visitor, he was all but standing to attention, fists clenched tightly at his sides.

Bulky in his rain-speckled overcoat, Superintendent Benson's face was unreadable. In the split second before he began to speak Chris felt his senses zooming in, his mind becoming almost preternaturally sharp. He saw the individual spikes in Benson's neat wet hair; a small scar beneath his right eye; the slightly askew knot of his tie; a callus, reddened by the cold, on the first knuckle of his ring finger. Everything seemed so crisp, so focused, as if at that specific moment the myriad intricate elements making up the equilibrium of the universe were fleetingly, exquisitely balanced.

And then Benson uttered his first words and the entire structure collapsed.

'Chris,' he said, his voice as measured as his footsteps had been, 'I think you'd better sit down. I'm afraid I've got some very bad news for you all.'

Chris didn't sit down; he fell. As if the tendons had been slashed in the backs of his knees, he dropped back onto the settee so heavily that he bounced. A terrible buzzing started in his ears; he thought he was going to faint. He was vaguely aware of Caroline beside him, slowly shaking her head, a look of utter, desolate horror on her face.

I don't want to know, he thought. *If you don't say the words they won't be true.* He wanted to shout this out, to scream it. But his throat was paralysed; he couldn't speak. And by the time he could it was too late.

'. . . bodies of Kieron and Matt were found in the grounds of Mitre House less than half an hour ago,' Benson was saying, his voice a soft, apologetic rumble. 'According to the coroner's initial assessment they had been dead about three hours.'

Why? Chris thought, appealing to a God he didn't believe in. *Why did you let my boys die?*

Beside him, Caroline whispered, 'How?'

Benson heaved out a huge and heartfelt sigh. 'Early indications are that they died of exsanguination. Blood loss. There were . . . wounds around both their throats.'

Caroline seemed colourless, reduced almost to invisibility by shock. But she kept asking the questions, breathing them out in a voice that was less than a whisper. 'Was it . . . an animal?'

'It's too early to say,' Benson replied. 'First indications are that it was not the same animal that killed the people in the woods.'

Your children will die, Chris thought. And in that moment he *hated* Nick Miller with every fibre of his being. He wished he had never met the man; wished he had never agreed to spy on his wife; wished with all his heart that he had never been at Mitre House to witness the death, ten years ago, of the child-killer Karl Mitterhaus.

It was bitterness and regret and fury that finally enabled him to rediscover his voice. Aware that tears were running down his face only when they began to splash on the backs of his clenched fists, he looked up at Benson.

'It wasn't an animal,' he said, his words thick, choked. 'We all know that, don't we?'

Sue Penney looked puzzled, but Benson merely stared back at him with eyes full of sorrow and fear.

'It was them,' Chris said. 'It was *them!* It was fucking *them!*'

Grief overwhelmed him and he slumped over, his head hitting the arm of the settee, sobs tearing painfully and raggedly out of him.

'Who?' asked Sue, bewildered. 'Who are you talking about?'

It was Benson who answered. 'The Circus of Nights,' he said.

It wasn't until almost half an hour later that they discovered that Sam was gone.

Twenty-Eight

'**D**o you trust me?'

'More than anything.'

Emil reached out. 'Then take my hand.'

Sam took it without hesitation. It was cold as ice, and yet conversely the very touch of his skin sent ripples of pleasure through her body. She felt as if she were floating on air as he led her through the red velvet drapes fronting the 'Mirror Of Life'.

'It's so dark,' she said once they were inside.

'You're not afraid of the dark, are you?'

'Not when I'm with you.'

She closed her eyes as she followed him through the darkness. They moved quickly, almost running at times. She felt carefree, abandoned, capable of anything. The darkness enveloped her, soft and caressing; it brushed against her skin like fur. Eventually the blackness behind her eyelids turned blood red, then orange, then golden.

Emil slipped his hand from hers. 'Open your eyes,' he said.

She did so, slowly, the light flooding her, replacing

the darkness. They were at the end of a golden, mirror-lined corridor, standing in front of the biggest mirror of all.

But she was alone. Or at least her reflection was. She looked to her right and Emil was there, standing beside her.

'You have no reflection,' she said.

'Does that bother you?'

Sam shook her head emphatically. 'No.'

He stepped in front of her, facing her. As always he moved like oil, like a panther, silently and effortlessly. He held out both hands this time, palms up. She placed her hands in his, her own palms down. She felt his strong fingers closing around her slender ones. His grip was gentle, but inexorable.

'Come with me,' he said.

'Where?'

Instead of answering her question, he stepped backwards – *flowed* backwards – dragging her with him. As if this were a dream, the glass of the mirror was suddenly no longer glass but a threshold, an open doorway. He stepped across it and she went with him, trusting him completely. As she too crossed the threshold she felt a dank chill that raised gooseflesh on her arms, and smelled something thick and cloying, rank like rotten meat. She experienced a twinge of resistance, of fear, but Emil's voice soothed it away.

'Don't be afraid. I have something important to show you.'

The golden light dimmed, as though a dense black cloud had passed over the moon. Sam felt rough, uneven stone beneath her feet, heard the hollow, echoing drip of water. The chill increased, penetrating her bones. She shivered. But still she allowed Emil to draw her deeper into the cold, stinking darkness. She trusted him. She loved him. He released one of her hands and swung her slowly round, as if this were a dance, a waltz, until she was standing once again by his side.

'See,' he said, gesturing at the sight before them; the sight which until now he had been shielding with his body.

It was an open coffin on some sort of pedestal. In the coffin was a middle-aged man, his hair grey and flowing, his eyes closed. He looked asleep rather than dead, and yet there was a spar of wood jutting from his chest. The blood which had flowed from the wound was black and long-congealed, but there was fresh blood, and plenty of it, still wet and startlingly red, on the man's skin.

If she had not been with Emil, Sam felt sure that the sight would have sent her screaming from the room. But he had wanted her to see it. Therefore everything was fine.

'Who is it?' she asked.

'He is my brother,' said Emil. There was pride in his voice, and also something else – defiance, perhaps?

Sam looked into the handsome but lined face of the man in the coffin, and then at Emil. 'But he's so much older than you.'

'Two years only,' Emil replied. 'But he is only partially restored.'

'Two years?' Sam didn't understand. This man looked old enough to be Emil's father. 'What happened to him?'

Emil's black eyes flashed. His face tautened with anger. 'He was murdered by peasants. But soon he will live again, and we shall have our revenge.'

'Live again?' said Sam. 'But how?'

The attack was swift and merciless. Before Sam could even scream, Emil had leaped upon her and fastened his teeth on her throat. He tore open her jugular vein, and then held her thrashing, dying body by the hair over his brother's coffin, watching in satisfaction as her lifeblood gushed and spattered over him. As Karl's flesh absorbed the blood of the sacrifice, Emil saw it tightening, becoming younger again, blooming with life. He sensed Karl's ruptured heart repairing itself, pushing out the jagged spar of wood which had temporarily suspended his life.

Yes, he thought. Soon Karl would live again, and side by side he and his brother would exact their revenge. Together they would tear this place and its people apart.

Twenty-Nine

'We have to act *now*,' John said.

There were seven of them gathered in the Blaines' red-walled sitting room. John, Nick, Lynn and Chris occupied the settee and armchairs, Anthony and Kate were on the floor, backs against the wall, holding hands, and Superintendent Benson was sitting, with his arms crossed, on a wooden chair which he had carried through from the dining room. Both Chris and Lynn looked hollow-eyed, shell-shocked, as if they had stared deep into the abyss and been irredeemably changed by what they had seen there. But they looked determined too, and angry. Chris in particular couldn't sit still. His knee jerked up and down; his body rocked back and forth; his hands clenched and unclenched. Unlike his wife, who had retreated upstairs with Sue Penney, and was currently lying in a darkened room, unwilling to face the world, Chris looked ready to go to war. John didn't know whether that made him an asset or a liability.

Surrounding them were achingly poignant reminders of a family life torn apart. Computer games under the

TV; family portraits on the dresser; a 'Good Luck With Your Exams' card on the mantelpiece. John had wondered whether it might not be such a good environment in which to hatch their plans, whether being reminded of what they had already lost might debilitate them, but in hindsight it seemed the opposite was true. Although their mood was grim, it was also charged with a righteous fury. If any of them had any doubts about the need not only to cut out the cancer that was killing their community but to do it quickly and ruthlessly, then all they had to do to strengthen their resolve was take a look around.

John had already proposed – and Nick, Lynn and Chris were in full accord – that the only method which was still open to them of carrying out the surgery effectively was to gather as many of Shettle's inhabitants as they could and march on the circus in the hope of forcing it out of their community, overwhelming it with sheer numbers.

'I know it's crude,' he said to Benson, 'I know it's lawless, and I know that it goes against every policing instinct in your body. But believe me, Alex, it's the only way.'

Benson pursed his lips. His arms were still crossed – the classic defensive pose. 'Is it, now?' he said.

'Yes,' said John, nodding, 'I'm afraid it is. No offence, but we've already been pussyfooting around for far too long, and as a result of that some of our people have died.'

'We have no actual evidence—' Benson began, but Chris butted in.

'My boys are *dead*, superintendent. My daughter is *missing*. Evidence or not, I know – we *all* know – who fucking killed them. Now, either you and your men are on our side or you're not, but either way we're going to drive those bastards out – or die trying.'

Lynn was nodding, but John held up a hand. 'Okay, guys, calm down. Let's not turn this into a slanging match or start bickering amongst ourselves.'

'John's right,' said Nick. 'We need a united front on this. If we start pulling in opposite directions it will play right into their hands.'

John nodded at his friend, grateful for his input. Since their visit to the circus that afternoon Nick had been quiet, preoccupied, and not only because of Alan, or the terrible news about Chris and Caroline's boys, or even the fact that today was the tenth anniversary of his wife's death. No, there was something else – and John suspected it had to do with Nick's reaction to Madame Serena's outburst earlier. He had asked Nick about it on the way to Chris's, but only briefly – there simply hadn't been time to discuss it at length. Nick, however, had fobbed him off with a shrug and a shake of the head and a muttered denial that it was anything important.

'Thank you, Nick,' Benson said now. Unfolding his arms he placed his hands on his knees and looked at Chris. 'I fully understand your desire for revenge, Chris, but, as I said before, I simply cannot condone vigilante justice. You talk about driving the circus people out, but how is that going to be achieved? They're not sheep. They're not going to run if you simply jump up and down and shout at them. If they're as ruthless – as murderous – as you claim, then they're going to resist, and that will inevitably lead to violence. If I allow mob rule to prevail, then people will get hurt, possibly killed.'

'People have already been killed,' Chris said bitterly.

Anthony held up a hand. 'Can I say something?'

There were a few nods. 'Go ahead,' said Nick.

'Why not just arrest them? Move in, arrest them, question them, put them in cells?'

Chris snorted. Benson said calmly, 'On what charge?'

'Well . . . suspected murder,' said Anthony.

Benson shook his head. 'I can't arrest people without evidence. And I certainly can't arrest them all. We don't have the resources. Besides, even if I *could* arrest them, I'd almost certainly end up having to let them go in a day or two.'

There were grumbles of resentment, frustration. Chris suddenly jumped up and shouted, 'This is ridiculous! While we're sitting here talking, God knows what they're doing to my daughter up there.' He looked ready to head off there and then, but once again John raised a hand.

'Can I suggest something? A compromise?'

Benson nodded. 'Go ahead.'

'Why don't we go up there with all the officers you can spare, but supplemented by a team of hand-picked men? Reliable men. Tough but disciplined, unlikely to fly off the handle at the slightest provocation. And once we're there we'll talk to them. We'll tell them we know what they're up to, and that they're not going to succeed. We'll demand that they remove the "sickness barrier". We'll make their position untenable.'

Lynn shook her head. 'They won't listen.'

'They'll *have* to listen. We'll *make* them listen. We'll have the advantage of sheer numbers on our side.'

'I want them punished for what they've done,' Chris said.

'They will be,' Benson said. 'If they were responsible for the deaths of your boys or for the people killed in the woods, then they won't escape justice. I promise you that.'

Sitting on the floor next to Anthony, and silent until now, Kate said, 'But we don't even know what they are.'

Everyone looked at her. She blushed, but continued, 'I mean, you're talking as if they're . . . normal human beings, but they're not, are they? They've got abilities that we don't understand. They can *do* things. Impossible things. What if they won't abide by our rules? What if they're too strong for us, however many men we send against them? What if . . . what if they can't even be *killed*?'

There was silence for a moment. Then John said, 'All we can do, Kate, is use the resources available to us. And if those resources fall short, then so be it. At least we can say that we tried.' Turning his attention to Benson, he said, 'Well, Alex? What do you think of my proposal? Extraordinary situations call for extraordinary measures, after all. Do we have a working plan?'

Benson looked at him hard for a moment, and then he nodded. 'We do,' he said.

Thirty

It wasn't exactly the peasants marching on Castle Frankenstein with flaming torches, but Nick couldn't help thinking that it was pretty close to the modern equivalent. It was full dark by the time a forty-strong contingent of police officers and local people arrived at the gate of Hobbes' Meadow in a variety of vehicles. Indeed, it was almost seven p.m., the proposed start time for the Circus of Nights' final performance.

There would *be* no performance tonight, however, final or otherwise. 'CANCELLED – BY POLICE ORDER' notices had gone up all over Shettle in an effort to keep people away. There had still been a few who had defied the notices, or had simply failed to see them, but they had been turned back at the top of Hobbes' Lane by a couple of Benson's officers.

Now their hand-picked band was all set for what Nick sincerely hoped would be a final and successful showdown. He stepped out of John's car and clicked on his torch, unable to shake the feeling that the last ten years had been leading inexorably to this moment. He was aware of the hubbub around him, of the apprehension, the nervous excitement, the barely restrained anger. And yet within the crowd he felt oddly isolated, alone with his thoughts.

He wasn't sure why he hadn't told John what had caused him to react with shock when they had been here a few hours earlier. Maybe it was because he wanted to be wrong. Or maybe, conversely, it was because he *didn't* want to be. When the ringmistress had raised her head and tearfully accused Alan of murdering her animals, her distress had been genuine, and consequently she had let her guard drop for a moment. And *in* that moment there had been, for Nick, a sharp and resounding echo of the past. For a split second the disguise had slipped and he had seen his dead wife, Anna.

Or had he? Even now he wasn't sure. The impression, so vivid at the time, had now acquired the quality of a dream, or an illusion.

Nick was shaken out of his reverie by a sudden purposeful clearing of the throat and a raised voice asking, 'Gentlemen, if I could have your attention?' He looked up. Benson was standing in front of the closed gate with his arms half-raised, like a conductor priming his orchestra.

The chatter died down. Faces turned in Benson's direction. 'Thank you,' the superintendent said. 'Now, before we start, I just wanted to make a couple of things clear. First I would like to reiterate that this is a police-led operation, and as such I expect you, as much as possible, to adhere to the letter of the law. Secondly, may I remind you that our primary and initial purpose this evening is merely to *speak* to the circus people and see where that gets us. To this end, myself and Dr Kersh have been elected as spokesmen for the group. I would therefore appreciate your patience and restraint while we conduct our discussions. What we *do not* need are people shouting out, hurling insults and making accusations. Is that clear?'

'Yes, Mr Benson, *sir*,' came a sarcastic response from the crowd, evoking a ripple of laughter.

Benson frowned. Hastily John stepped up beside him and raised a hand. 'Look, guys,' he said in his companionable way, 'we don't mean to treat you like schoolkids, but it's important that we establish a reasonable dialogue with these people if we can. If we go up there itching for a fight, they're more likely to dig in their heels, maybe even lash out. And to be honest, given the evidence so far, we don't know what they're capable of. It may be that . . . well, that they've got a few more tricks up their sleeves than we can deal with.'

'We've got a few tricks ourselves,' somebody muttered. There was a growl of assent.

John smiled, not only as if the speaker had made a joke but as if he appreciated it. 'True. But let's keep them there for the time being, shall we?'

There were nods. Grunts of general but reluctant agreement. Nick looked around, sensing the ugly mood and wondering how easy it would *really* be to keep the lid on things once the circus people showed themselves. As far as the men here were aware, the circus people's intentions were hostile. The meeting in the community hall that afternoon had made it clear that they had come to Shettle ostensibly to take revenge for the death of a child-murderer who had perished in a fire ten years previously, and to achieve that aim they had (somehow) physically isolated and scrambled the minds of an entire community. Six people had already died, three of them children, and a teenage girl was currently missing. And although none of these incidents had *officially* been linked to the circus, the consensus in Shettle now seemed to be that the Circus of Nights and those associated with it were responsible.

Nick knew that it was only the thinnest veneer of 'civilised' behaviour which was preventing the men here – 'disciplined' and 'sensible' though they were supposed to be – from storming into the enemy camp and setting it ablaze. He dreaded to think what would happen if things got out of control – but in part he welcomed it too, and that frightened him more than anything.

They set off across the field, the combined light of forty torches blazing the way ahead. They were not armed, aside from the police officers who carried their regulation batons. John and he had discussed passing around crucifixes but had thought that it was a step too far, that it might irreparably undermine their credibility. As they approached the big top, the police officers leading the way with Benson at their head, Nick half-expected the circus people to gather in front of them like an opposing army preparing to do battle. But there was nothing. Not a sound. Not a stir of movement.

He glanced to his right, to the haunted but determined-looking figure of Chris Blaine by his side. Chris had been more or less silent since the meeting in his front room had broken up a couple of hours earlier. While Benson, John, Lynn and Nick had made preparations for this evening's confrontation, Chris had slipped away to spend some time with Caroline. When he had reappeared it had been as if he had left his grief and his anger behind; either that or buried it deep within himself. It was eerie: he was like a ghost – there and not there. Nick was about to ask him if he was all right before realising what a wildly inappropriate question that was. So in the end he contented himself with a nod. Chris nodded back.

The big top had been opened up as if for business, and the canvas flaps tied back. As Benson approached the snout-like entrance and called out, Nick felt nervous. When no reply was forthcoming, the superintendent turned to address the men once again. It was decided that the group should split into two, one half to investigate the big top, the other to search the encampment of caravans and trailers round the back.

Nick, who was in the group detailed to enter the big top, would have favoured a more cautious approach, but Benson led them through the entrance tunnel like a gung-ho general at the head of an occupying army. Beyond Benson, Nick could see that the spotlights were on, each of them angled so that its bright beam of light shone down on the centre of the ring. What the spotlights were illuminating, though, Nick couldn't see at first; he was in the middle of the group and there were too many people in front of him. He was aware that there was something wrong only when Benson, at the head of the group, halted abruptly and emitted an exclamation of profound shock that then seemed to jam in his vocal cords, dwindling to a thin and somehow lacklustre groan.

Others around Benson were more articulate. Nick heard an officer mutter 'Fuck,' and a local man (Nick recognised him as Craig Tullston, an ex-soldier who now ran a farm shop) cried out angrily, 'The bastards!' As the bodies in front of him thinned out as men moved forward into the auditorium, Nick stepped up beside John who had come to a halt a few feet ahead of him. Now that he had an unobstructed view of the centre of the ring and was finally able to see what had caused such a horrified reaction in Benson and some of the other men, he went cold all over and a pulse started to beat hard in the base of his throat. Around him he was vaguely aware that others were also gaping in bewilderment, anger and fear, too horrified – like him – to speak.

Piled in the centre of the ring, lit up like an exhibit, were three dozen or more blood-spattered corpses. Within the tangle of arms and legs and open-mouthed, wide-eyed faces, Nick saw police officers, itinerant labourers and circus performers. Among the performers were clowns, the family of jugglers, the shaven-headed tiger woman, and – most sickening of all – the tiny girl in the tutu who had stood astride the galloping, circling horse. Grotesquely, even the horse itself was there, a little apart from the heap of human corpses, but slaughtered just the same.

John, who had been standing beside Nick, walked forward slowly and stepped over the knee-high barrier into the ring. As the overhead lights fell on him he seemed, simultaneously and weirdly, to become both more vivid and bleached of colour. As he circled the bodies, taking care to avoid the pools and spatters and runnels of blood, Nick again had the odd, almost dream-like impression that he was looking at an exhibit in an art gallery, something that was shocking and thought-provoking but not actually real. Despite everything he knew about Karl Mitterhaus, and all that he had learned about the Circus of Nights, he still found it hard to get his head around the cold reality of slaughter on such a brutal scale.

Concluding his examination, John walked back towards them, his face sombre.

'It looks as if they all died the same way,' he said.

'Which was?' Benson had rediscovered his voice, but it was gruff and cracked, like that of an old man.

'They had their throats torn out. Not cut. Torn.'

Benson stole a glance behind him. 'Like the Blaine boys.'

'There's something else, too,' John said, his eyes flickering to look at Nick.

'What?' Nick asked.

'Not all the circus people are there among the dead. Some are missing. Madame Serena, the dwarf, the strongman, Emil the acrobat, the trapeze artists . . .'

Nick knew what John was thinking, because he was thinking it himself. 'I wonder where they are,' he murmured.

Thirty-One

As soon as he caught a glimpse of the stark and terrible display beneath the unflinching beams of the big-top spotlights, Chris Blaine turned and high-tailed it out of there. He did it not because he was squeamish, but because he was terrified of finding out to whom one of those bodies might belong. His mind felt like a piece of elastic at full stretch. The only thing that drove him on, and that allowed him to keep his appalling grief at bay, was the possibility that he might yet save his sole surviving child. If, however, it tran-spired that Sam was among that awful stacked heap of human kindling in the centre of the ring, he honestly believed his mind would shatter like glass.

As soon as he stepped outside the icy air hit him like a slap and he gasped and staggered, his raw eyes filling with tears. They were tears not of grief – not yet – but of cold. He bent forward, hands on knees, blinking hard and shaking with reaction. His guts felt jittery, but he successfully fought the urge to puke. The rain in his hair and on the back of his neck was like stealthily probing fingers, but it helped to revive him.

He stood up slowly, wondering what to do. The thought of hanging around here and waiting for everyone to come filing out of the big top filled him with dread. If he didn't see Sam's body, or hear about her death, then she would remain alive. He knew that that was a desperate and pointless way to think, but it was all he had. He needed to remain purposeful; he needed to keep searching. He clung to the hope that if he searched long and hard enough, if he truly *believed*, then perhaps he would be rewarded.

But where? Round the back of the big top with the other group? No. The two groups would merge soon enough to exchange information – and besides, what if he went round there and saw *more* bodies stacked up beside the trailers and caravans? His gaze passed across the darkened trailers which, two nights before, had been selling hot dogs and popcorn and toffee apples. Maybe Sam was in one of those? Tied-up, frightened, but unharmed?

As soon as the idea occurred to him, it seized hold and wouldn't let go. He knew again, deep down, that it was the thinking of a desperate man. But at the same time he could picture Sam in his mind's eye so clearly that it was almost like a vision. She was lying on a dirty wooden floor, wrists and ankles bound with the same thick rope used to anchor the big top, a filthy twist of cloth clamped between her teeth and knotted tightly at the back of her head to prevent her from screaming. Her face would be dirty, but there would be clean tear-tracks down her cheeks. He hated to think of his daughter held against her will and terrified out of her wits. But she was alive, that was the main thing. She was *alive!* He looked again at the trailers. Which one would she be in?

Without hesitation he walked towards the 'Mirror Of Life'.

Thirty-Two

Anthony put 'Redux' on a triple word score and earned himself a whopping thirty-nine points.

Kate wrinkled her nose. 'Redux? Is that even a proper word?'

'Course it is.'

'What does it mean then?'

Adopting the overconfident expression he always wore when he wasn't one hundred per cent sure of something, he said, 'Well, it means . . . a revamp. Like if somebody brings back an old TV show.'

Kate looked at him dubiously. 'That sounds like woffle to me. What do you think, Lynn?'

Lynn opened her mouth, then closed it again. She looked down at the Scrabble board on the kitchen table and her brow crinkled in a frown. 'What does it matter?' she said. 'I can't even believe we're doing this. Playing bloody Scrabble with all this lot going on. Your dads are out there risking their lives, and my dad . . .' Her voice choked off and suddenly tears were brimming in her eyes. As the first one spilled over and trickled down her cheek she pushed her chair back with a screech, stood up and rushed out of the kitchen.

Kate and Anthony looked at one another in dismay. Anthony placed his hands flat on the edge of the table, meaning to push himself to his feet, but Kate put a hand lightly on his arm. 'I'll go. You stay here and clear the Scrabble away.'

Anthony looked for a moment as if he might argue, and then he nodded. 'Okay. I'll make some coffee. Be in in about . . . five minutes?'

'Make it ten.'

Kate stood up and hurried after Lynn. She hadn't heard the front door open, which was a good thing, because her immediate thought had been that Lynn's intention might be to join the men up at the circus. Of the three of them, Lynn had been the one who had protested most vehemently when Dad and Dr Kersh had insisted they remain in the house with the doors and windows locked.

'I'm not a child,' she had said.

'But that's just it, Lynn, you *are*,' Dr Kersh had replied in that soft, reasonable voice of his. 'Remember Mitterhaus's words? "Your children will die". That's you, Lynn. You and Kate and Anthony – and Sam too, wherever she is. You're their primary targets and as such we can't allow you to be in the front line, not for this. They've already taken Kieron and Matt. We're not going to let them take any more of you.'

Lynn hadn't liked it, but she had complied reluctantly, and for the last hour the three of them had been holed up in the house that Kate shared with her dad, waiting for news. Kate could understand Lynn's outburst about the pointlessness, the inappropriateness, of playing board games while not far away their dads might be risking life and limb to protect them. But on the other hand what else were they going to do? Sit and worry? At least Scrabble occupied their minds. And helped pass the time.

The kitchen was at the rear of the house, overlooking the small back lawn. The only other room on this floor, aside from a tiny toilet tucked under the stairs, was the sitting room at the front. To reach it Kate had to walk along a short hallway with the staircase on her right and enter the first (and only) door on her left. Beyond that the hallway opened out into a small front porch. From where she was, halfway between the kitchen and the sitting room, she could see the wooden front door with its eye-level half-moon panel of frosted glass.

Someone was on the other side of that glass. A dark, bulky shape. She could see them moving about.

She came to a halt, a pulse jumping into swift and immediate life in her throat. Her skin prickled. Although she hadn't turned the light on in the hall and couldn't possibly be seen through the frosted glass panel, she felt suddenly and horribly vulnerable. Maybe it was just paranoia but she got the impression that the figure on the other side of the door was being deliberately stealthy. Then her hunch was confirmed as the door handle went slowly down, then back up again – once, twice, three times.

Kate hovered, wondering which way to go. Forward to tell Lynn there was someone outside? Or back to the kitchen to fetch Anthony? Though her throat felt tight and her mouth dry, she forced herself to speak, or rather to call softly. 'Lynn? Anthony?'

The words were barely out of her mouth when the door burst inwards.

It was as if it had been hit with a battering ram. Wood splintered; the glass panel exploded; the hinges were wrenched from their moorings. The door swayed and then toppled into the hall, allowing cold air to rush into the house.

Out of the night stepped a giant. He had to duck his head to prevent himself bumping it on the lintel. His hands, the ones he had used to smash the door from its hinges, were like garden rakes covered in flesh. Because of his blue boiler suit, Kate didn't recognise him at first. And then she did. It was the strongman from the circus.

Anthony and Lynn came running from opposite directions as the strongman rose to his full height. Behind him Kate saw lights in the shadows, shining like the eyes of cats. Then the lights drifted closer, and she realised that they *were* eyes, and that they belonged to Michael and Helga, the trapeze artists from the circus. They stepped daintily into the house, and then moved aside like actors on a stage to allow the ringmistress in her dark glasses to step between them.

Last to enter was a figure clad in black, with eyes to match, who moved like oil. Emil the acrobat. His lips curled back in a silent snarl, and with a shock of fear Kate saw that, like those of the panther he resembled, his teeth were long and sharp.

Thirty-Three

D own the rabbit hole, Chris thought.

That was what it felt like when he stepped through the red velvet drapes and into an utter blackness that sealed itself behind him. He had no way of knowing how big the room he had entered was (if indeed it even *was* a room) but he ploughed on regardless. Under different circumstances he might have felt disconcerted and disorientated but on this occasion he felt, oddly, almost hopeful. If the circus people *were* holding Sam, then it stood to reason that they wouldn't make it easy to find her. They would do something precisely like this in an effort to get him to turn back.

But he *didn't* turn back, and at length his resolve was rewarded. He came to a pair of overlapping black curtains that felt like animal fur and pushed his way through them into blazing golden light. When his eyes adjusted he discovered that he was standing in a narrow corridor, both sides of which were lined with funhouse mirrors. He also discovered that the curtains through which he had entered the corridor were gone, leaving no discernible exit either behind him or ahead. Curiouser and curiouser.

Refusing to be deterred, he moved slowly along the corridor. At each mirror he halted and ran his fingers around the outside of the frame in the hope of discovering a hidden door – behind which he might find Sam, tied up and awaiting rescue. He was determined to press doggedly on to the end and had already decided that if he reached the last mirror only to find that too affixed securely to the wall, then he would try a different tactic. He would smash the mirrors. In fact, he would rip the place apart with his bare hands if he had to.

He had examined over a dozen mirrors when he sensed that he was not alone. Half-turning, he was astonished to see the white-faced dwarf in the jester's outfit standing boldly in the centre of the corridor about ten metres away. The dwarf was watching him with a contemptuous expression, as if Chris was doing something utterly pointless. It was this as much as anything that caused Chris's face to flush with sudden anger.

'Where's Sam?' he said, taking a step towards the dwarf. 'Where's my daughter?'

The dwarf sneered. 'Where you'll never find her.'

At that Chris's anger clicked all the way up to 'murderous'. With a strangled roar he ran at the dwarf, intending to kick and stamp the answer out of him, if needs be. The dwarf gave a high-pitched giggle, as if this was no more than a childish game, and scampered away. However, as far as Chris could see he had nowhere to run; ahead appeared to be nothing but a dead end. The dwarf had almost reached the final mirror on the right-hand wall, which was twice as large as the others, when he dropped something that Chris hadn't even noticed he'd been carrying. The object hit the floor with a heavy metallic clunk, but before Chris had time to register what it was the dwarf leaped at the final mirror.

Despite his desire to inflict severe pain on the little man, Chris clenched his teeth, anticipating the impact. He fully expected the dwarf to bounce back from the mirror – or perhaps even hit it hard enough to shatter it and be cut to ribbons by falling glass – but instead the dwarf seemed to disappear *into* the mirror.

Chris was so surprised that he stumbled a little before managing to regain his balance. Immediately he realised what must have happened: the final mirror wasn't a mirror at all, but a doorway. But when Chris reached it a second or two later he found that the mirror's surface *was* glass, after all. Or at least, something *like* glass; something equally as hard and smooth and cold. The difference, however, was that the glass in *this* mirror wasn't reflective – it was black. As black as the area immediately beyond the red velvet drapes had been. It seemed to absorb light, to be depthless. Staring into it made Chris feel sick and dizzy. He stretched out a hand, just to reassure himself that there was a solid surface in front of him.

The instant he touched it the mirror changed.

Now there was no longer blackness beyond its surface but some sort of room or cave. Dominating the room – or the section of it that he was looking at – was an open coffin on a stone altar or pedestal. Chris couldn't see much of the figure inside the coffin, but he did see something that sent cold, feverish tingles through him.

He saw a jagged spar of wood, stained black with old blood, jutting from where he guessed the figure's chest would be. That could mean only one thing. He was looking at the body of Karl Mitterhaus.

But that was impossible. Mitterhaus had burned to death, hadn't he? There had been nothing left of him but ash. So what was this? A vision? A bad dream? Mitterhaus through the looking glass? Chris was still pondering when two figures appeared, stage left, one walking backwards, pulling the other. The first figure, dressed all in black, was Emil. And the other . . . Chris gasped.

It was Sam.

He stepped forward, raised a fist, and pounded on the glass. Was this happening now? Or was it simply a recording? Or perhaps it hadn't happened at all? Maybe it was nothing but a vision, designed to taunt him?

'Sam!' he yelled. 'Sam!' There was no response from beyond the glass, no indication whatsoever that his daughter could hear him. He hit the mirror harder. Maybe he could smash it, break through? Emil had tugged Sam around now and was standing beside her. They were looking down into Mitterhaus's coffin. Chris could see their lips moving as they talked, but he couldn't hear what they were saying.

He saw Sam frown. Then he saw her say something that, from her expression, was clearly a question. But instead of answering, Emil suddenly lunged at her, lowering his head and tearing into her throat with sudden and shocking ferocity.

'*Nooo!*' Chris screamed as blood erupted from Sam's gashed neck. He threw himself at the glass, kicking and pounding, but it was impervious to his assault. Emil held Sam over the coffin by her hair as if she weighed nothing at all. As his daughter's blood spattered onto the body of Karl Mitterhaus, Chris looked around desperately for something heavy, something he could use to smash the glass. His glance skidded across the item that the dwarf had dropped, and then backtracked. No sooner had he realised what it was than he was running towards it, scooping it up.

It was a gun. Without even thinking about it, Chris ran back to the mirror, aimed it and fired. He expected the glass to shatter and raised his left hand to shield his face from flying shards, but instead the effect was akin to striking a match in a room full of gas. The mirror exploded, engulfing Chris in a raging fireball. He was aware only of closing his eyes, and then of sudden, mind-warpingly intense pain – pain so all-encompassing that he would not have thought it possible to experience it and remain alive.

He tried to scream, but his already melting lips had welded themselves shut. When they finally tore apart, he succeeded only in swallowing fire. Dropping the gun, which unbeknownst to him had left a burning imprint of itself on his palm, he wheeled away, his daughter forgotten. The only thing that occupied Chris's thoughts now was his own unendurable agony. On burning legs he began to run, instinctively trying to outdistance the fire that was already devouring him.

Thirty-Four

Nick had thrown up once and was thinking there was a fifty-fifty chance that he might do so again when the burning man appeared. He seemed to come out of nowhere, to plunge from the darkness. Instinctively, his body reacting before his brain was fully in gear, Nick tried to bolt, but instead ended up slipping on the wet grass and landing in the mud on his backside. As he went down he noticed that flames were lapping at the red drapes that served as the entrance to the 'Mirror Of Life' and realised that this was where the burning man had come from.

The man ran in a perfectly straight line for maybe three seconds, as if he had some definite destination in mind, and then seemed to lose all purpose. He staggered, wheeled to one side, and finally fell, the wet grass sizzling beneath him. It was when the smell – charred pork blended with something that was denser, meatier and utterly sickening – wafted over Nick that his stomach lost its fifty-fifty battle. He rolled over to his left side, dug his elbow into the mud so that he could raise his head, and puked until his stomach hurt.

By now several other men, most of them still shell-shocked by what they had seen in the big top, had started to drift outside. Even as Nick was puking he heard their cries of horror and alarm and became aware of feet pounding the soft ground beside him as they ran towards the burning man on the ground. Blinking tears from his eyes, Nick rose to his feet and staggered to join them, his empty stomach still rolling. Through his blurred vision, it appeared as if the group of half a dozen or so who had gathered around the burning man were beating him, adding insult to injury. But then Nick realised that they had stripped off their jackets and were trying to smother the flames with them.

It didn't seem to be making much difference, but then someone had the bright idea of running his jacket through the soaking wet grass to dampen it. That worked better, and within a minute or so – the group of six or seven having now swelled to around twenty – the flames were out, stifled beneath a thick layer of damp and smouldering jackets. As the fire died, the men began to peel the jackets away again, revealing the victim beneath. Some of them immediately recoiled from both the sight and the smell of him, clapping their hands over their mouths. Others turned and stumbled away to retch into the grass.

Nick's stomach was still rolling but he stayed his ground. The man in front of them was a blackened ruin. His skin, still smoking, had shrivelled and melted and *crisped* on his bones; his hair was gone; his lips had peeled back from his teeth, like crackling on a joint of pork.

He was still alive, though. That was the horrible thing. His limbs were twitching, his chest jerking erratically as if there was something in there trying to get out. Worst of all his eyes were moving. They looked like shrivelled prunes, but they were flickering from side to side. Nick had the sudden horrible idea that this was not a mortally wounded man but *something else*, and that it was not just observing but *marking* every one of the men who had denied it the blessed release of death.

Though Nick wasn't sure whether someone had passed word to John, or whether he had simply hurried across as soon as he'd realised what was happening, all at once he was there, pushing his way through the scrum of people. He dropped to his knees beside the badly burned man and immediately began to examine him. His face was grim, and although he said nothing Nick could tell by the look in his eyes that there was no hope.

Then the crowd gasped and jumped back as the burned man shot out a hand and grabbed John's sleeve. John, to his credit, was the only one who didn't recoil, nor even flinch. He simply looked down at the blackened claw and murmured, 'It's all right. You're among friends here. We're not going to hurt you.'

At the sound of John's voice the burned man began to twitch and jerk more violently. His mouth opened and closed and a guttural sound came from his throat. A few more men turned their faces away as saliva (or possibly blood) that was as black as oil trickled from the corner of his mouth and ran down his charred face.

'It's all right, don't try to speak,' John said.

The man's shrivelled eyes flickered again – and at that moment, with a flash of utter horror, Nick suddenly realised who he was.

'Oh God,' he said. He stumbled forward and dropped to his knees beside John. 'It's Chris. John, *it's Chris.*'

John said nothing. He simply half-raised a hand, as if to say: *Shh. Don't upset him.*

Chris was still struggling to speak. John, perhaps realising that it was pointless telling him not to, bent forward, putting his ear close to the fire-ravaged mouth. Chris made a few more guttural sounds and then his body was seized by a violent spasm. His arms and legs jerked as if he was having a fit, his back arched like a bow, and then he slumped back down in the grass and was still.

Nick looked at John. 'Is he . . . ?'

John nodded. 'Mercifully, yes.'

'What was he trying to say to you? Could you tell?'

John sighed. He looked calm, but tired. Incredibly tired. He rubbed a hand across his eyes and then he looked at Nick and nodded.

'He said "They killed her".'

Thirty-Five

Unlike Kate, Lynn recognised the strongman immediately, despite his boiler suit. As soon as she heard the crash of the front door she knew that the circus people had come for them. She ran out of the sitting room and into the hallway just as Helga, Michael, the ringmistress and Emil flowed into the house. To her right, halfway along the hallway, Kate was staring at the circus people in shock, Anthony running up behind her.

'Quick, you two, out the back way!' Lynn shouted. Without waiting to see whether they had taken her advice, she retreated back into the sitting room, pulling the door shut behind her. There was a settee to the right of the door. Adrenalin pumping through her system, she put all her weight behind it and managed to shove it forward – only a few inches, but enough to block the doorway. Then she ran across to the closed curtains covering the windows that overlooked the front garden and yanked them apart. The main window in the centre didn't open but the two smaller side ones did. To reach them she saw that she would have to scramble up onto a windowsill which had a double radiator attached to the wall beneath it. The windowsill was the height of her stomach but the top of the radiator was no higher than her thigh. Lynn was placing one foot on top of the radiator – a high step but a manageable one – and gripping the lip of the windowsill to haul herself up when the door flew open, sending the settee skidding halfway across the room.

She glanced back over her shoulder, expecting to see the strongman lumbering through the door, but it was Helga. It flashed across Lynn's mind that the tiny trapeze artist must be a hell of a lot stronger than she looked. Then Helga hissed at her like an angry cat, exposing long needle-sharp teeth, and with a strength born of panic Lynn hauled herself up and onto the windowsill. Her foot dislodged a tall glass candlestick, which fell to the floor and snapped in half, and a framed photograph of Kate in a flowery swimming costume standing in a paddling pool, which fell over with a clatter. As Lynn fumbled with the catch on the window, Helga rushed across the room towards her, fingers extended like claws. Without thinking, Lynn scrabbled at her throat for the silver chain which John Kersh had insisted she wear and drew out what was on the end of it – a silver crucifix.

Although she wasn't religious, it seemed that she didn't need even a modicum of faith to make it work. As the crucifix flashed in the light, Helga skidded to a halt, raising a protective arm, a look of genuine fear, even pain, on her face.

Somewhere in the back of her mind, Lynn was

thinking, *You've got to be kidding me*. But she held the tiny crucifix up with her left hand while fumbling at the window catch behind her with her right. Eventually she felt it give, the window sighing open. Still facing the cowering Helga, Lynn pushed it further, admitting a swirl of cold rain-flecked air into the house. She was about to manoeuvre herself out backwards when a hand reached in through the window, grabbed her left wrist and yanked.

Off balance and caught by surprise, Lynn toppled out of the window. It wasn't a long drop, no more than a metre or so, and there was nothing but grass below her, but she still landed square on her back with enough of a thud to knock the wind from her lungs. She lay gasping for a moment. Then a figure loomed over her and a face blocked out the night. At first Lynn thought the face had nothing but skull-like hollows where its eyes should have been, before she realised that it was simply the ringmistress, Madame Serena, in her dark glasses.

'Fuck off!' Lynn screamed and scrabbled for the crucifix once again. She found it and raised it with her left hand, thrusting it into the ringmistress's face. Instead of recoiling, however, the ringmistress simply snorted, reached out and yanked the crucifix from Lynn's grasp. The chain dug painfully into the back of Lynn's neck for a split second before snapping.

'That doesn't work on all of us, *dear*,' the ringmistress said, and tossed the chain over her shoulder.

Lynn tried to sit up, and as she did so she saw that the ringmistress had something in her other hand – a fist-sized chunk of rock. Before Lynn could take evasive action, the ringmistress drew back her arm and swung it towards Lynn's head. There was a sickening *clonk* of impact, a far-too-long moment of skull-splitting pain . . .

And then blackness.

Thirty-Six

'Quick, you two, out the back way!'

Lynn's voice unfroze Kate's legs. She turned to run back the way she had come and almost collided with Anthony who was barrelling up behind her. He grabbed her arms and swung her round in front of him, shielding her with his body as they ran back towards the kitchen. Behind him he could hear Emil and Michael giving chase, both of them snarling like dogs let off the leash and ordered to attack.

From the corner of his eye, Anthony glimpsed a hand that looked like a hook-fingered talon poised to take a swipe at his head. He ducked and the tips of his attacker's fingers raked across the back of his neck. He was so surprised when his attacker howled in pain that he half-turned to see what had happened. It was Michael, the trapeze artist. He had stumbled to a halt and was cradling a hand on which the fingertips were blistered and smoking.

Emil, who was just behind Michael, halted too. He looked at Michael's hand and then at Anthony, caution on his face. At first Anthony was puzzled – and then suddenly it clicked. Michael's hand must have brushed across the silver chain around his neck! He had laughed when his dad had insisted the three of them wear crucifixes – but he wasn't laughing now. Could it be true what his dad had claimed? Were the circus people *really* . . . what? Demons? Vampires?

'Head towards St Peter's!' Anthony shouted over his shoulder, thinking that he and Kate might be safe in the little church on the corner of the street. 'I'll hold them off.'

He reached beneath the collar of his shirt and pulled out the crucifix. When he held it up, both Emil and Michael hissed like cornered cats and backed away. As Anthony backed away too, towards the kitchen, Emil and Michael shuffled forward, shielding their faces with their arms like men in a sandstorm. So the crucifix had an exclusion zone of – what? Two metres? Maybe three? Well, that was okay. Anthony was happy to shuffle backwards all the way to the church if needs be.

But then at a sharp word and an impatient gesture from Emil, the strongman began to lumber towards Anthony. At first he defiantly stood his ground, holding the crucifix up higher, brandishing it directly in the strongman's face. It was only when it had no effect, when the strongman kept coming, that it occurred to him that maybe not *all* the circus people were vampires. Deciding that discretion was the better part of valour, he turned and fled.

As he ran across the kitchen he pushed chairs over in his wake. He was pleased to see that Kate had left the back door open; if he had had to pause to open it he would probably have been caught. He ran into the back garden and headed across the lawn without breaking stride, focusing on the gate set into the hedge at the bottom. That was open too, swinging gently in the chilly breeze which accompanied the rain that had now diminished to a light drizzle. *Thank you, Kate.*

With no idea how close his pursuers were, Anthony burst through the gate and ran up the little alleyway, known locally as the Ginnel. The Ginnel served as both a cycle path and a short cut between North End Road, where the Millers lived, and the High Street at the far end. It wasn't towards the bright lights of the High Street that Anthony ran, though. On the corner of North End Road, directly opposite a set of playing fields where he had spent a great deal of time kicking a football around as a kid, was St Peter's Methodist Church. It was a modern and unprepossessing concrete-and-glass structure with a wrought-iron crucifix above the door and a billboard outside that usually displayed some quasi-humorous religious slogan. This week's offering, black on luminous orange, was: LIKE POSTMAN PAT, GOD ALWAYS DELIVERS.

At the end of the Ginnel he risked a glance back. Emil and Michael were maybe five metres behind him, with the strongman lumbering along another ten metres or so in their wake. From the effortless way the two vampires were keeping up (neither were sweating nor even breathing hard) Anthony had no doubt that if he hadn't been wearing the crucifix they would have brought him down easily by now. It was heartening, therefore, to see that the panting red-faced strongman was clearly not built for speed. As long as Anthony could stay in front of *him* he might yet be okay.

On North End Road he turned right – and there was the church, thirty or so metres ahead. His heart leaped as he caught a glimpse of Kate. She was halfway up the gravel path leading to the church's ugly entrance porch (nothing but a flat concrete canopy supported by metal pillars), the gate she had just burst through swinging shut behind her. Even as Anthony watched, the shadows beneath the canopy swallowed her up. As they did so it suddenly occurred to him that the church door might be closed and locked – he hadn't thought of that – and he experienced a brief flutter of panic. But he was encouraged by the fact that Kate didn't reappear after a few seconds. Nor could he hear her either thumping on the door or pleading to be let in.

Five seconds later he was bursting through the gate and running up the path himself. Beneath the canopy the main door was mostly in shadow, though he could see a faint reddish glow from within the building shining through the stained-glass cross inset into the dark wood. At the door, once his hand was actually resting on the cross, he allowed himself the brief luxury of another glance back. Michael and Emil had paused outside the gate and seemed to be psyching themselves up to enter what Anthony supposed must be sacred ground, despite the lame quips and bad puns on the church billboard. Pounding along the street towards them, the strongman had dropped ever further behind. Anthony pushed the door open and entered the church.

The small square vestibule immediately beyond the

main door reminded Anthony of the waiting room at Shettle surgery. The carpet was red, the walls white. There were rows of identical metal-framed chairs with grey leather seats, and a low table in the centre was strewn with leaflets and magazines. The only way this room *differed* from a medical waiting room, in fact, was that instead of posters on the walls warning against AIDS and lung cancer there was a large wooden crucifix and a couple of framed paintings depicting what Anthony supposed must be Bible scenes.

Seeing the crucifix, Anthony nodded in satisfaction. To him it was simply an artefact fashioned out of wood, with no more significance than a chair or a table, but to Emil and Michael it was clearly a psychological – perhaps even magical – barrier. Of course, it would not prove a barrier to the strongman, which meant that he had to be Anthony's main concern. He hurried across to the double doors on the far side of the room, which led into the main body of the church, and pushed open the left one, softly calling Kate's name.

His words echoed up towards the ceiling in ghostly whispers. The interior of the church was mostly in darkness, aside from a dozen or so artificial candles in which low-wattage tulip bulbs burned. Most of the candles were affixed to the walls that ran the length of the room towards the chancel, though two flanked yet another crucifix. This one stood three metres high on a splayed base at the head of the nave. It was positioned dead centre where the Sunday congregation could sit on their pews and gaze up at it in awe.

'Kate,' Anthony called again. 'Are you there?'

A shadow, thicker than those around it, bulged from behind the crucifix, and one of the artificial candles dimly illuminated Kate's white, scared face.

'Thank God,' she said with no apparent irony. 'Are we safe here?'

'I think so,' said Anthony. 'From the vampires, at least.'

'Vampires.' She repeated the word with a kind of faint wonder, as if she couldn't seriously believe what was happening.

'The strongman's still out there, though, and he's *not* a vampire. I'm going to have to deal with him.'

Kate looked alarmed. 'What do you mean? You're not going back out there?'

'No.'

'What, then?'

'I need something heavy. This'll do.'

He hurried up the central aisle between the pews and across to the pulpit. At the base of the pulpit was a three-legged stool made of hard, heavy wood. He hefted it in one hand.

Kate looked at him in startled wonder. 'You're not going to fight him, are you?'

'I'm hoping it won't come to that.' Anthony gave the stool an experimental swing. 'I just hope this'll be heavy enough to penetrate his thick skull.'

Kate's look of startlement changed to one of horror. 'You can't mean that?'

'I'm afraid I do.'

'But you're not a violent person. You've *never* been a violent person.' She sounded almost disapproving.

He smiled faintly. 'This isn't the time for niceties, Kate. It's them or us. Literally.' When she opened her mouth to reply, he added, 'And there's no time to discuss it any further, either. He'll be here any second. Now get back down behind that crucifix and don't make a sound.'

Without waiting to see whether she would comply he hurried back along the central aisle between the pews, hoping against hope that the doors at the back of the room wouldn't fly open before he was in position.

They didn't. He pressed himself into the shadows against the wall next to the door he had come through and waited.

He didn't have to wait long. Over the rapid boom of his heart he heard the outside door thump open. It occurred to him that maybe he should have tried to barricade it in some way, though he felt pretty sure that if the strongman was determined enough – and with Emil and Michael to answer to, there was no doubt in Anthony's mind that the strong man would be *exceptionally* determined – he would be able to find his way into Fort Knox.

Anthony heard plodding footsteps crossing the carpet in the reception area. As they drew closer, he licked his dry lips and took a firmer grip on the stool. His hands felt a little sweaty, and he had a sudden awful image of himself swinging his makeshift weapon only for it to fly out of his grasp. He wished he had time to wipe his wet palms on his clothes, but he didn't. He tensed as the plodding footsteps halted outside the door.

There then followed such a long interval of silence that Anthony became convinced the strongman knew exactly where he was and what he was planning to do. He shrank back further against the wall, half-convinced that the cool plaster was pulsing in time with his heartbeat. All at once, without preamble, the double doors swung open and the strongman ducked through them. He stepped into the dimly lit church and looked around.

He didn't look behind him, though, and for that Anthony was grateful. Now that the moment had finally arrived, he found his doubts taking a back seat and his instincts kicking in. Just as he had imagined himself doing, he stepped away from the wall, swung the stool in an arc and smashed the thick edge of the rounded seat against the back of the strongman's skull. The strongman grunted, took a staggering step forward and went down on one knee, as if about to propose to his beloved. Noting with almost clinical satisfaction that blood was already running from a wound in the strongman's head and staining the collar of his blue boiler suit, Anthony swung the stool and hit him again.

This time the strongman went down like a heavyweight boxer KO'd by a brain-rattling punch. As he lay face down, blood pooling around his head, Anthony began to feel jittery with adrenalin. The blood-spattered stool slipped from his fingers and clattered to the floor.

'Oh my God,' Kate said, emerging from behind the crucifix. 'What have you done? Have you killed him?'

'I doubt it,' said Anthony. 'We need to tie him up.'

'But he's unconscious.'

'Yes, but he won't *stay* unconscious, will he?'

'But where will we—' Kate began. And then the doors behind them flew open.

They both spun round. The ringmistress stood there, arms outstretched, holding the doors open. Behind her Anthony was horrified to see Emil, Michael and Helga. True, they were shuffling along like explorers lost in the Sahara Desert, arms held up as if trying to shield themselves from the blazing heat of a noonday sun, but the fact that they were here at all, that they had crossed the threshold, proved that the so-called House of God was not the impregnable fortress that Anthony had hoped it would be.

Instinctively he scrabbled for the crucifix around his neck and held it up. The ringmistress sneered.

'That won't work on me.'

'Run!' shouted Anthony, grabbing Kate's hand. Together they turned and fled towards the back of the church. Anthony had no real plan, just the hope that they might find a door at the rear of the chancel that would lead outside. They were halfway down the central aisle when he heard what sounded like the fluttering of wings close behind them. As he turned his head to see what it was, Kate wrenched her hand out of his grasp and screamed.

To his horror, Anthony saw that a dark, winged creature was attacking her head. It looked like a bat – but it was huge, its body as fat and plump as a rat's, its wingspan as wide as a seagull's. Kate was screaming and flapping at it with her hands as it scrabbled at her scalp, its claws partly entangled in her hair. Without thinking, Anthony reached across, grabbed it with both hands and squeezed its fat furry body. The creature screeched, then opened its rat-like snout even wider and sank tiny razor-sharp teeth into the back of his hand. Howling in pain, Anthony wrenched the creature out of Kate's hair and dashed it to the floor. Without waiting to see whether he had injured it, he ran on.

Kate, however, didn't. Reaching the three-metre-tall crucifix, she pounded to a stop and ducked behind it. Knowing that it would provide no protection against the ringmistress, Anthony skidded to a halt and turned.

'Kate!' he shouted. 'Come on! We've got to . . .'

And there his voice trailed away as his brain did what amounted to a mental double take. Because lying on the ground in the centre of the nave between the two front rows of pews was not the bat-like creature that had attacked Kate but Helga the trapeze artist.

She was on all fours, shaking her head like a dazed animal. Anthony saw her look up groggily – and then he saw her face contort with primal terror at the sight of the huge crucifix towering above her. Immediately she began to writhe and scream as though in terrible agony. Her face changed again, her bone structure seeming to *flow*, to become sharper, her eyes turning red and bulging from their sockets, her lips peeling back to reveal long needle-like teeth.

At the sight of such a hideous transformation, Kate screamed too and instinctively thrust out her hands to shove herself back from the crucifix. So violently did she do so, however, that the crucifix first rocked on its base and then, slowly at first, began to topple forward. As the huge metal cross fell towards her, Helga released the most terrible sound Anthony had ever heard – a screech of such mortal, excruciating terror that it seemed to paralyse him, to lock every muscle in his body.

The trapeze artist raised a slender arm in a final, pitiful attempt to ward off the inevitable – and then the crucifix crashed down on her. Her screeches of agony were inhuman, almost unbearable to hear, but mercifully short. As black smoke rose from beneath the felled cross and a terrible charnel-house stench filled the air, Michael, still standing at the far end of the room, above the strongman's unconscious form, howled and clapped his hands to the sides of his face. To Anthony's horror and astonishment, he began to shrivel and decay, his flesh turning brown like dead leaves, his hair falling out in clumps, his legs giving way with a snapping sound like that of old, dry twigs.

'My children!' the ringmistress shrieked. 'My children!' She threw herself to the ground beside Michael and tried to cradle him in her arms. But he was little more than dry bones and desiccated flesh now, and the instant she tried to lift him he dissolved into dust.

Kate gaped at Anthony, her face a mask of shock. 'What happened?' she whispered.

Anthony shook his head; his voice was feeble. 'I don't know. Some kind of . . . symbiotic link, maybe.'

As if she had heard them, the ringmistress raised her stricken face. Pointing at Kate she screamed, 'You killed them! Your own brother and sister! And you killed them!'

Kate's eyes were wide. She looked utterly bewildered. Shaking her head, she murmured, 'I don't . . .'

The ringmistress jumped to her feet and began striding down the aisle towards her. 'Haven't you realised, you silly little bitch? Don't you know who I am?'

She tore off the headscarf, allowing her russet curls to tumble free. Then she peeled off the dark glasses and threw them aside. Her face exposed, devoid of make-up, she stared up at Kate defiantly.

Kate stared back for a moment. And then all at once she paled, her mouth dropping open. 'Oh my God . . .'

'What is it?' Anthony asked.

Kate looked almost cataleptic with shock. Her lips moved feebly. 'It's . . . my mother . . .' she whispered.

'*What?*'

Before she got the chance to elaborate, Anthony heard a blood-curdling growl behind him. Spinning round, he realised that with everything else that had happened in the last few minutes he had completely forgotten about Emil.

The black panther, crouched low, muscles rippling beneath its velvety fur, gazed at him for a split second, its yellow eyes impassive.

Then it leaped.

Thirty-Seven

It was the rattling that woke Lynn. She felt like a dice being shaken in a cup. She opened her eyes and immediately wished she hadn't. The movement, tiny though it was, triggered a deep, sickening throb in her left temple. Her skin felt stiff there, and sticky, as if she'd spilt something in her hair which had dried partly – paint, maybe. She blinked, focusing on the confusion of shapes in front of her. She saw big black boots attached to legs clad in a thick blue canvassy material that made her think of workman's overalls. Then a memory flashed through her mind – the circus strongman smashing down the Millers' front door and stepping into the house – and with that everything else came flooding back.

She'd been hit, hadn't she? The ringmistress had whacked her on the side of the head with a rock. So where was she now? Lying on a hard surface, inside something that rattled with the strongman watching over her. As surreptitiously as she could, peering through half-closed eyes so as not to give away the fact that she was conscious, she looked around.

Metal walls. A low ceiling. The rise and fall of a guttural-sounding engine. It didn't take a genius to work out that she was in the back of a van.

So she'd been kidnapped, not killed. Which was better, obviously, though still not ideal. From her dad's notes Lynn was only too aware why the circus people had come to Shettle. She'd read Karl Mitterhaus's words so many times that they were now writ large in her mind: *Your children will die . . . to give me back my life.* She could only guess, therefore, that she was being taken somewhere specific, that they were going to make a big deal out of killing her. Which meant that if she got even a half-chance to escape she had to take it. If she was determined about anything at all, it was that she would not give in to these bastards without a fight.

Though her head was throbbing and her back felt stiff (either from falling out of the window or lying on the floor of the van), the rest of her seemed pretty much okay. She wiggled her toes and fingers experimentally and was pleased to find that she hadn't been tied up – evidently her kidnappers were arrogant enough to suppose that she was no threat to them. She wondered how fast the van was going, whether the back doors were unlocked, and if so, whether she would have time to scramble across, open them and leap out before the strongman could react. He was sitting against the van wall with his knees drawn up and the tip of his left boot only a metre or so from her head – but maybe the grumbling of the engine had lulled him to sleep? It was unlikely, she knew that, but not impossible – and she had to explore *every* possibility.

Moving infinitesimally slowly, Lynn tilted her head just enough so she could look up at the strongman's face. She had decided that if his eyes were closed she would go for it, because what did she have to lose? But his eyes were open, albeit gazing vacantly into space. What surprised Lynn, however, and also provided her with a brief thrill of savage glee, was that the collar and shoulders of his boiler suit were dark with blood – his own, evidently, judging by the fact that he was holding what appeared to be a church hassock, also bloody, against the back of his head.

At some point, clearly, someone had given him a good whack on the back of the bonce. She hoped it was Anthony or Kate. Speaking of which, where were they? As if on cue, she suddenly heard Anthony's voice behind her.

'Where the hell are you taking us?'

He sounded indignant rather than cowed. *Good for you*, thought Lynn.

From the front of the van came a harsh bark of a reply. It was the ringmistress's voice, but she sounded both angry at Anthony (for something specific? What the hell had been happening while Lynn had been unconscious?) and viciously gloating at the same time.

'We're going back to where it all began. We're going to complete the circle.'

'Complete the circle?' Anthony replied. 'What the hell is that supposed to mean?'

This time it was Emil who answered. His voice was chillingly matter-of-fact. 'You will all die to restore my brother to life.'

Lynn heard Kate begin to weep, which was a relief – at least it meant she was alive – and Anthony's outraged reply: 'You can't do this! You'll be stopped!'

The ringmistress laughed, nastily and raucously, but Lynn heard it only as background noise; she was thinking hard. Back to where it all began. That could only mean one thing. So if she could get word to the cavalry . . .

Knowing she was taking a big risk, she inched her right hand slowly up the thigh of her jeans. She felt a giddy sense of relief, and not a little hope, when she felt the hard rectangular bulge of her mobile phone in her pocket. Painstakingly she slipped her hand into her pocket, pincered the slim metal shape between her thumb and forefinger, and carefully slid it out. Her heart thumping hard, she palmed the phone, angling it slightly so she could see the display screen.

Thumbing the 'Menu' option, she selected 'Phone Book'. She scrolled down to 'JohnKersh' and rapidly but carefully tapped in a message: **Captured. Mitre house**. As she pressed 'Send', a huge hand swooped down and twisted the phone from her grasp. She jumped and cried out, and then, knowing the game was up, propped herself up on her elbows and watched in dismay as the strongman, his face impassive, crushed her phone in his massive fist as easily as if it was made of plasticine.

Thirty-Eight

'We can't just leave them here,' said Benson.

John sighed in exasperation but tried to remain patient. 'I'm sorry, Alex, but I don't see that we have any alternative. We don't have the storage facilities in Shettle to cope with an incident on this scale, and until we find a way through this damn sickness barrier we can't take the bodies any further afield. To be honest, even the hospital morgue in Wenthorpe would struggle to accommodate *this* many fatalities. There are over forty people dead in there.' He pointed at the big top, his trembling hand the only indication of the terrible strain he was under. 'That's the equivalent of several motorway pile-ups.'

Benson shook his head, causing raindrops to fly in an arc from the brim of his cap. 'I know you're right, John, but . . . it's just not decent.'

John almost smiled at the old-fashioned word. 'Decent is the very last thing it is,' he agreed. 'But these creatures we're up against . . .' He shook his head, unable to express the sheer depth of his abhorrence.

The sense of purpose and righteous indignation of

less than an hour before had been severely dented. Confronted by the carnage in the big top and then by the appalling death of Chris Blaine, many of the men who had been selected for tonight's mission were now standing or sitting around, looking pale, defeated and shell-shocked. Some had rallied; a few had taken the deaths as a personal affront and seemed more determined than ever to confront and defeat the enemy. It was this group, accompanied by a haunted-looking but doggedly determined Nick Miller, who were currently turning the circus upside down in a fruitless search for survivors of the slaughter, or clues to where those who had perpetrated it might have gone.

John, along with Benson and several of his men, had been involved in the grim task of laying out the dead in neat rows and identifying as many of them as possible. They all knew that tampering with a crime scene before forensics had been over it with a fine-tooth comb was against procedure, but these were exceptional circumstances. For the foreseeable future a skeleton crew of local plods and a community doctor pretty much constituted the entirety of Shettle's available resources, and until that changed they would just have to muddle along as best they could.

Benson expelled a huge sigh and adjusted his cap, causing more water to trickle from its peak. 'I don't mind telling you, John, that I'm finding it difficult to get my head round this. I mean, if the circus people are responsible for these killings, why murder their own?'

'Because the circus was just window dressing,' John replied, 'and the killers were just a small clique within it. Once the other performers and the workers had served their purpose they were disposed of, along with everyone else.'

'Disposed of,' murmured Benson, an incredulous look on his face. 'I've seen some things in my time, but I've never come across anything this . . . this callous before. I mean, forty people! How do you kill forty people like that? The killers must have . . . held them at gunpoint and used this missing panther as a weapon.'

John shook his head. 'Panthers aren't that neat – you saw the bodies of those killed in the woods. And if the killers had guns, as you suggest, why didn't they use them? Why go to such elaborate lengths?'

'To make a statement, perhaps?'

'That doesn't make sense and you know it.'

Benson's outburst was born of frustration. 'Well, what do *you* suggest?'

John's voice was quiet. 'Despite all the evidence, I still think you're looking at this the wrong way. You're still assuming that the killers are human.'

'What else *can* I assume? All this talk of vampires . . . it's just ridiculous!'

John shrugged. 'If it helps, think of them as some super-evolved offshoot of humanity we don't know about yet that perhaps gave rise to *stories* of vampires. I mean, who knows? That may be true.'

Before Benson could reply a figure came running across the muddy grass towards them. It was Nick Miller. As he reached them he took off his rain-speckled glasses and wiped them on a handkerchief which he fished from his pocket.

'Anything?' asked Benson.

Nick shook his head. 'The place has been completely abandoned.'

Anxiously John looked at his watch. 'We should be getting back to the kids. We've spent too long here already.'

The words were barely out of his mouth when his phone chimed in his pocket. He fished it out. 'It's a text from—' Then his face fell. 'Oh, Christ.'

'What is it?' asked Nick.

John held it up so that Nick and Benson could read it. 'We've got to go.'

Thirty-Nine

'**B**ring her.'
Emil, standing by Karl Mitterhaus's coffin, pointed at Kate.

'No!' shouted Anthony, draping a protective arm across her body. But the dwarf, holding a knife whose blade was almost as long as his own arm, sniggered nastily and lunged forward. Slashing down, he opened a neat slit across Anthony's knuckles. Anthony cried out and snatched his hand back instinctively as the blood started to flow.

The strongman lumbered forward, shoved Anthony against the wall and grabbed Kate by the arm. 'No,' she pleaded, struggling pointlessly as she was dragged across the stone floor towards the waiting Emil. 'Please, don't.'

Desperately Anthony turned to Anna, who was leaning against the rear wall, beside a manacled corpse that was all but a skeleton, a grim expression on her face. 'How can you let this happen? Kate is *your* daughter! Your one remaining daughter!'

Anna refused to meet his eyes and said nothing. But the dwarf stepped forward, telling him to shut up and waving the now-bloodstained knife in his face as a reminder of what would happen if he didn't.

Emil's lips curled back as Kate was dragged towards him. His panther-like fangs seemed to spring from his mouth, dribbling with saliva. The whites of his eyes flushed red and he gave a low, satisfied hiss from deep in his throat, like a gourmand clapping his eyes on a mouth-watering main course. Kate was still crying and struggling, even beating ineffectually at the strongman's arm with her free hand, but she was as helpless as a maggot on a hook.

She whimpered when she got her first proper look at Karl Mitterhaus in his coffin, a jagged spar of wood jutting from his chest. Although the silk lining of the coffin was drenched in what appeared to be relatively fresh blood, his corpse, curiously, was not.

'He looks well, don't you think?' murmured Emil. Kate cringed back as he leaned towards her. His breath stank of raw meat. 'He has already absorbed the blood of three of his killers' children. Now you shall add *your* blood and allow him to live again. It will be a just sacrifice – and a noble one.'

'That's your opinion,' Lynn called. She was standing against the stone wall, beside Anthony. 'I can't say *I* share it.' She turned her attention to Anna, who looked troubled, her eyes downcast. 'And I don't think you do, either, do you, Anna? Are you *really* going to stand by and watch this psycho kill your daughter just so he can resurrect his child-murdering brother?'

Anna met Lynn's gaze briefly. She looked almost ashamed. 'Perhaps . . .' she began.

'Go on,' Lynn prompted.

Anna's voice grew stronger. She looked at Emil. 'Perhaps there *is* another way.'

Emil barely glanced at her. He was breathing hard, his eyes almost completely red; the bloodlust was upon him. 'There is no other way,' he growled.

'But she's my *daughter!*' Anna protested.

Emil sneered. 'Helga was your true daughter. Your *pure* daughter. This creature killed her.'

His hand shot out and grabbed Kate by the throat. Desperately Lynn blurted, 'How *can* Helga have been Anna's daughter? She was the same age as Kate.' Turning to Anna again, she said, 'Can't you see? They're manipulating you, trying to trick you. They've been manipulating you for years. Helga *can't* have been your daughter, Anna. Kate is your only *true* daughter. And you're allowing him to kill her.'

Emil sneered. 'What do *you* know about *us*, peasant? We are not like you. We are strong. We do not spend half our lives as vulnerable children. We develop quickly. We are the ultimate survivors. Even when we die we are not truly dead.' His red-black eyes flickered back to Kate's terrified face. 'As I shall prove.'

Kate gave a strangled scream as his mouth opened wider. Just as he was about to lunge at her throat, Anna screeched *'No!'* and dashed forward. She shoved Kate hard in the back, catching Emil by surprise. Kate was wrenched from Emil's grasp and went sprawling on the stone floor, bruised but intact. Enraged and overcome with bloodlust, Emil sprang at Anna, bearing her to the ground. Pinning her to the cold, rough stone, he snarled like an animal and sank his teeth into her throat. Anna's eyes opened wide with shock as Emil began to drink, making disgusting slurping and sucking sounds. Then her eyes flickered and glazed, and her body went limp.

'Mistress . . .' muttered the dwarf in dismay. He was half-turned away from Anthony, watching proceedings with horror. Anthony took advantage of his distraction by stepping forward and kicking the knife out of his hand. The dwarf yelped as the blade spun away into the darkness and hit the wall with a metallic clatter. Instantly the little man's features twisted with rage and he hurled himself at Anthony. Anthony took a step back as the dwarf flew at him and, using the little man's forward momentum, he grabbed his arms, spun round, and smashed him against the stone wall. Lynn winced as the dwarf hit the wall head first. There was a terrible crunching *snap* and the dwarf slumped to the ground dead, his neck broken.

'Watch out!' Lynn shouted. Anthony turned – too late. The strongman lumbered forward and wrapped both his massive hands around Anthony's throat. As Lynn dashed across to the other side of the crypt to retrieve the knife, the strongman lifted Anthony off the floor. Unable to breathe, Anthony punched and kicked at the strongman's body, but he might as well have been attacking a tree. His vision began to fade as red lights popped like fireworks inside his skull. The last thing he saw as darkness closed in were the strongman's pale grey eyes peering blandly into his own.

328

Forty

Exactly ten years since he had last been here, John Kersh drove in through the gates of Mitre House. A decade ago it had been daylight, the sky deepening towards dusk; now it was a starless, rainswept night. A decade ago the car behind him had been driven by Chris Blaine, the private investigator hired by Nick Miller to investigate his wife; now Chris was dead, and John's car was part of a convoy led by police Superintendent Alex Benson. A decade ago Mitre House had stood, in all its dark and evil majesty, peering down at them at the end of its winding, weed-choked driveway; now the house was no more, and where it had once stood was nothing but a fire-blackened crater in the ground.

Despite the differences, though, there were enough parallels between the present and the past to give John the eerie feeling that the terrible events of that day had never really relinquished their hold on him. Now, as then, his friend Nick Miller was beside him. Now, as then, the shadow of death hung over their community. Now, as then, they were heading for a confrontation with something unspeakably depraved and corrupt.

At least in this case they *knew* what they were about to face, whereas ten years ago they hadn't. John tried to convince himself that this was a *good* thing, that it would give them an advantage in the final battle, but his argument sounded so hollow, even to himself, that he couldn't bring himself to voice it.

Just as they had ten years ago, the gnarled leafless trees seemed to reach spavined limbs towards them as he drove his car between them. In the headlights the trees appeared to lurch and jitter, their trunks acquiring the texture of dusty bone. Despite knowing that the house would no longer be there, John still found it a shock when they reached the gravel forecourt to encounter nothing but a few crumbling reminders of the building that had once stood. From Nick's reaction it was clear that he was similarly affected. Leaning forward as if to confirm the evidence of his own eyes, he murmured, 'God, there's even less of it left than I expected.'

The dozen or so vehicles stopped in a haphazard line and for the next thirty seconds or so the night was filled with the choppy sound of car doors opening and closing. Despite the mood of shock and defeat at the big top, the text from Lynn had galvanised the group back into action and there was a renewed mood of purpose and determination among the men. Torches were switched on and weapons which had previously been left behind on Benson's orders were now retrieved from car boots and the backs of vans. There were no firearms, but there were spades and crowbars and baseball bats. One man – Cliff Hoskins, who owned a sporting-goods shop that had been ram-raided so many times that the council had now erected concrete bollards in front of it – had even brought along a crossbow.

Benson eyed the weapons doubtfully but said nothing. Clearly their discovery inside the big top had changed his opinion about vigilante justice. As John and Nick hurried up to him, he gestured around him and said, 'As you can see, the place seems deserted. Of course, it could be that Lynn's captors are still on their way here. Or even that her text was discovered and she's been taken elsewhere.'

John had already thought of that. It had also crossed his mind that Lynn might not have sent the text at all – that it could have been a ruse to mislead them.

Nick, however, was shaking his head vehemently. 'I'm sure they'll be here somewhere. This is where Mitterhaus died. If they're planning on resurrecting him they'll do it here. They'll want to bring things full circle.'

John saw the tight, beady-eyed expression on his friend's thin pinched face and knew that his argument was based not on logic, nor even a gut feeling, but simply on a desperate need for it to be true. He knew this because he felt the same. The lives of his son, of Nick's daughter, and of Lynn Michaels, who had opened their eyes to the true intentions of the Circus of Nights, were absolutely dependent on it being the case. If Lynn's text turned out to be a dead end then all would be lost.

'I suppose we could organise search parties,' Benson began.

'You do that. I'll lead the first one. We'll start down here.' John was already walking towards the edge of the crater. Raising his voice, he said, 'Who'll join me?'

As a few of the men, including Nick, moved forward, John gestured towards Cliff Hoskins. 'Cliff, would you come too – just in case?'

John, Nick, Cliff Hoskins and five other men, including two police officers given the nod by Benson, clambered down into what had once been the cellars of Mitre House. As John shone his torch around, one of the constables asked, 'What exactly are we looking for, Dr Kersh?'

'I don't know,' admitted John. 'But let's look all the same.'

Less than five minutes later someone gave a low whistle off to his left. John looked up and saw torch beams converging on what had once been the north-west corner of the house. He picked his way urgently but carefully through the debris of blackened rubble, and arrived to find the men gathered around a man-sized opening in the stone wall.

A thrill went through him. This was it. He knew it. He glanced at Nick, on the opposite side of the doorway, and saw the same shine of expectation and apprehension in his eyes.

'From here on in we need to be as quiet as we can,' John whispered. 'The element of surprise could be all-important. We should all turn our torches off.' Leading by example, he turned off his own. 'Our enemies are . . . formidable. They have abilities that we don't fully understand. You all saw back at the circus what they're capable of and how ruthless they are. Don't make the mistake of assuming they have the same strengths and weaknesses of normal men. If they attack you, don't hold back. Show them no mercy – because they won't show you any.' He glanced at Cliff, and then at the crossbow. 'You understand me?'

Cliff nodded.

John wanted to tell them more, to make them fully aware of what they were up against, but he knew if he started spouting about vampires he would lose all credibility. His hand stole up and touched the place in the centre of his breastbone where the crucifix was hanging under his layers of clothing. Silly superstition or a genuine charm against evil? If Lynn (and presumably Kate and Anthony) had been captured, then evidently their own crucifixes hadn't done *them* much good.

'Everyone ready?' he whispered. There were nods in the darkness. 'Okay. I'll go first. Then Cliff.' As one of the police officers started to speak, John raised a hand sharply. 'I know what you're going to say, but that's how it's going to be. That's my son in there, and I really haven't got time to argue.'

So saying, he ducked his head and stepped into the passage. It was narrow and dank and smelled of rot and mould. He expected it to be pitch black, expected to have to feel his way along, but to his surprise it was not entirely dark. There was light up ahead. Just a faint, flickering glimmer, but light all the same.

For the first ten or fifteen metres the light didn't change, and although he could see it clearly he began to wonder whether it was an illusion. Then gradually it brightened, acquiring shape and definition. Another fifteen metres and John was able to tell that it was candlelight and that it was coming from a larger space beyond the end of the passage. Now he could see the rectangular shape of the doorway, ten metres ahead. He paused briefly to look round and place a finger to his lips. Just behind him Cliff Hoskins, his face an impressionistic rendition of glowing orange planes and craters of black shadow, nodded grimly.

John turned back and was about to resume his stealthy progress when, from up ahead, there came a faint, strangled scream, followed by a screeched word – 'No!' – which seemed to ricochet down the passage. Immediately John started to run, scrabbling for the chain around his neck. Behind him he heard pattering feet, like a multiple echo of his own rapid footsteps. His mind raced as the end of the passage lurched closer. He knew that once they were through the doorway he would only have a second or two to assess the situation and act.

A couple of seconds later he burst from the passage into a dimly lit stone chamber about the size of two tennis courts. Stepping to the left to avoid blocking the entrance, he quickly took in the scene before him. In the foreground, ten or so metres away, was a coffin, with a body lying in it, on a stone dais. On the floor beside the coffin, the acrobat Emil was crouched on all fours over the prone and motionless form of the ringmistress, tearing at her throat in a way that reminded John of a lion devouring a gazelle. Just beyond Emil he saw Kate, lying on her back, using her elbows and heels to scrabble away from the scene, an expression of utter horror on her face.

On the far side of the room, though, was – for John – the most appalling sight of all. Both of the strongman's hands were wrapped around his son's neck and he was holding him up in the air like a rag doll, strangling the life out of him. John was appalled to see that Anthony's face was purple, his eyes bulging, his legs kicking feebly at the air.

'Cliff!' John yelled, pointing at the strong man. The sports-shop owner, who had entered the chamber behind him, needed no further prompting. Stepping forward, he raised his crossbow, took aim and fired. The bolt left the track like a streak of fire, candlelight reflecting off the shaft as it flashed across the room. John noticed that there was already a bloody gash in the back of the strong-man's head a split second before the bolt entered it.

Instantly the strongman dropped Anthony, who fell to the floor in a crumpled heap. As the giant spun round as if to confront his attackers, John saw with a combination of lurching revulsion and primal glee that the bolt had passed straight through the man's skull and was now protruding from the punctured egg of his left eye. For a second or two, though, the strongman seemed to find the horrifying injury little more than an irritation. He gritted his teeth and took a clumping step forward, his hands clenching and unclenching convulsively. Then his legs simply buckled and he crashed to the ground, the bolt popping out of the hole in the back of his head as his face hit the floor. The strongman's tree-trunk limbs twitched and thrashed for a moment, and then he was still.

John headed towards Anthony, vaguely aware of the rest of the men pouring into the chamber behind him. But as he ran past Emil a hand whipped out like a striking snake and wrapped around his ankle. John went down heavily, the impact knocking the wind out of him. Nevertheless he managed to twist onto his back, once again instinctively scrabbling for the chain around his neck. Emil loomed over him, clawing his way up his body towards his face. If John had any lingering doubts about the existence of vampires and demons, the sight of the acrobat at that moment swept them all away.

Emil's eyes were blood red, his pupils tiny pinpricks of black. The expression on his face was bestial, his mouth a wide snarl of blood-coated fangs, his chin and throat spattered with gore. There were twin pulses beating on both sides of his temples and his black hair hung down like a shaggy mane. As he opened his mouth yet wider in a predatory snarl, John finally succeeded in freeing the silver crucifix from his layers of clothing, and, not knowing whether it would do any good, thrust it at Emil's face.

The result was spectacular. Emil recoiled like a scalded cat, hissing and clawing at the air. As he reared back, John glimpsed someone in his peripheral vision rapidly approaching from his left. He turned his head to see Lynn, wearing a grimly determined expression, a blood-stained knife in her hand. Drawing back her arm, she stabbed Emil so savagely that John heard the thud of the blade burying itself in the dense meat of his back. Emil lashed out in defence, his arm moving so quickly that John perceived it as nothing more than a streak of movement. Batted away like a troublesome fly, Lynn pinwheeled backwards, her feet skidding rapidly from under her.

Still brandishing the crucifix, John tried to pull himself out from beneath the weight of Emil's body. Though the vampire was hissing and diverting his face from the silver cross, he was still kneeling on John's legs. The silver chain to which the crucifix was attached was cutting into the back of John's neck, and preventing him from holding it at arm's length. He was fumbling at the back of the silver chain with his left hand, trying to free it, when he became aware of a number of people converging on him – Nick, a local man called Terry Blake and one of the police officers.

Nick ran straight past him, but Blake and the police officer grabbed Emil's arms and tried to haul him up and away from John. With a panther-like roar, Emil spun and lashed out again. There was a cry and a wet spattering sound and suddenly Blake was staggering backwards, his stomach ripped open and his intestines splashing onto the floor like a mass of writhing pink eels. As Blake collapsed with a look of shocked surprise on his face, the police officer, who had been fortunate enough to receive no more than a gashed arm, slipped in the offal and fell, hitting his head on the stone floor and knocking himself unconscious.

And then suddenly here was Nick again, with something in his hand. With Emil still half-turned away, Nick stepped forward and with no hesitation whatsoever rammed the object into the centre of Emil's chest. He jumped back smartly as Emil whirled round, screaming like a wounded animal. John registered the object protruding from the vampire's chest at the same instant that Emil looked down at himself and did likewise. It was a wooden spar of blood-stained wood – the same spar, in fact, which had been used to subdue Karl Mitterhaus ten years previously. John suddenly realised that the body in the coffin, which he had glimpsed when he had entered the room, must belong to Mitterhaus, and that Nick must have pulled the spar from Mitterhaus's body in order to use it on Emil.

Two-for-one! he thought wildly. *Special offer!*

He watched with a mixture of horror and fascination as Emil died.

First the vampire aged and withered, his hair turning white and falling out, his skin darkening and shrivelling like an old apple. Then his lips peeled back from his teeth in a macabre grimace and his eyes sank into the gaping pits of his eye sockets. His limbs twisted and tightened as they dried out and his fingers curled in on themselves. A moment later Emil simply collapsed, like a precarious sand sculpture undermined by the incoming tide.

With a grimace of distaste, John scrambled out from beneath Emil's powdery, remains. He rose to his feet, dusting himself down and looked at Nick. 'Thanks.'

Nick nodded and managed a shaky smile. 'Kate's okay. Lynn too.'

'What about Anthony?'

Nick was about to reply when something over John's right shoulder caught his attention and caused his eyes to widen.

John turned, just in time to see Karl Mitterhaus sitting up in his coffin. It was not the young man that Alan Michaels had put down with a stake through the heart ten years ago, and neither was it the withered creature that Mitterhaus had become in death. This version of the child-killer was somewhere between the two, still powerful and athletic despite his heavily lined face and the grey streaks in his thick, flowing hair.

John didn't know for sure but he guessed that the blood of the Blaine boys, and possibly of their sister Sam, had partially restored Mitterhaus to youth, a process which would presumably have seen completion with the deaths of Anthony, Kate and Lynn. However, although Mitterhaus had been denied the full flush of youth, he appeared to have absorbed enough young blood (perhaps coupled with Nick's removal of the spar of wood from his chest) to achieve resurrection.

As Mitterhaus rose from his coffin, John once again raised the crucifix around his neck. Mitterhaus flinched as if slapped, turning his head away with a snarl. As he did so, someone stepped in front of John – Cliff Hoskins, once again levelling his crossbow. With the crucifix now shielded by Cliff's body, Mitterhaus bared his teeth and lunged forward, sweeping out a long arm and slapping the weapon aside just as Cliff fired.

The blow was so strong that Cliff's arm snapped like a twig, causing the crossbow to fly out of his hand. The bolt went high and wide and the crossbow itself spun through the air and hit John squarely in the temple, opening a gash across his forehead. John grunted and went down, the crucifix slipping from his hand. With panther-like grace, Mitterhaus sprang from his coffin, hands outstretched, and hit Nick square in the chest. Nick too went down, with Mitterhaus on top of him.

As John sat up, fingers probing dazedly at the gash in his forehead, someone stepped over his body and snatched up the crossbow, which had landed at the base of the dais. It was Lynn, who had picked herself up after Emil had knocked her off her feet and was now doggedly limping back into the fray. John saw Lynn grit her teeth with effort as she pulled the string of the crossbow back to notch tautly against its trigger catch. He wanted to tell her that if she couldn't get a spare bolt from Cliff, who was now writhing on the floor, nursing his busted arm and looking white as a sheet, she might find one sticking out of the back of the strongman's head – if she didn't mind pulling it loose, that was.

Lynn, however, didn't need a bolt. Stepping across to Mitterhaus, who was still pinning Nick to the floor and looked all set to tear his face off, she put the crossbow over his head like a strange necklace and pulled the trigger. Released from the catch, the string shot forward – and decapitated the vampire as neatly as a guillotine.

Mitterhaus's severed head flew off and hit the floor beside Nick's own head with a coconut-like crack before bouncing once and then rolling to a stop. Nick shoved Mitterhaus's suddenly limp body away from him in disgust as blood began to gush from the stump of the neck into his face. Clambering to his feet, he gave Lynn a goggle-eyed look from behind his blood-spattered spectacles and then suddenly grinned.

'That was . . . inspired,' he said.

She half-laughed, half-sobbed. 'That was for my dad.'

'No, Nick's right. That *was* inspired.' They both turned to see John sitting up, his back to the stone dais, dabbing at the gash on his forehead with an already blood-soaked handkerchief. He reached out a shaky hand. 'Now, if someone will help me up, I'd like to see how my son is.'

They rushed forward and pulled him to his feet. They had barely done so when Kate threw herself into Nick's arms.

'Dad,' she sobbed. 'Thank God you're okay.'

'Ditto,' he said, before his voice choked off and they wept in each other's arms.

Aided by Lynn, John hurried over to Anthony. He was still slumped against the wall, unconscious, though his eyelids were fluttering. The bruises on his neck, where the strongman had tried to throttle him, were purple-black and already swelling. John remembered how Mitterhaus had inflicted similar injuries on him ten years ago to the day. *Parallels*, he thought again.

'Anthony,' John said gently. 'Son, it's me.'

Anthony began to mutter. His eyes fluttered open.

'Hi,' Lynn said, grinning. 'Welcome back.'

John was not so ecstatic – not yet. He was worried that Anthony might have been deprived of oxygen for so long that he had suffered brain damage. He waited anxiously as Anthony's stare fixed on him and slowly focused, watched his son's lips move silently for a couple of seconds. Finally, in a hoarse whisper, Anthony said, 'Dad? What are you doing here? What's happened? Why've you cut your head?'

John couldn't help it – he laughed out loud and wrapped his arms around his son. 'It's over,' he said. 'The vampires are all dead.'

Anthony swallowed and winced. 'You mean I've missed all the fun?' he croaked. 'Typical.'

Epilogue

John and Nick stood side by side, watching as the big top was dismantled. Soon all trace of the Circus of Nights would be gone. For ever, with luck.

With the deaths of Emil and Karl Mitterhaus, not to mention the other vile creatures that had invaded their community, the so-called 'sickness barrier' had evaporated like morning mist. As a consequence the authorities had finally been able to move in, and the bodies had been taken away that afternoon in a fleet of ambulances sent from Wenthorpe and beyond. Including their friend Chris Blaine, forty-three people had died up at the circus. Chris and Caroline's three children, the three who had died in the woods, Alan Michaels and poor Terry Blake, whom Emil had murdered just seconds before Nick had pierced his black heart, had pushed the final death toll to over fifty. John suspected it would be a long time before Shettle came to terms with its loss, but he was sure that eventually, given time, it *would* recover. He looked at Nick and placed a hand on his shoulder.

'You okay?'

Nick smiled, but it didn't reach his eyes. 'Never better. You?'

John grimaced and looked away. 'Feeling a bit guilty, to be honest.'

'Guilty?' said Nick, surprised. 'Why?'

'Because I'm the only one who's come out of this intact. You've lost Anna. Lynn's lost her dad. And Caroline . . .' He heaved a huge sigh. 'It hardly bears thinking about what *she*'s lost. God knows how she'll cope.'

Nick was silent for a moment. Then he said, 'It's not a competition, John. And you're not to blame for any of it. When it comes down to it, it's just the luck of the draw. Life's lottery. You had as much to lose as everyone else, but you didn't hold back. You stood up to be counted like the rest of us.' He shrugged and smiled. 'Listen to me. Cliché man. But it's true. Life's just random. There's no pattern to it.'

John recalled the thoughts he'd been having last night – about the circularity of events. About parallels.

'You're probably right,' he said. 'I just hope that it's finally over.'

'It is,' Nick said decisively. 'We burned them, remember? Reduced them all to ash.'

Superintendent Benson might have protested had he not been otherwise engaged in organising transport and treatment for the wounded but to John and Nick it had seemed the right thing to do. They had agreed that it would have been wrong to leave the remains of Emil and Karl Mitterhaus for forensics to pore over – wrong and possibly dangerous. And so, after supervising the evacuation of the group – including the removal of their own dead and wounded – from the underground chamber, John and Nick had gone back and dropped lighted candles into Mitterhaus's silk-lined coffin. They had waited for the fire to take hold and then they had left. It had been a cleansing act, an act which John had hoped would signal a final end.

But still he couldn't stop thinking about parallels. Ten years ago that day too had ended in fire – and look what had happened.

Shaking off his doubts, he forced a grin and slapped Nick on the back. 'Come on – I'll buy you a drink.'

'Wouldn't mind a coffee,' Nick said. 'Something hot to take away the chill of the day.'

'A coffee it is,' said John.

The two friends turned and trudged away. Behind them, beneath a shroud-grey sky, the big top slumped and sagged like a vast creature expelling its dying breath.